The Anti Cinderella

To Shannon
Live in a world of possibilities!
Tawdra Kandle

TAWDRA KANDLE

The Anti-Cinderella

ISBN-13:978-1718785632
ISBN-10:1718785631

Cover designer: Meg Murrey
Formatting: Champagne Book Design

How many girls can say their first kiss was with a prince in the British royal family?

I was fourteen and he was sixteen, and yes, it was magical. But that kiss didn't exactly change my life. To tell you the truth, I didn't even think about it—or Nicky Windsor—for the next ten years . . . until fate, in the guise of my grandparents, brought us back together again.

Now everything has spun out of control. I'm ducking reporters and photographers when I try to leave home. My friends act as if I'm someone they don't know anymore. The whole world seems to be watching me, wanting to see some kind of modern Cinderella story.

But trust me, I'm no man's princess. I'm more comfortable in tennis shoes than in a tiara, more likely to rock a bucket than a ball gown, and more liable to fall on my face than to pull off a graceful wave.

The only thing that keeps me from running away and hiding is Nicky. He's all I've ever wanted in a man: hot, hunky and head-over-heels in love with me. I think I feel the same way. I think I want to be with him forever.

But the idea of life with the royal family terrifies me. Even if I have found my one and only, can I handle what comes after our happy ending?

Dedication

Many years ago, my grandmother told me stories about two little princesses, Elizabeth and Margaret, igniting my lifelong love of all things royal.

And so this book is dedicated to the memory my Nana, Marian Shute Thompson, with great love and gratitude for this and so much more.

Chapter One

"Woooohooo! Hot mama walking alert." Shelby, my roommate and best friend in the world, waved her hand in front of her face in an exaggerated fanning motion as she lounged in the doorway of my bedroom. "Damn, girl! Sometimes I forget how good you clean up."

"Funny. Very funny." Rolling my eyes, I balanced myself on one foot. "I need your input. Which shoes work best? Option one . . ." I switched feet, lifting the first one up behind me. "Or option two?"

"Hmmm. It depends. Are you going to a club? Or is this date a quiet affair at an elegant restaurant?" Shelby wiggled her fingers, grinning at me wickedly. "C'mon. Tell me all the details."

I blew out a breath. "Neither one. And get real. Where would I find either a club or an elegant restaurant within thirty miles of us? Tonight is a command performance at my grandparents' house."

"You're going to visit Honey and Handsome without me?" Shelby frowned, pushing out her bottom lip. "I thought you loved me."

"I do, which is why I'm not taking you with. This isn't the fun kind of H squared visit. It's a formal dinner. It's going to be long and boring." I shook my foot. "Shoe answer, please."

"Uh, the first one. It's cute, but it's not trampy."

"Excellent. That's exactly what I was going for." I kicked off the shoe that hadn't made the cut and found the match to the one I was wearing. "Tell me again why I put myself through this shit."

"Because your grandparents are funding your graduate school career and keeping you fed, with a roof over your head?" Shelby tilted her head. "Those seem like wonderful reasons."

"Yeah, that's right." I turned a little, checking myself out in the full-length mirror. My black dress was silk, sedate and stylish, the most important three S words for this kind of occasion. "Plus, there's the whole thing where I love them."

"What's not to love? Honey and Handsome are the coolest people I know. No one who'd just met them would ever guess that they're both in their seventies."

"Or that they've been married for over fifty years." I frowned, concentrating on fastening my earring.

"Yes! They're so dang cute together. Remember when they came here to help us move in, and we caught them making out in the kitchen?"

I held up one hand. "I don't want to remember that, thanks. Eww. You might find it adorable, but it's not something you want to see if they're your grandparents."

"I guess I can see that." Shelby was silent as she watched me dig through my backpack, pulling out essentials like my driver's license, cash, tissues and mints and depositing them into a small evening bag. "What's the occasion tonight? Why did they ask you to come to one of their fancy dinners?"

"I'm not entirely sure," I scowled. "Honey was being a little cagey when she called to tell me. She said they wanted me to be there because of my unique point of view on the subject at hand, or something like that. It probably has to do with ecological sustainability. They like to have me there as back-up so it seems like they have the latest research on conservation."

"Are you saving the moose this time?"

I snorted. "Totally possible."

"Well, whatever the cause, I know you'll end up having a blast. Your grandparents never throw dull parties."

"Yeah. You're not wrong. I'm not afraid of being bored. I just don't want to smile and act happy around a bunch of rich people. Even if they might someday consider donating millions to one of my projects." I patted my bag, took one more look in the mirror and straightened my shoulders. "All right. I'm set, I guess. Do I look okay? Will I do?"

Shelby scrutinized me with narrowed eyes. "You will. You're gorge, babe. You'll knock them all dead. And who knows?" She gave me wide, dramatic eyes. "Maybe one of them will bring his hot and sexy grandson, who just happens to be rich as hell, and your eyes will meet across the crowded room—"

"Ugh!" I stuck out my tongue at her. "Just stop. You'll get my hopes up, and when no one under the age of seventy is there, I'll have to drown my disappointment in some of Handsome's best whiskey. That never ends well."

"Hey, it could happen. And if it doesn't, at least your grandfather's whiskey is primo." She leaned in to kiss my cheek. "Have fun. Drive safe. Make good choices. Give the two H's my love."

"Will do. See you tonight."

I stopped at the tiny front closet by the door to grab my long rain coat. Yes, it was late April, but this was Maine, and although today's high temperature had broken the sixty-degree mark, as soon as the sun set, the chilly air would get downright frigid. I'd lived here long enough that I didn't mind the cold so much, but my dress tonight was sleeveless, and there was no way I was going to shiver when I could avoid it. The rain coat wasn't exactly haute couture, but it would do the job.

Opening the door to the hybrid compact Shelby and I shared, I tossed the evening bag onto the passenger seat and eased behind the wheel. I was unreasonably grumpy about this dinner. My grandparents were wonderful, amazing people, and I adored them beyond reason. One of the reasons I'd chosen Grant's graduate program was because the school was close enough to Honey and Handsome's summer home that I could visit when they happened to be living there. But I wasn't in any mood to play nice just now, when I'd spent all day mucking around in a muddy field, working on the research for my final project.

The sun was drooping low in the sky, but I still needed my sunglasses, thanks to the eye-level glare. I knew this route by heart, since I'd been driving it for two years now. Still, this time of evening was when the moose liked to come out and play, and God knew I didn't need to hit one of those monsters tonight. So I kept my car to a reasonable speed, sliding my eyes right and left as I passed wooded areas and open fields.

Darkness settled slowly, and I finally shed my sunglasses a few minutes before I reached the turn that led me down my grandparents' driveway. Their home was large, but it wasn't ostentatious. No one would ever guess that these two had founded and still owned—and were actively involved in—one of the largest organic juice and sandwich businesses in the country. Honey Bee Juices had won accolades over the years for its business practices, growing methods and passionate commitment to conservation and activism. I was proud not only of my family's success and efforts to do the right thing, but of the fact that they used their wealth in practical ways.

This estate, for instance, housed a group of horticulturists for a month in the summer, men and women of all ages who won scholarships to a camp where they were taught the latest methods for natural gardening. Not only that, but Honey and Handsome always opened their home to anyone visiting the nearby college—the one I was currently attending.

"Nothing we have is truly ours, Kyra," Handsome liked to tell me. "Everything is held in trust. And if we don't share, what's the point in anything?"

My grandparents were, without doubt, the coolest, kindest and most compassionate people I'd ever known. Growing up, I'd spent a lot of time with them—not because my parents were absent or neglectful, but because we worked and played as a family so often. Both of my parents worked in the juicing business, and I was always there, too, listening, watching and learning.

It was natural that I became close to my grandparents, of course, who had wanted me to call them Grammy and Grampy. But even as a toddler, I'd had my own mind. I'd noticed from a young age that my grandmother always referred to her husband as Handsome, while he called her Honey almost without fail. If it was good enough for the two of them, it worked for me, too, which was why all of their grandchildren—and their grandchildren's friends—henceforth used the same names for our grandparents.

I smiled as I stopped the car and climbed out, my heels crunching on the gravel of the drive. Handsome and Honey gave selflessly to all of us, whether it was time, attention or education. They didn't lavish us with gifts, exotic trips or designer clothes, but my grandparents were the reason I was now in my last year of graduate school at Grant. They'd covered the tuition and bought the adorable little cottage that Shelby and I shared. I worked hard to keep up my grades, and Shelby and I were responsible for all the maintenance on our home, in addition to the improvements Handsome requested, but that was a small price to pay for the freedom to study and live without worry.

That was why I never really balked when H squared, as Shelby teasingly called them, asked me to make an appearance at one of their gatherings or fundraisers. They didn't force the issue, ever, nor did they invite me to any social affair that would make me uncomfortable. Truth be told, I almost always ended up having a good time and meeting interesting people.

Which, come to think of it, made me wonder why my car was the only one in the circular drive as I climbed the steps of the porch. Usually, other guests' vehicles would be here, too, by now; I was running late, as I usually was. Everything was quiet, and for a moment, I wondered if I'd somehow misunderstood my grandmother and gotten the date wrong.

"Kyra, are you planning to come inside, or should we deliver your dinner on a tray to the porch?" Honey's voice behind me held more than a hint of laughter. "You look like you're lost."

"I was beginning to think maybe I was." I turned around to face the front door, where my grandmother stood. "Where is everyone? I know I'm not early. That just isn't possible."

"You're just exactly right on time." Honey drew me into a tight hug and kissed my cheek. It was impossible to believe, looking at her, that she was over seventy years old. Her skin was smooth, her eyes clear, and the hint of white in her hair was well-camouflaged by her natural blonde. The smile on her face held just a hint of mischief, which made me pull back a little, my eyes narrowing in suspicion.

"Honey, what are you up to?"

"Up to? Whatever are you talking about?" She affected innocence, but I knew better.

"Honey . . . you told me this was a formal dinner with some people you wanted me to meet. Tell me you're not scheming about something else."

"I never scheme, sweetie. And maybe you misheard me. I said it was a formal dinner, and you might meet someone interesting." She gave a little nod, and I remembered that she was right. That was exactly how she'd phrased it.

"You're not making me feel any better." I followed her into the foyer. "How many people are you expecting? And where is everyone?"

"Already sitting down, waiting for you." Honey inclined her head, indicating the direction of the dining room. "Your grandfather is entertaining."

"Oh, brother." I giggled, leaning conspiratorially against Honey. "That means long-ass stories, doesn't it?"

She bent her head so her mouth was next to my ear. "'When I was first coming up with the recipe for pineapple sunshine, the juice that put us on the map . . .'" Her impression of Handsome made me laugh even harder.

We walked across the foyer and down the wide hallway that led toward what my grandparents called the public side of the house—where the large, formal dining room, the conference rooms and the ballroom were all located—but to my surprise, Honey steered me to the left and opened a door.

When I hesitated, she only smiled. "Since it's just the four of us, I thought it would be cozier to eat in the family dining room." When I didn't move, she patted my back. "Come on, now, no one's going to bite you. Don't you trust me?"

"All of sudden, not so much." I frowned, but I allowed her to move me along.

This part of the house was comfortable and warm. The sitting room where I'd played dolls as a kid flowed into the kitchen and dining room. As we rounded the corner, I heard the sound of my grandfather's laughter mingling with someone else's voice.

I didn't know who it was—not really—but for some reason, my heart began to pound, and I felt a little lightheaded. There was something familiar—something in me that recognized the tone and timber of the voice.

We rounded the wall that hid the table from my view, and I came to a sudden, abrupt halt. Sitting at the table next to my grandfather, leaning back in his chair as though his being here was the most natural thing in the world, was a man I thought I'd never see again—not in person, anyway.

He looked so different—and yet, of course, not that very different. He wasn't the boy I'd known ten years before. He was a man now. Still, although I hadn't been in the same room with him—or even in the same city, to the best of my knowledge, since I was fourteen, it wasn't as though I hadn't seen him. I hadn't sought out glimpses of him, but they'd been impossible to avoid on magazine covers at the grocery store checkout counters or splashed over social media.

Yet, he was more a stranger than a friend now. Too many years divided us, and those years had taken us in opposite directions. Neither of us was who we'd been back then on the Florida beaches.

And then he saw me, and the way his eyes lit up was heart-rippingly familiar. A smile spread over his face, and slowly he rose to his feet.

"Hi, Ky."

CHAPTER Two

Ten Years Earlier

"Kyra! C'mon. Honey says if we want, we can walk downtown and get ice cream. You coming?"

I hesitated, glancing at the boy sitting next to me on the beach blanket. He was staring out at the ocean, his eyes distant and remote. I knew that if I said his name, he'd glance over at me, and I hoped I'd see the flare of admiration . . . and something else that I didn't dare name even to myself. Not yet.

But if I asked him if he wanted to go with my sisters to get ice cream, it would break the spell. He might say yes, but more likely, he'd shake his head no and tell me to go ahead without him.

I didn't want to go without him. Oh, I loved ice cream—I loved it so much that most days, I begged Honey and my mom to let me go get a cone after dinner. But something had changed this summer, and ice cream somehow didn't hold the same allure as it once had.

I'd known Nicky since I was six years old. At first, he'd been just another of the many playmates who flitted in and out of my life throughout early childhood. There were plenty of those, because I spent so much time with my parents and grandparents, and they, in turn, often entertained business associates, fruit growers and managers of our many stores. Honey and Handsome liked to mix business with pleasure, so it was natural that they had their meetings at their beach home, inviting attendees to bring along their families to enjoy the beautiful grounds and the ocean.

But Nicky wasn't connected to Honey Bee. He came for three weeks every summer to stay with his grandmother, whose home was next to ours. For a long time, for most of our days together, I'd had no idea that he was anything other than just a kid who talked a little funny and had some very precise ideas about building sand castles. It had only been about four years ago that I'd realized that my summer vacation buddy Nicky was known to the rest of the world as Prince Nicholas.

Even then, it hadn't changed anything. He was still just Nicky. He came to Florida for those weeks in the summer because his grandmother was American. She had left the United States decades before to marry the Earl of Umbria, but before she had been a countess, she'd been Honey's best friend, which was why the two women had homes next-door to each other on the Florida coast.

"Kyra!" My sister's patience, never one of her strong suits, was at an end. "Come on! Honey's waiting."

"You go on." I twisted to face Lisel. "I don't want to go."

Her face went blank with shock and then twisted with the kind of frustration reserved for sisters. "But Kyra—"

"Go on. I'm fine." I turned my back to her and prayed she'd cut her losses and leave now, before this got embarrassing.

After a few seconds, I heard her huff out a breath before she stomped away, muttering under her breath. Thankfully, whatever she was saying was unintelligible.

"You could've gone with her." Nicky didn't look at me as he spoke. "You didn't have to stay here because of me."

"I wasn't staying here because of you." The lie slipped easily from my lips. "I just didn't feel like ice cream. It's not always about

you, Nicky."

One side of his mouth twisted up into the half-smile that this summer had begun to set my insides to shaking. "You're always good to remind me of that fact. Thanks."

"Any time." I bumped my shoulder against his and tried to think of something witty to say. Tonight was Nicky's last night with me, since tomorrow, he'd be flying up to Boston with his grandmother, where they were taking a private tour of Boston College before they returned to the UK.

Until last year, I'd never paid attention to when Nicky arrived or left. He'd show up one day on the beach, and it would be a happy surprise when he joined my sisters and me as we played. And then three weeks later, he just wasn't there, and someone would say, "Oh, yes, they went back home." On the beach, in the summers, time had no meaning to the young.

But last year, when I'd been thirteen, everything had changed. Suddenly, I'd found myself hyper-aware of Nicky, of the way he moved, of the way his bathing suit fit and how his chest was now broad and the way his blue eyes smiled when he did. I knew the minute he arrived on the sand every morning, and I knew when he left.

And this year had been even worse. I could feel Nicky's presence, even when I wasn't looking at him. His voice was deeper, and when he spoke, the timber of it echoed so deep inside me that I could hardly breathe. I tried not to look at him, to moon around him, as my mother called it, but it wasn't easy.

I'd treasured each day jealously, since I'd asked, in what I'd hoped was an off-hand manner, when he was scheduled to leave. It was killing me to think about being here alone after he'd gone. I wondered if I could talk Honey and Handsome into taking me on a trip to England sometime during the school year. I had my argument ready, all about the educational benefits of a tour of Europe.

"You could write to me." I spoke out loud before I realized it. "You know, you could write letters to me. So we could keep in touch."

"Aw, Ky." He shook his head. "Guys don't write letters."

"That's not true," I protested vehemently. "History is full of great letters, and most of those were written by men. Probably only because no one thought to save the ones women wrote, but still. Lord Byron wrote to his Teresa, and John Keats to Fanny, and—" I held up one finger in triumph. "Even your ancestor Henry VIII wrote letters to Anne Boleyn."

Nicky laughed. "You had me until the last one. I don't usually claim Henry VIII as my favorite relative. Not a very good example, as he later separated poor Anne's head from her body. No amount of beautiful love letters makes up for that kind of treatment."

"All right. I'll give you that. Well, then . . . Shakespeare!" I grinned. "You can't argue with that one."

"Did the Bard write love letters? I don't remember."

"The sonnets have to be letters. Or at least I think they are." I smiled dreamily. "'Let me not to the marriage of true minds admit impediments.'" I gave a little sigh. Shakespeare had been my happy place ever since freshman English this past year. I'd begun gobbling up all of his works, aided and abetted by my grandmother, who had a weakness for him, too. Glancing sideways at Nicky's face, awash in amusement, I back-peddled a little. "Anyway, I wasn't talking about love letters. Just regular letters. Like, 'Hey, Kyra, how are you? I'm here in England, where I'm . . .' And then you tell me what's going on with you, and I write back and do the same."

"I don't know." He frowned. "Maybe it was only people who lived a long time ago who were good correspondents. And I might not have been right about men in general and letters, but this guy doesn't write letters." He pointed at his chest. "I'd fail you miserably."

"I don't agree. I still think you're wrong, too, about writing. I

know plenty of guys who are still alive and kicking who write letters." I was bluffing, of course. Although, come to think of it, my grandfather wrote me beautiful letters.

"Oh, really?" Nicky quirked a brow my way. "You know plenty of guys, do you?"

For the first time in my life, I felt a small thrill of feminine power. "Yes, I do. Lots and lots. Tons of cute and funny guys."

Now I had his full attention. Nicky folded one knee back, bending it at an angle to his body, and shifted to face me. "Do you have a boyfriend, Ky?"

"No." Being coy was one thing, but honesty was important to me.

"Do you want to have a boyfriend?" He tilted his head, examining me.

I wanted to respond with a question—Are you applying for the job? But I wasn't sure I could handle the answer.

"I don't want a boyfriend just to say I have one." I scooped up a handful of sand and let it sift through my fingers. "Some of the girls I know want that. They don't care who the boy is—they just want to be able to say that."

"But not you." There was a bit of surprise in his tone.

"No." I shook my head. "I'd only want a boyfriend if it was the right person."

"Ah." Nicky nodded. "That's . . . mature."

"What about you?" I wasn't sure I wanted to hear the answer to this question.

"No boyfriend for me." He winked at me, and I rolled my eyes.

"You know what I mean. Do you have a girlfriend?"

"Don't you think you'd know if I did?" There was a thread of irony in his voice. "She would be on magazine covers. I don't want to do that to anyone. Especially after what happened to my sister."

I winced. While I knew about Nicky's family, more often than not I forgot that his parents, his grandparents and his sisters were on the world stage. But there wasn't any avoiding the media coverage of his oldest sister and her fiancé.

"Honey told me Alex is staying down here even after you go." I nibbled my lower lip.

"Yeah, she thought the space would be good. A break from . . . just everything, I guess. It can be suffocating. Not only all the attention from the press, which is horrible enough, but my parents and the rest of the family, they don't know how to handle her. They don't know what she needs—none of us do, to be honest. So it's better for her to be here. Maybe she'll get over it."

"Maybe." I wasn't as optimistic as Nicky. Losing the man she loved to a tragic accident didn't sound like something a woman got over—not quickly, certainly, and maybe not ever. Even at the age of fourteen I knew that much.

"I don't see how I could ever put someone through the nightmare of being linked with me." Nicky scowled. "It's brutal. And it's not fair to a person who wasn't born into it."

I had no idea how to answer that. I couldn't make a good argument against his statement, as I didn't have any experience with the life he led. But for reasons I couldn't explain, I didn't like what he was insinuating.

"If your father and your grandfather thought that way, you wouldn't be around," I pointed out. "And maybe if the person cared about you enough, the other stuff wouldn't matter to her."

Nicky didn't answer me, but his frown deepened and his brows drew together. The waves crashed against the sand, and the last beams of the day's sun glowed wanly. I wished desperately that I could think of something to say that would make him see me. Every once in a while, I had the feeling that he did—his eyes would warm, and his smile would seem to hold some kind of secret, as though it was only for me. But those times were rarer than I would have liked.

"I'm going to miss you, Ky." He said the words so softly that I almost thought I'd imagined them. For a moment, I just held onto that and basked in it, not only in what he'd said, but that he'd used the name no one else did. My family wasn't big on nicknames—aside from affectionate titles for grandparents, obviously—and so no one ever called me anything except Kyra. Only Nicky had ever—and always—called me Ky.

And then the meaning of what he'd said sank in. Nicky was going to miss me. I chanced a sideways glance and realized that he was watching me again. Studying me. Waiting for a reaction.

I ran the tip of my tongue over my lips. "I'll miss you, too."

"Sometimes I wish . . ." He trailed off and shook his head. "Doesn't matter, does it? My grandmother says something—if wishes were horses, then beggars would ride. So they don't help."

"But maybe—I could visit you. During the year, you know. I've never been to England. Or you could come back here." When he remained silent, I added, "Or we could write."

"I don't have the freedom to just take off for trips that aren't planned in advance. I'll be in school, and my term holidays are already set. And I wasn't lying before. I'd be a lousy letter-writer."

I nodded as reality swept over me. "Okay. Yeah, you're right. That was just—I wasn't thinking."

"Ky." Nicky sounded so tired. "It's not that I don't want to—you're my friend. Sometimes I think the three weeks I'm here, with my grandmother and you—that's when I'm who I really am, and the rest of the year, I'm just playing at being someone else. But when I go back there, Florida feels very far away. Like a dream. So to write to you, or to try to keep in touch—to believe I could see you or visit and it would be anything like the summer—it wouldn't work."

"Okay." I swallowed hard. "Yeah. Summer—um, things. Friendships. Whatever. They don't usually work the rest of the year, do they?"

He lifted one shoulder, as if that was some kind of answer. I closed my eyes and hoped that I wasn't going to cry. That would be ridiculous. I wasn't crushing on Nicky. We were friends. He was my friend, and it was only natural that I'd think he was cute. I'd think the same about any guy I only saw once a year, when I was on vacation.

A breeze blew over us, and I shivered. Twilight had fallen, and it was fully dark over the ocean, so that I could see stars begin to twinkle just above the line where the water met the sky.

"Ky." Nicky whispered my name, and he touched my cheek with one finger, using that gentle caress to turn me to face him. He was close, those vivid blue eyes staring down into mine. What I saw there was confusion and uncertainty and something else that I thought might be want. Need. But I was too young to be sure. No one else had ever looked at me the way Nicholas Windsor was looking at me right now.

My heart thudded against my ribcage. Nicky's fingers slid over my cheek, brushing my jaw before he cupped the back of my neck, wordlessly urging my head to tilt up. In the moment before my eyes slid closed, I saw the way his eyelashes fanned against his skin. I inhaled the scent that was unique to Nicky, a mix of suntan lotion, some kind of light cologne and man-smell. I thought about everything he'd said and how his fingers felt against the back of my head, and I worried that maybe I was sweaty back there, from where my hair had lay while the sun was still high in the sky.

And then his lips touched mine, and all other rational thought ceased. I didn't worry, I didn't stress and I didn't think. I only felt the way his mouth pressed into me and the tickle of his breath as he exhaled through his nose. Every nerve in my body jumped to life and exploded in a new and joyous dance.

He eased back a little, gazing down at me before he breathed out my name once more.

"Ky." When he kissed me again, his tongue teased my closed lips until I parted them slightly. He didn't thrust his tongue into my mouth; he only traced the sensitive inner flesh with a gentle sweep. I didn't know what to do—should I meet his tongue with mine? By the time I'd made up my mind to try, Nicky had pulled back.

He was still right there, close enough that I thought he might kiss me again. I hoped he would. My lips tingled, and it felt as though my skin was buzzing, longing for more. I tried to remember the stories about making out I'd heard from other girls or read about in books. Would he want to touch me? I wanted to be brave enough to press my hands into his chest, to skim them down his back and to lean my body against his.

Behind us, from one of the houses, a voice called, breaking the spell between us. I thought it was probably someone looking for Nicky, since I knew that if Lisel and Honey had returned from the ice cream shop, they'd just walk back onto the beach to find me.

Nicky muttered something under his breath, releasing his hold on me as he flipped his wrist over to check his watch.

"Kyra, I'm sorry. I have to go inside. My flight tomorrow is early, and I promised my grandmother I'd eat with her tonight."

"Oh, sure." I forced a smile and hoped he couldn't hear the pounding of my heart. "Of course, you should go in. It's fine. I'm fine."

"I know you are." Nicky brushed my hair back over my shoulder. "I just wish—part of me wishes that I'd done this the first night I was here. And the other part of me is glad I waited, because maybe it would have ruined our time together. Maybe I shouldn't

have—you know."

"I'm not sorry you did." I held his gaze steadily. "I wouldn't want my first kiss to be with anyone else but you, Nicky."

"Your first kiss." His mouth quivered between a frown and a smile, as though he wasn't sure whether to be pleased or upset. "Kyra, if there was a way—"

"It's okay." I blinked rapidly, furiously fighting back the tears I hated. "It's okay. Really. You have to go. I'm fine. My grandmother and Lisel are going to be back in a minute, too."

He nodded and stood up, pulling me to my feet as well. "I'll try to write. I can't promise, but . . ."

"Then don't. I'll see you next summer. It's all right, Nicky. I'll see you next summer."

He pulled me into a hug, but I could already feel him drawing away. "Goodbye, Ky."

"Bye, Nicky. See you next year." He released me, and I watched him turn away and jog up the beach toward the lights beyond the dunes. For a few long minutes, I stood still, hugging my arms around my ribs, holding onto the magic of this moment.

When I began trudging in the direction of my grandparents' home, I wasn't one bit sad. I'd just had my first kiss. It had been as perfect as any girl might dream it to be. And although I knew I wasn't going to see Nicky any time soon, next summer would come quickly. I'd be a year older, and so would he, and maybe . . . maybe there would be more kisses.

I'd see him again. Next summer.

CHAPTER Three

"WHAT ARE YOU DOING HERE?"

I didn't take any time to think before I blurted out the words. What was going through my mind tumbled out of my lips, which wasn't anything new. As Shelby often said, my filter was faulty.

Nicky didn't seem surprised by the greeting. "Well, your grandparents heard I was going to be in the area, and they very kindly invited me to dinner. And then they thought it would be fun for us to see each other again, since it's been a while."

"Ten years. But who's counting?" I flipped my hand over. "Not me."

"I can see that." He grinned. "Aw, c'mon, Ky. Aren't you even the least bit pleased to see me?"

I rolled my eyes, but at the same time, I felt my initial shock giving way to pleasure. This was Nicky, after all, my childhood playmate and my very first crush. After the disappointment of the summer after our first—and, as it turned out, our only—kiss, I'd come to a place of acceptance as I'd grown up. The more aware I'd become of who Nicky was to the world at large, the less real that night had seemed to be.

Within a year or so, I'd realized that the kiss—that magical fairy-tale moment in my life—couldn't have meant to him what it had to me. He was a freakin' prince in England, and I was just a kid. Just Kyra Duncan, the scrawny kid from the states.

I'd gotten over it—and him—years before. I didn't even think about him, beyond an occasional smile when I caught his image on the cover of a magazine. So while I was not thrilled about being hoodwinked by my grandparents, I wasn't altogether unhappy to see Nicky.

"Maybe just a little bit," I conceded, feigning grumpiness. "As long as you're not going to get pushy about sand castle design or call me Kyra-Myra. I won't put up with that crap."

My grandfather laughed. "Not quite the warm and tender reunion your grandmother was envisioning, Kyra. But I'd expect nothing less of you."

"Thanks, Handsome." I paused behind my grandfather's chair to lean over and give him a warm hug and a kiss on his cheek. Out of the corner of my eye, I saw Nicky rising to stand. When I straightened again, my hands resting on Handsome's chair, my childhood friend held out his arms.

"For old times' sake?"

I heaved a sigh, but it was more for dramatic effect than anything else. "Fine. But I'm going on record that I'm not happy about this, Honey." I shot her a glare. "You made me dress up. You said I had to wear heels. I won't forget that."

"Aren't I worth the effort?" Nicky's hands ghosted down my arms, his touch gentle as he drew me against him for a hug. The deep sniff I took was instinctive; I remembered how he used to smell so good, and he hadn't lost that in the last decade. As he embraced me tighter, I was keenly aware of his hard chest and the muscles in his arms. Nicky hadn't gone soft, but that wasn't a surprise, either.

I let my eyes close and pressed my hands into his upper back, returning the hug. I felt the tickle of his breath over my neck, and I thought I heard him swallow, too. I wondered if he was remembering the last time we'd been this close—or if he'd forgotten it altogether.

"Well, sit down, sit down," Honey fussed, skirting the table to take her own place. "Mrs. Muller made us a lovely dinner, and she's been chomping at the bit to bring it out."

I disentangled myself from Nicky and stepped back to take my seat across the table from him. "It smells good. And I'm famished."

"Of course, you are." My grandfather chuckled. "I don't know where you put it all, sweetie. You must have a hollow leg."

I winked at him. "It's clean living, Handsome. That, and good genes."

"Those come from your grandmother's side of the family. But you can't stay still, either. That's at least part of the equation."

"True." I shook my napkin into my lap and turned my attention to our guest. "So, Nicky. Catch me up on life. What've you been up to since you were sixteen?"

He quirked one eyebrow at me. "Seriously?"

I feigned amazement. "Of course. Hey, I'll go first. I finished high school—not with honors, exactly, but with good enough grades to get me into a decent college in Florida. I decided to go south because I was tired of the winters in Philadelphia, and I figured Honey and Handsome's place on the beach would be a good spot for studying."

My grandfather snorted, and I ignored him.

"While I was in college, I finally gave in to the love I'd been denying all of my life . . . science. Namely, plant biology and sustainability practices. I majored in bio, and then these totally cool people who birthed my father—" I grinned at my grandparents. "They offered me a full ride to the graduate program of my choice, provided I kept up my grades and worked for them after I finish my degree. My friend Shelby, who I'd met at school in Florida, was applying for a scholarship at Grant, up here in Maine. I thought, what the hell, maybe I should try the extreme north, after spending four years in the extreme south. I got in, and so did Shelby. We've been living up here, studying and generally behaving ourselves, since then. We graduate next spring—we're just finishing up the current term now." I spread out my hands on the table. "And that's what I've been doing for the last ten years. Your turn."

When Nicky didn't immediately respond, I added, "Come on, now. Fill me in. I mean, you don't think I've been reading about your life in magazines or following your groupies on social media, right?"

He huffed out a short laugh. "Touché. All right. I went to Eton, where I eventually finished with two A-levels, in history and biology. After that, I went to St. John's College at Oxford." One side of his mouth lifted into a half-smile. "And since then, I've just been a playboy, flitting around from beach to ski resort, charming women and fending off the envy of other wealthy noblemen everywhere. As one does."

"Oh, Nicky, don't be so modest." Honey shook her head. "You are one of the hardest working people I know." She turned to me as the housekeeper waltzed into the dining room with serving bowls. "Nicky is the patron of Waste

Not, the organization in the UK that fights hunger, and he's on the international board of No Hungry Child, which works to eradicate childhood hunger worldwide."

"Speaking of hungry people . . ." Mrs. Muller clunked down a bowl on the table and patted my shoulder. "I made your favorite new potatoes, Kyra. And the broccoli here, it's what you brought me over the other day from your greenhouse."

I smiled. "Thanks, Mrs. M. It all looks delicious."

"You have a greenhouse?" Nicky picked up his fork, sliding a glance my way. "That sounds ambitious."

"It's not my personal greenhouse. It's just where I work at the college. Or one of the places where I work." I helped myself to a healthy spoonful of potatoes. "But enough about me. What brought you across the pond?"

"Oh, a few things. Meetings about a conference NHC is doing in the fall. Visits to some potential sponsors for Waste Not." He gestured toward my grandfather with a jerk of his chin. "And a very illuminating chat with the owners of one of the most charitable and passionately altruistic companies I know."

I stabbed a potato and took a bite. "They're pretty great. I'll give you that."

"I think Honey Bee Juices could only benefit from a partnership with Waste Not." My grandmother sipped her wine. "It kills me to think of how much perfectly acceptable food is often wasted because of regulations and policies." When Handsome began to interrupt, she lifted her hand. "I know, I know. Those rules are there for a reason. I understand that. But the rules don't say we have to trash fruit and veggies that we can't use in our juices. They only say we can't serve them to paying customers. I'm excited about the idea of having a way to put what we can't use to a better purpose."

"That's exactly what we're trying to communicate to other businesses." Nicky grinned. "Auntie Maggie, you'd be a wonderful spokesperson for Waste Not. I'm tempted to kidnap you away to London and introduce you to some of our restaurant owners over there."

"Hey, now." My grandfather glared. "Keep your hands off my woman, buddy. Prince or no prince, my Maggie isn't going anywhere without me."

"Yes, sir!" Nicholas raised his hands. "I promise, I'd take you both."

We all fell silent for a few minutes as the food moved around the table. I snuck a couple of peeks at Nicky as we ate. Ten years had definitely been kind to him. He actually looked better here, in person, than he did in the pictures I'd seen. There was something broader and more magnetic about his presence. Or maybe that was just me, bringing my old crush vibes back to life.

The sleeves of his white dress shirt didn't do much to disguise the muscles in his arms. I wondered if they came from hours at some hoity-toity gym. Most of the guys I knew at Grant earned their bulk through hours of labor, in the fields or the gardens or with the livestock they raised. I couldn't imagine Prince Nicholas using a shovel to move compost and manure or a fork for turning over the earth.

Still, he didn't seem too polished or glossy. I tried to picture him in the greenhouse or tromping around the gardens with me, and I couldn't quite get there.

"What exactly are you studying in grad school, Ky?" As if picking up on my thoughts, Nicky smiled at me as he cut into the chicken breast Mrs. Muller had set onto his plate. "Biology, you said?"

"Bio was my major in undergrad," I corrected. "My masters will be in sustainable crops and farming practices."

"Which fits in nicely with her future employment." Handsome winked at me. "One of the changes we've made in the last five years is that we've acquired our own small farms and orchards for sourcing fruits and vegetables. It makes sense both economically and ecologically. Kyra's going to help us make those new properties more efficient and sustainable. More healthy crops and less food in landfills."

"That sounds interesting." Nicky leaned back in his chair, studying me. "Maybe I'll kidnap you, too. I can think of quite a few people in England who'd like to hear more—and others who might not like it, but need to listen."

"Tell him about your study, sweetie." Honey nudged me, but before I could say anything, she launched into her own explanation. "Kyra did research into something called intentional non-interventionism. She's conducting her own experiments and studies for a research paper. It's fascinating."

"Nothing like a grandmother to give something a big build-up," I remarked dryly. "Honey, you're going to go with me to present my paper to the advising faculty, right? I think I'll need your enthusiasm to help sell it."

Honey laughed. "I have confidence that it will stand on its own merits, sweetie. Now explain it to Nicky."

Nicky rested his elbows on the edge of the table and gazed at me, interest and amusement in his eyes. "Yes, tell me all about this. Slowly and in plain English, please, so I can follow along."

I gave a little shake of my head. "Don't try to play the

dumb royal card, Nicky. I remember you as being a smarty-pants when we were kids. You were always trying to convince me that you knew more than me about everything, from books to math to . . ." I narrowed my eyes. "Sand castle design."

"How long are you going to hold the grudge about that, Ky? I was right. You were wrong. It was eleven years ago. Get over it already. I have." His teasing smile dared me to argue.

"Ha!" I crossed my arms over my chest. "Easy for you to, uh, *get over it*. You won the contest. And then you gloated for the rest of the summer."

"It wasn't really the rest of the summer. I believe I left Florida two days later."

The corner of my mouth curled up. "It just felt like it to me, I guess. Also, that was the first thing you brought up the next summer, as soon as you got there. You never let me live it down."

"Eleven years, Ky. Eleven. I think it's time to let it go. Surely you've had other more important things happen to you in that time. Right?" He was laughing at me, and the old rivalry I'd felt from our childhood sprang to life inside my chest. Ten-year-old Kyra was dying to come out and throw down.

I drew in a deep, calming breath. I wasn't going to let him goad me into immaturity. "Definitely. We'll let bygones be bygones."

He cocked his head, and I thought I might have surprised him a little. "You were about to tell me about your project."

"Yes." I folded my hands on the table and willed my focus to what consumed all of my attention these days. I could talk about the research for hours, but I'd been working on coming up with sound bites that could explain what I was doing without boring the listeners. It was crucial to be able to share the information with potential donors and grant sponsors if I wanted to continue my project after graduation.

"We're calling this intentional non-interventionism, which sounds complex—but it's really incredibly simple. For generations, farmers and gardeners have been looking for methods to make planting and growing better. We want more efficiency, more return on what we plant, healthier seeds—all of that. It seems to make sense. We've fertilized and pruned and manipulated the soil . . . and the result is that the plants today have become dependent on our processes."

A small frown formed between Nicky's brows. "Okay. Is that a bad thing?"

"In and of itself, no, not exactly. But ultimately, we're destroying the land." I leaned forward, my passion barely banked. "When I was in college, I picked up a book about natural farming by a man named Masanobu Fukuoka. He worked on his father's land in Japan, putting an idea he'd had into practice. He farmed all during World War II, and then later, what he'd learned spread all over the world. And much later—before he died—he was active in trying to reclaim desertified land—you know, land that was once fertile but that has, over time, become a desert. To rehabilitate it and to stop the spread."

Nicky's face lit up. "I've heard of Fukuoka, but I haven't delved too deeply into his work. Exactly how does this relate to your own research?"

I shifted in my chair. Sometimes I got so excited about this that it was hard to sit still. "The idea of natural farming is wonderful, of course. It makes so much sense. But it's not as simple as it sounds. We can't just stop doing what generations of farmers have been implementing for hundreds of years."

"Why not? Why can't we let things happen naturally?" Nicky rested his chin on his hand. "I thought that was the point."

"It is—but it doesn't work that way. Not exactly. What Fukuoka discovered was that the plants had become dependent on our intervention. They don't remember how to grow and thrive without it anymore."

Handsome was watching me, his eyes warm with pride. "Give him the animal analogy. That was what made it click for me."

I nodded and turned my attention back to Nicky. "Think of plants that have been carefully cultivated for centuries as domesticated animals. Like dogs. Once upon a time, dogs were wild. They lived apart from humans and were capable of fending for themselves—they could hunt and protect themselves. But you couldn't take a thoroughly domesticated animal now, toss it back into the wild and expect it to behave exactly like its undomesticated counterpart, could you? Instinct is there, yes, but in so many cases, it's been trained out. When wild animals have to be brought into captivity for whatever reason, the humans interacting with them try not to let those animals become dependent on them, or else they have trouble making the transition back into their habitat." I sat back, lowering my hands to the table with an audible thwack. "It's the same way with plants. If they've been trained to be dependent on us, they don't remember how to grow on their own."

"But how do we untrain them?" Nicky was watching me closely.

"That's what my research is all about—finding new methods to *not* intervene, to be intentional about non-intervention.

We have to go back and teach the plants how to reclaim their ability to thrive without our help."

"And you have, what, greenhouses? Fields? Filled with plants in training?" He raised one eyebrow.

"I have a field, yes. Two of them, actually. No greenhouses—I mean, not for this project. I use greenhouses for other things. Like growing vegetables early in the season, especially in Maine, where the temps aren't exactly cooperative this time of year."

"Can I see?"

I stared at him, not quite understanding. "I'm sorry?"

"Your fields, where you're doing your experiments. I want to see them."

"Why?"

"Why what?"

"Why do you want to see them?" I laid my fork on my plate and slid my chair back a little.

"Kyra, don't be silly. You should take Nicky over there and let him see what you're up to. He'd find it interesting."

"I doubt it." I was feeling slightly ganged-up on. "It's not—it's just dirt and plants. Trees. It's unorganized and messy. It's not the kind of place. . ." My voice trailed off.

"Not the kind of place I'd enjoy? You mean because I'm a prince?" Nicholas skewered me with a cool stare. "Because I don't like to get my hands dirty?"

"No." *Yes.* "Because it wouldn't mean anything to you if you're not involved in the research. My best friend is my roommate Shelby, and I haven't dragged her down there, because she's not part of the project."

"You took me to see it," Honey pointed out helpfully. "And I'm not part of it, either."

"You're my grandmother. You had to be nice about it." I rolled my eyes.

"I'm your friend, aren't I? Maybe your oldest friend. Shouldn't that give me field-viewing status?"

I snorted. "You were a summer friend who I used to see for three weeks once a year. And I haven't seen you or heard from you in over ten years, so no, that means nothing to me."

"Kyra." Handsome shook his head. "Take him over there. Why are you being so stubborn?"

"Stubborn is what Ky does best." Nicholas held my eyes, challenging me to argue. "But seriously, I'd be very grateful if you let me see what you're doing. Believe it or not, the idea of natural farming dovetails with my work. Maybe I'll learn something I could bring back to England with me."

"All right. Fine." I couldn't think of any other logical reason to tell him that he couldn't come to the garden. I also wasn't exactly sure why I was so resistant to the idea, except that I was afraid seeing more of Nicky might be dangerous to my emotional equilibrium. It wasn't likely that we were going to revive our old friendship—we were different people who lived in worlds that couldn't be any further apart. The last thing I needed was to forget that fact. "But you have to be subtle about it. I have other people involved in this project who are usually hanging around the fields, and then there are students working on their own stuff in other plots. So be cool. Don't show up with an entourage or a motorcade. Oh, and just . . . wear regular-people clothes, okay? Don't get all duded-up."

"Duded up?" One of his eyebrows quirked up as he stared at me. "What the hell is that supposed to mean?"

I flipped my hands over. "You know. Like what you're

dressed in now. That's not appropriate attire for walking around in the mud and muck."

"Ah." Nicky nodded at me thoughtfully. "I'll tell my valet to set out my best dungarees."

My face must've reflected my dismay, because he erupted in laughter. "I'm joking, Kyra. I don't have a valet. And I know what jeans are. Don't look so alarmed. I promise, I'll do my best not to embarrass you."

"Yeah, sure." My voice reflected my skepticism.

"Is anyone ready for dessert?" Mrs. Muller poked her head into the dining room. "I have a pie and ice cream ready to bring in."

"Perfect timing, Jeannette." Honey sat back, her gaze moving between Nicky and me. "I think pie is just what we need."

I was thinking that something stronger would've been more helpful—maybe tequila—but I forced a smile as I handed the housekeeper my plate.

One day. One quick visit to my field. And then, after that, I could go back to forgetting Nicholas Windsor.

CHAPTER Four

"HEY, KYRA." ED SCOTT, MY PROJECT PARTNER, WAS squatting alongside a plot of turned soil, from which small green seedlings were poking their sweet little heads. He glanced up as I approached. "Is it just me, or is there some spring in the air today?"

I laughed a little. "Spoken like a true New Englander, Ed. It's just barely forty degrees. In Florida, this would be considered winter weather."

He stared at me from under the brim of his Boston Red Sox cap. "Feels like spring. No snow on the ground. Sun's shining, and the sky is blue. Doesn't seem like winter anymore."

Sometimes, teasing was lost on guys like Ed. "Yeah, guess you're right." I dropped to my haunches. "What're you working on?"

"More soil samples. I'm planning to put together the preliminary report on the control field this weekend, so I want to make sure we have accurate numbers on the minerals and nutrients."

"Good thinking. I'll pull a few on the natural farming plot tomorrow." Scooping up a fistful of the rich black dirt, I let it sift through my fingers. "And we start the second wave of planting on Monday. Will you think I'm a total geek if I admit I'm a little nervous about that?"

"Nah. It's exciting." Ed smiled briefly. "And this is your baby. Your idea. You want everything to go well."

"Yeah, I do." I stood up and wiped my hands on the worn denim covering my thighs. "Ed, have you given much thought about what you'll be doing after graduation?"

One of his shoulders lifted in an eloquent statement. "Not too much. I'd like to go for my doctorate, but I don't think I could handle those student loans on top of what I already have."

"Oh. Yeah, I get it." I did understand, even if I felt a pang of guilt. I was well aware that I was damned lucky that my grandparents had underwritten my education. I had the kind of freedom few of my classmates did. There wasn't any pressure for me to take a job that I might not like but that would pay the bills.

"Probably have to hope for an offer from one of the big companies, for a few years at least." One side of his mouth twisted up. "Does that make me a sell-out, d'you think?"

"No. It means you'll do what you have to do, even if it's just for a little while. You can always keep up with the stuff you enjoy more on the side." I drew a line in the dirt with the toe of my boot. "Or maybe something else will come up, and you won't have to make that decision."

"I guess. Maybe." Ed sounded doubtful. "There just aren't that many opportunities for people with our degree. Not yet, anyway." He rose to stand next to me and squinted over my shoulder. "Who's that coming over here?"

I turned to follow the direction of his gaze, and my stomach dropped. I couldn't make out the face, but I recognized the easy gait and the build. "Oh. Oh, um, I ran into an old friend last night, someone I hadn't seen a long time. I told him a little bit about what we're doing here, and he asked if he could stop by to check it out. He won't be staying long."

"Okay." Ed brushed off his hands. "I'm going to get back to work. Yell if you need me."

"Sure. Thanks." I stepped over to the path of packed dirt and made my way toward the far edge of the field. I wasn't sure whether I was relieved that Nicky was here or annoyed that he'd remembered to come.

The night before, he'd changed the subject as we ate the pie, and I'd begun to hope that maybe he'd just been messing with me, getting a rise out of me, or maybe pretending to be interested in my work. I'd tried not to be disappointed about something I'd never really wanted anyway.

And then as I was leaving, lingering just inside the door to hug Honey and Handsome, Nicky, who was staying with my grandparents at their house, held out one hand, palm up.

"Give me your phone."

I frowned. "Why?"

Nicky wiggled his fingers. "I want to put my number into your phone so that you can send me the address for your garden. What time will you be there tomorrow?"

I tilted my head. "How do you know I'll be at the fields tomorrow? Maybe I don't go every day."

"But you will be, won't you? So give me the address and tell me the time. I'll be there in the proper clothing."

Part of me wanted to argue so that I could avoid seeing Nicky again. It had been a lovely surprise this evening, and I wasn't going to give my grandparents a hard time for arranging the dinner, but the truth was that I'd enjoyed myself too much with him. I'd remembered all too clearly how much fun we'd had as kids. I'd liked him all over again, and this time, I understood with perfect clarity why nothing real or lasting could ever happen between us.

Still, I knew that Honey expected me to behave myself. She'd raised me better. Swallowing a sigh, I'd laid my phone in Nicky's hand and let him punch in the numbers.

"Promise you'll text me the info?" He'd passed it back to me with a twinkle in his eye.

"Do you doubt my word, Nicky? If I say I'm going to do something, I will do it." To make my point, I'd tapped in the address. "I plan on being there between seven and eight. That's AM, you know."

He'd only smiled. "Luckily, I'm an early riser. See you there, Ky."

"Beautiful morning," he called now as he approached me.

"Spring is in the air," I replied, thinking of Ed's assertion with amusement.

Nicky squinted and gazed up at the sky. "Not sure I'd go that far."

"I know. I was joking. The locals up here don't seem to get my weather humor." I rested my hands on my hips. "I wasn't sure you were serious about coming today."

His lips curved into the ghost of a smile. "I always keep my promises, Ky. I want to see what you're working on here. Your enthusiasm last night was contagious."

"Sure, it was." I shook my head. "Seriously, Nicky. I appreciate that you're trying to be nice, but whatever my grandparents might have told you, I don't need the validation. I'm very secure about what I do."

"I'm not here out of a need to make you feel good, Kyra, nor am I here because your grandparents pressured me. I honestly want to find out more about your work, and—" He paused and shrugged. "I wanted the chance to spend a little more time with you."

My heart skipped a few beats, and I had to tell it sternly to settle down. "That's sweet."

"Not really. It's true."

I had no idea how to answer that. "Well . . . okay. Let me show you around here. What there is to show anyway."

"Perfect." Nicky reached into the pocket of his jeans and pulled out sunglasses, which he slid onto his face. "I'm at your mercy."

I had a sudden flash of having this man at my mercy in a totally different situation and had to cough to bring myself back to reality as we wandered over the rich black dirt.

"Over here is the control plot. We have tomato and pepper plants in the first rows."

"Is it a little early for those?" Nicky leaned down to run one fingertip over a bright green leaf.

"No, this is the right time. We plant, and we pray there's not another long freeze. One night or two that happen sporadically are fine, but nothing prolonged." I watched Nicholas walk down the rows, trying not to notice how well the worn jeans fit his ass. My fingers curled just a little, and I wondered how that backside would feel in them.

"And the trees over here?" He pointed to the far end of the field. "Are they part of your experiment, too?"

"Yes. We know more about how natural farming works with trees, because the results are much clearer. Pruning, for example, is a huge intervention that changes how trees grow.

Once they've been pruned, they can't thrive without it."

"Ah." Nicky nodded, rubbing his jaw. "Last night, you called what you're doing intentional non-intervention. If pruning is an intervention—and you say it's a big one—what else is there?"

"Soil enhancement. Fertilization. Even irrigation, which is probably the oldest form of intervention we know. Here, in our control plot, we follow the traditional guidelines. We add nutrients to the soil, and we use some organic pest deterrents. We try to keep things as non-chemical as possible, but we're definitely intervening."

"And on the other plot?" I couldn't see his eyes, but his voice sounded as though he was interested. "What do you do there?"

"Pretty much nothing." I led him past the trees and down the path until we reached the experimental section. "I chose this particular plot because it's lain fallow for over five years, with no fertilization or supplemental minerals. We turned the ground with a broad fork and planted the seeds. Since then, we've only observed. I'll be running some soil tests in the next few days to verify that nothing has been manipulated, but that doesn't affect the plants."

"What about insects and other outside threats—animals and so on?"

I pointed to the far corner of the wide field. "We have fences all around as well as some sonic deterrents. It doesn't keep everything out, but it does help. We also plant onions and garlic on the perimeters of each plot to try to deter the rabbits."

"But not, I would think, the bugs." Nicky squatted to examine one of the pepper plants.

"No," I agreed. "We've planted basil, thyme and sage in alternating rows with the tomatoes and peppers. They attract insects that prey on the destructive bugs."

"Trap cropping?" He grinned up at me.

"Yes." I smiled back, a rush of pleasure sweeping over me. "Look at you, knowing your stuff."

"Full disclosure?" Nicky stood up next to me. He was closer than I expected. "I've been researching new farming techniques for the last year. I'd heard bits about the natural farming, but I haven't seen it in action—and what you're doing is more extreme than anything I'd imagined."

I tilted my head and nudged my sunglasses down my nose to stare at him. "Why have you been researching farming techniques and why didn't you say more last night? You let me think . . ." I stopped.

"I let you think what you were ready to believe anyway, that I'm the guy you read about in magazines—"

"I don't read about you in magazines. I don't read magazines." I crossed my arms. It was true. I didn't actually *read* the articles. I just looked at the covers. Closely.

"All right. Still, you can't deny that you made assumptions about me. And since I don't think you could have possibly based that opinion on the boy you knew when I was only sixteen, I have to wonder how and why you came to the conclusion that I'm some shallow idiot."

"I . . ." I didn't have a good answer to that question. "I shouldn't have assumed anything. You never acted like a spoiled brat when we were kids. You were always the sweetest and most generous boy I knew."

He chuckled. "Are you only saying that because I shamed you into it? Because I made you feel bad for not expecting more of me?"

"No." I rocked back on the worn heels of my boots. "I said it because it's true. You were never anything but a good friend to me. You didn't make me feel like a baby, ever, even though I was younger than you. And if you've been researching farming, you must have a good reason."

"I do." He turned away from me, his eyes scanning the fields around us. "This is real, you know? The soil. The plants . . . all of it is real and reliable. It's one of the reasons I like the work. But there's more." He swiveled his head and slipped off his sunglasses. "I want to tell you about it."

I smiled, fissures of pleasure zinging up my middle. There was no way I could help myself. Nicky sounded so much like the boy I'd known ten years ago.

"I want to hear about it."

"Good. Excellent." He jammed his hands into his pockets. "Have dinner with me tonight."

"What?" Taken by surprise, I stood there with my mouth gaping. "Tonight?"

"Yes, tonight. I've got a lunch meeting in Bangor, so I'm spending the night at a hotel there. I have a suite. Come have dinner with me there."

"No." I took a step backwards, away from him. "I couldn't do that."

"Why not?" Nicky stepped forward. He wasn't letting me evade him. "I want to talk to you. I want to get to know you again, Ky. Come to my hotel, and I'll have dinner sent up for us. It'll be just the two of us."

I couldn't catch my breath. "Nicky . . ."

"Do you know that no one calls me that anymore?" Reaching out, he laid his hand on my arm. "Not anyone. Back when we knew each other, that was my name. It was how my family knew me. But then they stopped. Now they all call me Nicholas. When you say my name, it reminds me of those summers and the way we used to be."

I hunched my shoulders, wrapping my arms around my middle. "But that was a long time ago, and we're not kids anymore. I can't eat dinner with you in your hotel room, Nicky. What if someone saw me?"

He winced, and I felt so horrible, I rished to explain myself.

"I didn't mean it that way. I didn't mean it about me. I only was saying if anyone saw me going into your room, they might wonder why you're spending time with someone like me."

Nicky was silent for a moment, his cheek twitching a little. "Kyra, first of all, no one's going to know who you're coming to see. I don't have people watching my every move." He paused. "That's not really true, because I have security, but I mean, there're no photographers or anything. Not on a trip like this. And even if there were, I wouldn't care. I don't go around worrying about what people think of me. That would be a full-time job, and it would likely drive me insane."

"But—" I was yet to be convinced that this was a good idea.

"But nothing. Come to the hotel. We'll eat and we'll talk and then you'll go home. I'm not inviting you with plans for seduction in mind. I promise. We were always friends, weren't we? Why can't we be friends still? Or again?"

I tossed up my hands. "I didn't think you were planning to seduce me, Nicky. Good God, I'm not stupid. I'm just not sure it's a good idea."

"If you can't give me any reason better than that to say no, I think you're going to have to say yes. I'm at The Charles Inn. My suite is 870. I'll order dinner for seven o'clock, all right?"

"Nicky." I shook my head, but then he smiled at me, his lips turning up slowly as his eyes went warm and promising.

"C'mon, Ky. We'll talk farms and dirt and techniques and plants, and you'll have such a good time, you'll forget you had second thoughts. I promise."

I heaved a deep sigh of defeat. "Fine. Fine! I'll go eat with you. But I'm not staying long. I have an early class tomorrow morning, and I hate driving in the dark."

"Do you want me to have a car sent so that you don't have to drive?" He frowned.

"Is that supposed to be a joke? Like last night, when you said you had a valet?" I didn't want to jump to any more conclusions.

"No, of course not. I don't have a valet, but I can arrange a ride for you. That's not so weird, is it? Don't people do that? I could send a town car to pick you up."

"I guess so." No one I knew did that, but then again, it wasn't difficult to find cars for hire these days. "But no, thanks. I'll be fine to drive myself home, as long as I don't have to leave too late."

"I'll have you back home before the clock strikes midnight, Cinderella." Nicky winked at me.

"Thanks, but I'm not fairy tale material. If I were anyone in that story, I'd probably end up as one of the mice who get zapped into coach drivers by the fairy godmother. That's definitely more my speed."

"Oh, Ky." Nicky laughed. "You are the least mousy woman I've ever known."

"You don't know that. You knew me years ago, but maybe I've lost my mojo since then. Maybe I'm ridiculously shy and quiet, and I sit at home binge-watching *The Gilmore Girls* every night."

"The what girls?"

"American television." I shook my head impatiently. "My point is that you really have no idea who I am anymore."

"That's why I want you to eat with me tonight, so we can get reacquainted. Then, if you decide I'm not worth your time and attention, or I find out you've gotten boring, we can walk away. No hard feelings. How about that?"

"All right. I'll see you at seven. With no expectations."

"Absolutely none. Zero." Nicky replaced his dark glasses, and I couldn't see his eyes anymore. "You have my number. Text me if anything comes up, but I don't expect it will, do you?"

I shook my head.

"Good." Bending, he brushed his lips over my cheek in a chaste kiss goodbye. He barely touched me, but it was the closest we'd been since that night on the beach when he'd taken my breath away. I felt a little dizzy, but apparently, Nicky wasn't similarly affected, since he strode down the path toward the small clearing where our cars were parked.

I was so focused on watching him leave that I didn't hear Ed approach from the other side of the field.

"Did your . . . uh, friend like our work?"

"Hmmmm?" I glanced at him, scowling. "Oh. Yes, I think he did."

"Does he go to Grant?"

I barked out a laugh. "No, he's not from around here at all."

"Ah." Ed rubbed the back of his neck. "He just looked familiar, is all. I feel like I've seen him before, so I thought maybe it was around campus. Or town."

"I doubt it." I didn't think Ed was secretly pouring over the kind of celebrity magazines that featured Britain's Prince Nicholas on the covers, but there was no escaping the pervasive media coverage of the royal family, even over here, even in the wilds of Maine. While my classmate probably wouldn't be able to put his finger on exactly who the handsome visitor to our experimental fields was, something was dinging in his consciousness.

"Huh." He lifted one shoulder, giving up. "You have a little more time, or you heading out now? I was thinking of measuring the trees on the control plot, and I could use a hand."

"Sure. I have a few minutes." I trudged behind Ed and tried to push from my mind the sheer terror I was feeling over the prospect of having dinner alone with Nicky.

Chapter Five

The Charles Inn was not a fancy hotel by most of the world's standards, but in Bangor, Maine, it was considered pretty dang ritzy. That was an actual phrase I'd heard one of my professors use about the Inn, and it made me smile as I walked through the low-ceilinged lobby with its overstuffed leather chairs and genteel worn tables. No chandeliers or glitz here. It was classic New England understated elegance.

There were a few small groups in the lobby bar, but otherwise, everything was quiet, which didn't surprise me for a midweek night. I noticed a couple of men sitting in chairs near the elevator, and by the way their eyes tracked me, I assumed they were part of Nicky's security detail. I had vague memories of the men and women Nicky had called his 'police people' when we were kids in Florida. They'd never been intrusive, but I'd often been aware of their presence. I could remember Honey and Handsome talking about them, too, with Nicky's grandmother.

Now, the two men gave no indication of surprise as I pushed the button and waited for the elevator doors to open. No one asked me where I was going, and I wondered if Nicky had let them know to expect me.

I stepped into the car and stood stiffly as it rose with a groan, stopping finally on the eighth floor. I didn't know what the other levels were like, but here, there were not many doors. It wasn't hard to find 870. As I raised my hand to knock, the knob turned, and the door swung wide.

"Hi, Ky."

Nicky was in jeans again, but these were different. The denim was so faded as to be nearly white, and I could tell it was soft as butter. The pants were slung low on his narrow hips, and the gray T-shirt he wore with them hugged his torso like a besotted lover. The arms that were revealed by the short sleeves on that tee were muscled and tanned. My fingers rose to my chin, just to make sure I wasn't drooling.

"Come in. Dinner hasn't been brought up yet, but it should be here shortly." He laid one hand on my back, between my shoulder blades, guiding me through the doorway and shutting the large oak door behind us. Glancing down, I saw that his feet were bare, which was strangely yet completely erotic.

The suite wasn't any fancier than the rest of the hotel. The room we were in was small, with a love seat and an armchair around a coffee table. Just beyond the connecting door, a huge four poster bed dominated the main space. I spied a suitcase on one of those wooden folding racks and a pair of shoes beneath it.

The whole scene was somehow strangely normal. I didn't know what I'd expected, but it wasn't this.

"I wasn't sure exactly what to order for you." Nicky was standing back, his eyes steady on me, watching me take it all in. "I tried to remember what you liked to eat when we were kids, and all I came up with were pizza and hamburgers. We used to eat them just about every day for lunch, do you remember?"

"Of course I do." I braced my hands on the back of the armchair. "They're still my favorite foods. Those, and the hot dogs we roasted over the open fire in your grandmother's garden."

"I'd forgotten those. You ate yours slathered in mustard." He wrinkled his nose.

"Mmmmm. That's how it's best. I still eat it that way."

Nicky chuckled. "Unfortunately, those were not on the menu here. I decided to go with the filet, since that was the most highly recommended. I hope that was all right."

"I love steak." I didn't know what else to say. Being tongue tied wasn't usually one of my problems, but then again, I also didn't spend much time with men who happened to be princes.

"You're nervous." He frowned. "Kyra, why are you nervous?"

My response was a knee-jerk reaction. "I'm not nervous."

"Oh, okay." He shoved his hands into his back pockets. "Then there's another reason your fingers are digging into the imitation leather of that chair."

I eased my grip. "Is it really imitation leather? Huh. And here I thought royalty commanded the real stuff."

Nicky shrugged. "I actually have no idea. Maybe it is real." He hesitated. "Is that what's spooking you, Ky? The whole . . . royal thing? I joked about it before, this morning at your gardens, but is that really bothering you?"

I tried to laugh it off, but even to my own ears, I sounded phony. "Should it? I mean, is there some kind of protocol

I'm not observing? Something I should be doing? I saw two guys downstairs, and they didn't quite fit in. I assume they're your bodyguards. Or whatever you call them. And when I saw them, I wondered if I was expected to . . . I don't know. Bow to you? Call you sir? Like, would they notice if I did the wrong thing?"

"Kyra, no." Nicky stepped closer to me and took both of my hands in his. "First of all, the protocol shit is more hype than it is reality. Aside from the Queen, the rest of us don't expect it. We don't need it. None of my friends call me sir—they'd laugh themselves sick if I told them I wanted that. No one bows. Well, except at very formal events, like state dinners or that kind of thing. Second, you're American, which means none of it would apply to you anyway. You fought a war a couple of centuries ago to earn the right to ignore it."

I nodded. "Okay, then. So no bowing or curtsying or anything like that, right? And it's all right if I call you Nicholas?"

"No." Releasing one of my hands, he tilted up my chin with his fingers. "I'd rather have you call me Nicky. It reminds me of everything that is real and solid when you do."

I stared into those warm blue eyes, and for the twinkling of a second, I saw something that made my heart pound hard. But before I could act on it, before I could move closer to him as my body was eager to do, there was a knock at the door behind me.

"Room service!"

The spell broken, Nicky dropped his hands and exhaled. "Dinner is served, I guess." He moved around me to open the door, and I stepped back to get out of the way as the attendant wheeled in the cart. I noticed that one of the men from the lobby stood next to the door, watchful as the teenaged girl navigated the table. His eyes flickered up to meet mine briefly, but there was no expression there. I could've been a sofa or a painting on the wall for all of the interest he demonstrated.

Nicky chatted with the girl while she uncovered plates and laid out the food. She kept glancing at him, and there was no doubt in my mind that she knew exactly who he was. Still, she kept her voice casual and her words light. I was envious of her ability to pretend she wasn't making small talk with a prince.

She cast me a long, appraising look, her eyes wandering down over the plain black long-sleeved shirt I was wearing with my jeans. Apparently, she didn't find me worthy of curiosity because she turned her attention back to Nicky.

"Is there anything else I can get you?" She smiled at him, and I could see that although she was hiding it pretty well, she was still dazzled. It wasn't surprising; how often did any celebrity, let alone a member of the royal family, come around Bangor?

"No, thanks. I think we're all set." When she didn't leave, he cleared his throat, adding, "Ah, Matthew will take care of you. Thanks again."

The guard held out his hand. "Right this way, miss."

"Oh." Frowning, she allowed herself to be led into the corridor, while the security guard—Matthew, I guessed—shut the door behind them.

"Well, that was slick." I smirked at Nicky. "I take it you don't handle tips and gratuities?"

He rolled his eyes, and his cheeks went slightly red. "Sometimes I do—I mean, I do carry money. But when I'm on official trips, I don't. This one is sort of a little of each. I'm making connections for both of the organizations I represent, and I'm also going to represent the Queen at a few luncheons in Canada next week. So—yeah, Matthew handles tipping." He reached down to fiddle with the linen napkin on the table.

"Does that embarrass you?" I cocked my head. "Having someone else take care of things like that? Being who you are?"

"It doesn't usually." He shook his head. "I'm generally very comfortable in my own skin, Ky. I am who I am—for better or for worse. I don't ask for special treatment. I can usually get around without anyone taking too much notice of me. But if who I am—who my family is—freaks you out, then—yeah, I guess it does embarrass me, a little. Or at least it makes me uncomfortable."

"I'm not freaked out." I stared down at the set table between us. "I guess . . . I'm not sure why I'm here or why you wanted me to come. If it's because you want to talk about farming and food and sustainability, then I'm fine. I can do that all day long. Or if it's that you want to be nice to me because we were friends when we were kids—okay. It's not necessary, but okay."

He ran his hand through his hair. "I thought I was clear this morning. Yes, I want to talk about food and farming. But I also want to get to know you again—partly because we were friends before, but I think I'd want to know you now even if I hadn't then. I like you, Kyra. I always have. But now there's something about you that makes me want to know more."

I couldn't decide if that response should calm me or make me even more jittery. He hadn't offered a real answer, but I decided that I wasn't going to get any more out of him just now. "Well, our food's getting cold. Let's eat, and you can pick my brain about sustainable farming. I'll promise not to be nervous, and you can relax about being royal. We'll just enjoy ourselves." I dragged the armchair around to face the table.

Nicky's smile stretched across his face, and he came over to help me with my chair. "I can live with that."

". . . so I've been working with business owners and members of our government to change the laws, so that there are incentives for restaurants and groceries to donate their usable, safe leftovers to those who need it. It's reprehensible to me how much food is wasted while people go hungry."

"Absolutely." I nudged aside my empty plate and leaned forward. "That food ends up in landfills, where it's not doing anyone any good. One of my projects in college—when I was an undergrad—was trying to show how to get rid of leftovers in the most planet-friendly way. First, they should go to humans in need—then, if that's not desirable, to animals, and then to compost. The last place food should go is to the dump. Did you know it takes twenty-five years for a head of iceburg lettuce to decompose?"

Nicky's eyes went wide. "There it sits, instead of feeding a hungry child."

"Exactly." I paused. "Except I'm not sure iceburg lettuce is what I'd feed a hungry child, but you know what I mean."

Nicky laughed. "I hated salad when I was a kid, so I totally understand what you're saying. We're learning, too, that teaching people how to eat better and providing them with the food necessary for that change makes a huge difference. We tend to give cheap food to those living in poverty, and that only compounds health problems and sets them up for trouble further down the road."

"Do you have community garden space available? I've read that giving people ownership over their food choices by letting them grow vegetables has been hugely successful."

"We've got some, and we're working on acquiring more." Nicky nodded. "But all of this is on a small scale so far. That's fine, but eventually, I'd like to see larger farms that can sustain more hungry mouths. That's where your natural farming comes in—along with the idea of reclaiming desertified land. If we could accomplish that, we could take on world hunger—not just what's happening in Britain."

"This is why I get excited about what I'm learning." I sat back in my chair, kicked off my shoes and curled my legs under me. "It could make a real difference in the world."

"Exactly." Nicky grinned at me, and suddenly, we were there—in a moment of complete serendipity and agreement, existing on the same level and speaking the same language. The pull I felt toward him—it was too strong to be simple attraction—was enough to make me go soft and gooey in all the right places. His dark blond hair fell over his forehead, and he brushed it away from his eyes. The flex of his arms as he did it made me want to lick the ridges and kiss every valley. I could almost sense the warmth of his breath over my neck, feel the strength of his hands as they traveled down my body . . .

"Want some dessert?" Nicky rose to his feet, spoiling my perfectly good daydream. "I didn't order anything, but I always keep chocolate on hand when I travel, so I have a few bars in my bag."

"As long as we're solving the world's problems, chocolate can only help." I stretched out my legs to stand, too.

"Could you roll the table to the hallway while I get it? The hotel staff will be by to pick it up shortly."

"Sure." I replaced the covers on the empty plates—the food had been delicious—and lowered the sides before I opened the door to guide the cart out of the room.

"Thanks." Nicky dropped onto the loveseat and patted the cushion next to him. "Have a seat, and I'll share my stash with you."

Giggling, I sat down, too, making sure to keep a safe distance from him. I didn't trust my traitorous lips not to kiss a path up his neck to his mouth without my consent—or his.

"Do you remember when we used to make s'mores with Handsome?" I accepted a square of dark chocolate and popped it into my mouth.

"I do. You used to steal my chocolate even then." He pretended to glower at me.

"I don't remember that." I totally did, but no way was I copping to that. "I was just thinking about how precise you were—with building the graham crackers, the marshmallow and the melted chocolate. It had to be in the exact right order, or you'd get all upset."

"I like things the way they're meant to be." He reached over and tapped me on the tip of my nose. "*You* used to end up covered in chocolate, as I recall."

"Because I hate marshmallows, and so I'd hold onto the chocolate squares until everyone was eating their s'mores, and it would melt in my hands."

"You were adorable, though." He bit into the bar.

"Adorable was so *not* what I was going for in those days. I was hoping for sophisticated and mature." I finished the bar Nicky had given me.

"That would've been tough to pull off with the chocolate moustache you wore."

"Thanks." I sighed. "We had fun back then, didn't we?"

"We did." Nicky settled back into the corner of the loveseat. "I used to look forward to those three weeks all year long."

"Me, too." I traced the seam of my cushion with the tip of one finger. "Until the year you didn't come. I didn't know you weren't going to be there until the end of the summer. I didn't ask anyone, but I heard Honey and your grandmother talking. That was how I found out."

"Yeah." His head dropped onto the back of the sofa. "That year . . . it was insane. Alex was still getting over Grayson dying. She'd been here with Gram, and then at the start of that summer, she decided to come home. I'd had my first year at Eton. I was young and stupid, and I told my father I wanted to travel. He let me go to Australia for two months . . . but the cost was that I had to give up my weeks with Gram."

"I heard that you'd traveled." I turned to my side and curled up my legs again, folding my arm and laying my head on it as I gazed at Nicky. "I knew why you didn't come that summer. But I didn't realize you'd never come again."

"Neither did I." He pressed his lips together. "I planned to come the next year, but . . . you know, things went on. It changed. I fell out of that rhythm of life, you know? I wasn't living on the routine my parents had set up for us years before. I was doing my own thing. By the time I settled down a little more, the chance to go back had passed me by." A shadow of pain crossed his face.

"I'm sorry about your grandmother." I reached over and laid my hand on his knee. "I still miss her. You know, Honey and I had just seen her the weekend before she passed. I was in college, and we'd surprised her, Honey and me. We went to tea at her favorite spot. We talked and laughed and visited . . . she told me old stories. When I left, she kissed my cheek and told me that she loved me. I told her that I was lucky to know her. That I was glad I'd spent my summers with her as a second grandmother. Two days later, Honey called and told me the news."

"She was . . . magnificent, wasn't she?" Nicky smiled, but there was an underlying sadness. "The last few years, I didn't see her as much as I should have. We always think we have all the time in the world, don't we? But we don't."

"It's true."

We were both silent for a few moments, lost in our memories of the past and of a woman with laughing gray eyes and an undying sense of mischief.

"I'm sorry I didn't come back after that summer, Ky." My hand was still on Nicky's knee, and he covered it with his own. "I'm sorry I didn't write to you or try to keep in touch. I wanted to." He paused. "The truth is that I'd spent the entire three weeks of that last summer we were together trying to work up the courage to kiss you. I was furious with myself that it took me until the last night. I kept thinking of what could have been, if I hadn't been such a slacker."

I laughed softly. "We had a good time, regardless. When I think back on those summers, all I remember are the good times. We didn't have any worries or cares, did we? Just the beach and ocean and food and games—and sandcastles." I narrowed my eyes.

"We did. And maybe if I'd kissed you earlier, it would have ruined our fun for that year. I don't know. Still, I had every intention of writing you letters once I got home. I had them all planned out, these romantic pages, saying everything I hadn't had the guts to tell you in person. But then I got back home . . ."

". . . and you forgot me," I finished for him. "I was a distant memory."

"No," Nicky disagreed. "I didn't forget you. I never did. But you became a little fuzzier in my mind. You were two years younger than me, and I was only sixteen. It wasn't like I was going to fly over to see you at school holidays or expect you to come to see me. I figured we'd see how we both felt the next summer."

"The summer that never came." I sighed. "Well, as you said, we were kids. Don't worry, Nicky. I didn't sit around moping over you. I missed you the next year, but I wasn't pining with a broken heart. I got on with life."

"Good to know. I think." Lifting my hand, he held my fingers in his palm, staring down at them. "I have to leave tomorrow morning. I have those engagements in Toronto—the official part of the trip. I'll be busy for the next seven days."

I tried to smile, but I couldn't deny the burn of regret, the disappointment of being left again. That was ridiculous; I knew full well that Nicky had his own busy life, and it didn't mesh at all with mine.

"You'll have fun. I hear the Canadians are a wild bunch."

He snorted. "I'll get through it. But then afterward, I'm coming back here for one more meeting that couldn't be scheduled during this time. It's a lunch thing, and then I don't leave again until the following day. Will you have dinner with me that night?"

Glad anticipation zinged through my heart, but I had to

tamp it down. I couldn't build up hopes and dreams that didn't have a chance. I might not be able to survive their inevitable knocking-down.

"Do you think that's a good idea, Nicky?"

"I absolutely do." He didn't hesitate at all. "I want to see you again, Ky. I'm not done talking with you. I'm not done getting to know you again. I'm not done with you, period." He twined our fingers together. "I'm not sure I want to be done with you."

"You mean, you want us to be friends again?" I had to be clear. If I didn't clarify what Nicky meant, I might be at risk for making huge leaps that would end with me being hurt.

"Of course. I also think maybe I want to explore the idea of us being more than casual friends." He smiled, so suddenly and impishly that I couldn't stop myself from smiling back. "Go on a date with me, Ky."

"A date?" I sat up straighter, tugging my hand back. "Are you crazy?"

He shook his head. "I don't think so. Why is that so shocking to you? Why does it seem to alarm you?"

"Because I'm me, Nicky, and you—you're you. You're not just my old buddy Nicky, who used to be my summer crush. You're Prince Nicholas. People know you. They recognize you. They expect you to date women who are super models or famous actresses or professional athletes or rich business-women. I don't fit those molds."

"I know you don't." He leaned forward to recapture my hand. "It's just one of your many charms."

"You don't understand." I tried to take my hand back again, but this time, he wasn't letting go. "I'm not the kind of girl who boys notice as a rule, Nicky. I'm friends with guys.

I'm their pal. I've had boyfriends, but nothing's been serious. Not ever. I'm the fun girl. I'm the casual girl. That's all great, but it's not the kind of woman who should be dating a prince."

"Don't worry about the kind of woman who should be dating a prince. Think about the type of woman who should be dating *me*." He paused, his eyes going narrow. "Wait a moment. Back up a little bit. Did you say I was your—summer crush?"

"Um, yeah." I shot him a teasing smile. "I kissed you, didn't I? Would I have done that if I wasn't having some pretty intense fourteen-year-old feelings?"

"That kiss . . ." Nicky lifted my hand and brushed his lips over the knuckles. "I thought about that kiss for a long time after."

"Did you?" His admission made me absurdly pleased. "I did, too. I had happily-ever-after scenarios playing in my head for a full month after."

"Only a month?" He quirked an eyebrow. "I'd have thought that kiss might have rated at least a year of fantasy. You wound me, Ky."

"It was my first kiss." I met his eyes, holding mine steady. "It was really the most perfect first kiss any girl could wish to have. But still—I was fourteen, but I was a practical girl. When you didn't write or get in touch, I was smart enough to move on. Or at least to tuck that memory away."

"Your first kiss." His thumb drew mindless circles on the back of my hand. "I didn't remember that."

"Didn't you? I told you that night. And it wouldn't have been hard to tell. I wasn't exactly a font of experience." I rested my head on the cushioned back of the loveseat.

"Nor was I," Nicky retorted. "That wasn't my *first* kiss, but it was among the first. I thought you did pretty well. Now that you say it . . . I remember. But I never would've guessed."

"I was fourteen, dude. And raised by protective parents and grandparents. I didn't just go around kissing any boy."

Nicky turned over my hand and as I watched, my pulse quickening, he pressed his lips into my palm. "I'm honored that I was your first."

I swallowed over the lump rising in my throat. "You were a hard act to follow. Pity poor Steve Callway, who had to be my second. He didn't stand a chance."

"Steve, huh?" Nicky snorted. "Sounds like a loser."

"No, he was nice," I protested. "But I was fifteen and not that interested. He took me by surprise, and I hauled off and hit him. So you definitely got the better response when it came to kissing me."

Nicky tossed back his head, laughing. "You punched a boy who kissed you? Why?"

"Like I said. I was surprised. He didn't ask me first." I lifted a shoulder. "The next time, he knew. He asked, and I didn't hit. It was a much more satisfying experience for both of us."

"Ky?" He played with my fingers, his touch on the sensitive skin between them making me shiver. "If I kiss you, will you slug me?"

I was very still, almost afraid to move. "You'd have to take your chances and find out, I guess."

"The first time . . . I didn't ask permission, did I? But you didn't hit me the way you did, uh, Steve."

"No, you didn't." I gave the barest shake of my head. "And I didn't."

"When I kiss you again, Ky . . . and I plan to do that . . . I won't ask. I'll take you by surprise." A crooked smile curved his mouth. "And I bet you won't punch me."

"You're willing to take that risk?" I smirked. "I'd watch out. I have a mean right hook. Just think how mortifying it would be to have to explain to the press why you have a black eye."

His gaze never leaving my face, Nicky moved across the space that separated us until he was looming over me, one arm braced on either side.

"I'll take my chances." Lowering himself just slightly, he touched his lips to my forehead. "When the time is right—and it's not going to be tonight, so you can relax—but at the right time, you won't even think about swinging at me." He smiled, but his eyes were filled with intense heat. "You won't be able to think about anything but me. I promise you that."

CHAPTER Six

Nicholas: *Have you ever been to Canada?*

Kyra: *Of course. Honey and Handsome have always had their house in Maine. We used to visit and drive up to Montreal all the time.*

Nicholas: *Really? I've never actually been to Quebec.*

Kyra: *Why not? I thought people from your family were always making appearances in Canada.*

Nicholas: *I don't know about always, but yes, we do visit fairly frequently. But not Quebec very often. They don't like us so much there.*

Kyra: *Ohhhhh. You mean, the whole French-English thing? I get it. Well, you should go sometime, when you're not there officially. It's very cool.*

Nicholas: *I'll keep that in mind. What are you doing?*

Kyra: *Right now? I'm writing a report.*

Nicholas: *Are you at home?*

Kyra: *Yep. Sitting in my jammies, curled up on the sofa. Shelby's watching old episodes of Grey's Anatomy, and I'm trying to focus on what I'm doing. Also, I'm having a beer.*

Nicholas: *That whole text raises so many questions. First of all, what are jammies?*

Kyra: *PJ's. Pajamas. Loungewear. Comfy clothes. What I live in when I'm not out in the world.*

Nicholas: *Ah. Something sexy?*

Kyra: *That's an inappropriate question, Prince Nicholas.*

Nicholas: *Uh huh. Answer it anyway.*

Kyra: *Bossy much? But fine. For me, jammies are yoga pants and T-shirt, with a hoodie right now because it's chilly in here. Not at all sexy.*

Nicholas: *I bet you make it look good. Second question: what is Grey's Anatomy?*

Kyra: *TV show about a hospital. Very intense and emotional.*

Nicholas: *Oh, a chick show. All right. Third question: why are you watching television while you're doing schoolwork?*

Kyra: *I do all my work with TV on. And this isn't exactly challenging. It's just a simple planting and growth report. No big deal.*

Nicholas: *Hmmm. Still sounds distracting.*

Kyra: *Or maybe the guy texting is distracting me. Ever think of that?*

Nicholas: *That seems unlikely. Last question: what kind of beer are you drinking?*

Kyra: *Corona with a lime. Yum.*

Nicholas: *Sounds good. I'm sitting in my hotel room with a scotch. One luncheon is over, and then I have a dinner tonight.*

Kyra: *Fun.*

Nicholas: *Not really. But it's my life. I'm looking forward to being back in Maine in five days.*

Kyra: *Why? Because you're excited about the meeting for your organization?*

Nicholas: *No, because I'm excited about having dinner with a beautiful, interesting and intelligent woman.*

Kyra: *And here I thought you were having dinner with me.*

Nicholas: *I am, doofus. You're the beautiful, interesting, intelligent woman.*

Kyra: *Doofus? Where the hell did you hear that word? It doesn't sound very British.*

Nicholas: *Oh, some kid taught me to say that when I used to visit in the summers. She called me that once after a competition on the beach.*

Kyra: *Oh. Huh. She doesn't sound very nice. But I bet she was right about whatever she was saying.*

Nicholas: *Are you saying that I really am a doofus?*

Kyra: *I'm sure you're not. Only that day, maybe you were. A little bit.*

Nicholas: *As much as I'd like to argue that point, I have to go over my speech for tonight. And you need to finish your report. Chat later?*

Kyra: *Yep. Chat later, doofus.*

Kyra: *I had a totally unreal moment today. You told me about your speech the other night, and then today, I was standing in the student commons and they had some fluff news show on the TV. Like celebrity gossip? And there you were. It was bizarre.*

Nicholas: *Ah. Bizarre, as in you laughed, or bizarre as in you were completely freaked out and don't want to see me?*

Kyra: *Bizarre, as in it was a little surreal. It didn't freak me out. And of course I want to see you. I was promised a dinner date.*

Nicholas: *And a dinner date you will have. Three more days. What kind of food do you like to eat? Aside from chocolate and chicken fingers and hot dogs, of course.*

Kyra: *Well, we established that I like steak, too. Hey, do you trust me? There's actually a really cool restaurant not too far from where I live. If a miracle happens and it's warm enough, we could eat outside.*

Nicholas: *I trust you. I told you that I'm willing to take my chances when it comes to you, Ky.*

Kyra: *Oh, the pressure of that trust . . . okay. I'll make a reservation. Does 7 work, or later? Or earlier?*

Nicholas: *7 would be perfect. Make the reservation in your name, if you will, and send the name and address of the restaurant. I know it's a bother, but I have to let my security know where we're going.*

Kyra: *It's not a problem. I'll send it tomorrow morning, once I have the reservation made. <changing subject> I forgot to say before, even though it was bizarre to see you on TV, you looked good. And your speech (what I saw of it) was excellent. Nice job.*

Nicholas: *Thanks. It's not my normal topic, but I wasn't there on my own behalf, so I did my best. Did you happen to see the part where I winked at the camera and gave a thumbs-up? That was for you.*

Kyra: *You did not do that. No way did you do that.*

Kyra: *. . .did you??*

Nicholas: *Of course not. But I had you there for a minute, didn't I?*

Kyra: *No. I never bought it for a minute. But now I'm rolling my eyes at you.*

Nicholas: *This is a picture of a guy who's happy to be boarding a plane and heading back to the states.*

Kyra: *Hey, he's kind of cute. Get his number for me, will ya? ;)*

Nicholas: *He appreciates your compliment. What are you doing?*

Kyra: *Just got home from working in one of the project fields. Not mine, but one of the group projects for a class. It rained for the last day and a half, and the field was completely mud. I was covered from head to toe.*

Nicholas: *Was or are? I'd like a picture of that.*

Kyra: *Was, smartass. I just got out of the shower, and I'm sitting down with a bowl of quinoa. About to watch a movie with Shelby.*

Nicholas: *Are you in your—what did you call them? Your jammies?*

Kyra: *You know it, dude. Yoga pants, hoodie and my favorite slippers. Hold on.*

Nicholas: *What is that? On your slippers?*

Kyra: *Frogs. Shelby's sister sent us matching pairs for Christmas last year. Aren't they cute?*

Nicholas: *Hmmm. Lovely. They look comfortable.*

Kyra: *They totally are—and warm.*

Nicholas: *Shelby's your roommate, right?*

Kyra: *Roommate, best friend . . . she's it. She's my person. We met when we were freshmen in college down in Florida. Her dad is a professor at the university, and her family adopted me for home-cooked meals and so on.*

Nicholas: *She sounds like a good friend.*

Kyra: *She is. I don't know what I'll do when we graduate—she wants to work in the southwest, and I plan to stick around here. Or go back to Florida. One or the other.*

Nicholas: *What do you plan to—damn, they just called for boarding. Have to run. Will text you tomorrow to confirm for dinner.*

Kyra: *Okay. Safe flight, Nicky. Can't wait to see you tomorrow.*

Chapter Seven

I'd first visited The Meadows shortly after its grand opening. Honey and I had gone there to eat dinner, because she'd read a review of the new restaurant and wanted to check it out. I was excited because our region of Maine had a dearth of farm-to-table eateries, and this one looked promising.

My initial impression of Gav Barrett, the chef and owner, had not been positive. He was a brash New York City transplant who didn't mince words or worry about cultivating friends. But the food was so amazing that I kept going back in spite of him. The more I got to know Gav, I realized that what I'd taken for arrogance was actually passion for getting things right, whether that was a certain dish or the experience of his customers. We'd bonded over a shared love for fresh food, and now he welcomed me as a friend whenever I managed to get over there for a meal.

Still, I was a little nervous about dining at The Meadows with Nicky. While the idea had seemed to be a good one at first, as the day of our date rolled on, I began to worry. After all, Nicky could eat anywhere in the world. He'd been in restaurants I'd only dreamed of enjoying. I hoped he wasn't going to find my choice boring and colloquial. It was one of the many aspects of the upcoming evening that I was agonizing over and second-guessing as I sat on the sofa, waiting for my date to pick me up.

I'd spent an hour trying to figure out what to wear. *An hour*. That was unheard of in my life. I never cared about my clothes. Whatever was handy and easy was what I put on my body. But tonight was different—special. So I'd flipped through the part of my closet that contained what I thought of as Honey clothes—the dresses and outfits that my grandmother would approve of for professional or formal dinners and events. But they all looked too stuffy. I'd been about to concede defeat and pull on my least-scruffy jeans when I'd spotted the tags dangling from something my mother had sent me last month.

I'd been moping about the endless Maine winter and sniveling to Mom about missing Florida. Two days later, I'd received a package that contained a soft cotton dress. It was a black and white floral print and had adorable cap sleeves and a flirty skirt that hit me mid-thigh.

Her note was typical of my mother's relentless optimism.

Kyra~Spring is coming, sweetie. I saw this and although it's not your usual style, it would look perfect on you. Wear on the first day it's warm enough—and keep faith. Winter might be long, but it always ends. Love you, Mom

Today just happened to be that day: the temperature wasn't exactly indicative of summer, but it was close enough—and much warmer than it had been since last September. With a sweater, I could make this work. I wouldn't freeze.

And just maybe, I'd look like the kind of girl who should be eating dinner with Nicky Windsor.

"Hey, I'm leaving!" Shelby sailed around the kitchen doorway and through the living room, halting briefly to stare at me. "Kyra, are you wearing a dress again?"

"Yes." I shifted unhappily on the chair where I'd perched. "I told you that I'm going out tonight."

"Right," she said slowly, frowning. "This is the guy you've been texting with? The one who met you at the garden last week?"

"Uh huh." I kept my eyes down. "He's an old friend. Someone I knew when I was a kid. It's not a big deal."

"Kyra, you dressing up twice in the same month is a big deal. Unless someone died. Which would also of course be a big deal, but in a different way."

"Mmmmm." I tried to sound noncommittal. Nicky hadn't exactly come right out and asked me to keep our reconnection a secret, but I had a hunch that he didn't want me blabbing it around to the world, either.

Plus, I hadn't wanted to tell Shelby about Nicky. Not yet. For now, whatever was between us—whether that was rekindled friendship, a meaningless flirtation or something more—was just ours. I didn't have to explain it to anyone. I didn't have to handle questions that I didn't know how to answer yet. I liked it this way.

"Okay." Shelby shrugged. "You know where I am if you need to talk to me. I'll see you tonight, won't I? You're not going to run off with your secret lover?"

"Oh, please." I snorted. "He's not a secret lover. He's not a lover at all. We're just—"

"Old friends." Shelby nodded. "Right. Well, I'm off to supervise the bio lab. I hope you have more fun than I do—whatever it is you're planning to do tonight."

"Bio lab is a hoot." I tried to subtly shift the subject away from my date. "We always had a good time."

"Yes, but we were not idiot undergrads. I'm fairly certain the ones in this class are seriously trying to develop some kind of biological weapon. They're devious, and they're also stupid. But in an evil way. They're like baby evil geniuses who don't have basic survival skills. I think they're seeing how far they can go before they push me over the edge."

I laughed. "No one said that being a TA was all fun and games, right? Woman up, babe. Go tell those bio babies to toe the line."

"Right. Sure." Shelby sounded hopeless. "And you enjoy your date." She pointed a finger at me. "Tomorrow . . . we're having a chick night, with wine and chips and Katherine Heigl movies. And you, my friend, are going to spill about this man you've been seeing."

"I haven't been *seeing* him." I began to argue with her and then saw the glint in her eyes. "Okay, fine. Chick night. Wine, chips, and spilled beans. It's a date."

She winked at me. "Later, K. Have fun tonight. Hang a sock on the door if I need to turn my head in the morning, so your fella can do the walk of shame in peace."

"Not going to happen!" I yelled, but she was already out the door and jumping into the car.

Once she was gone, I went back to chanting the mantras I'd been saying all day.

This is not a real date. It can't go anywhere. Nicky is a prince. You are you. He's a friend. You can have fun. But he lives in England, and you do not. Keep it light and don't expect anything to come out of this. Live in the moment.

"Live in the moment," I muttered. That's what I was

going to do. I was acting silly with all this nervousness. Nicky was just—Nicky. He wasn't as hot as what I'd built up in my mind. He was just a guy, and the fact that he'd given me my first kiss was why I had this crazy sentimental attachment to him.

A car turned into my driveway, kicking up gravel, and my heart went into overdrive. I jumped to my feet, smoothing the skirt of my dress over my legs, and snatched my small black purse from the coffee table. And then I froze, because I had no clue what to do next. Nicky had texted me earlier, asking for my address and promising to pick me up at six-thirty. But what did that mean, exactly? Was I supposed to wait for him to knock and meet him at the door, or should I go out now, so that he didn't have to leave the car? We lived far enough back from the main road that no one was going to spot him, and our nearest neighbor was too far away to see our house. But maybe he wouldn't want to chance being seen.

Before I could make up my mind, he was at the door. From where I stood, I could just barely make out his profile, the way he shifted from foot to foot as he waited for me. He was wearing a dress shirt—the sleeves rolled up above his wrists and the collar open—with khakis and a pair of brown loafers. His throat worked as he swallowed, and I wondered if it was possible that Nicky was nervous, too.

The chance that he might be gave me the strength to walk to the door and open it. Nicky's eyes met mine, flaring with surprised admiration as he took in my dress and heels.

"Wow." A slow grin spread over his lips. "Look at you. I didn't expect . . ." His voice trailed off.

"Didn't expect what? You didn't think I'd actually put on real clothes to go out to dinner with you?" I tilted my head.

"No, I didn't expect your legs to be so damn perfect." He leaned back a little and made it obvious that he was checking me out more closely. "I remember them from before. That summer, I was always afraid someone would catch me staring at your legs when you were wearing shorts. Or a bathing suit. Or maybe I was afraid you wouldn't notice me doing it."

"I didn't. Not really." Gripping the door knob, I hung on to it as I glanced up at Nicky through my eyelashes. "I hoped, and I dreamed, but I never managed to convince myself that it was real. And then later, when you were gone, I figured I'd been imagining everything."

"You didn't." He reached down to skim the back of his fingers over my cheek. "Ten years ago, Ky, you were cute, and you made me want to kiss you. But now, you're breathtaking. I still want to kiss you. But I'm not sure I want to stop there."

My head spun a little, wondering if he was going to suggest skipping dinner and going right to dessert—which could happen here in my bedroom. I also wondered if I'd have the courage to say no when most of me wanted to feel him, to touch him . . . to taste him.

Before I could wander too far down that trail of thought, Nicky stretched out his hand, offering it to me.

"C'mon, Ky. We better go now, before I give in to my baser instincts and try to convince you to stay in."

I slid my fingers between his, pausing only long enough to shut the door behind me and lock it. As we walked toward his rental car, Nicky tightened his grip and leaned down to brush a kiss over the top of my head.

"I didn't say it well when you opened the door, Kyra, but you look amazing tonight. So beautiful. And full confession . . . part of me did wonder if I'd find you in your jeans and garden boots."

I rolled my eyes, stepping back as he opened the passenger door for me. "I know how to behave, Nicky, and I know how to wear the right clothes. Just because I like sneakers more than stilettos doesn't mean I can't figure out which ones to wear when."

"Never thought you couldn't, sweetheart." One of Nicky's eyebrows waggled at me. "But I wasn't sure you'd deem me worthy of the trouble it would take to lose the jeans for one night."

"If anyone could make me lose my pants, it would be you, Nicky Windsor." The words tumbled out of my mouth before I could stop them, but the expression on his face made my own mortification totally worth it.

"I'm not going to forget that, Ky."

I was certain my cheeks were blazing red. "Let's try our best. Sometimes my mouth engages before my mind can stop it. Shelby says my filter is for crap."

Nicky crossed his arms on the top of the open car door and grinned down at me. "I call that refreshing." He winked at me before he closed the door and rounded the car to take the wheel.

"Refreshing, huh?" I slid him a glance as he pulled the seatbelt around to fasten it and turned the key in the ignition.

"Absolutely. I live my life surrounded by people who say whatever they think I want to hear. There are very few whom I can trust to tell me the truth. I like that you're someone who says what you're thinking." He turned in his seat to look over his shoulder, backing up to pull out of my driveway. "Can you tell me where we're going?"

For the next few minutes, I concentrated on giving Nicky

directions, pointing out turns. Our roads were generally pretty quiet around here; the biggest cause of traffic jams in this part of Maine was a moose who wouldn't move off the road. Consequently, when I realized that a small black car was mimicking our turns and lane changes, I didn't think I was being paranoid.

"Nicky, that Ford is tailing us."

He glanced in the rearview window. "Mmmmm. And doing a good job of it, too." One corner of his mouth tipped up. "It's my policeman, Ky. I talked security into letting us drive alone to the restaurant, but I can't escape them altogether." His hands tightened on the wheel just slightly. "It's part of the package that comes with spending time with me. Sorry."

"Don't apologize." I reached over the console and touched the back of his hand. "I'm just relieved it's not some evil villain who's after you—and me by extension."

Nicky chuckled. "No evil villains. Just a vigilant group of men and women who stick with me whether I like it or not."

"Do you ever try to ditch your guards?"

He shrugged. "Not anymore. I did when I was younger. And then . . . Grayson died. Suddenly, it wasn't fun and games anymore, you know? One of Alexandra's policeman was killed trying to protect my sister and her fiancé, and it hit me very hard that these people—they risk their lives every day on the off-chance that some maniac will try to make his name by offing a member of the British royal family. Just because I, personally, have never been in a situation where I was threatened doesn't mean that the sacrifice is any less real. That's why I try to respect their work now. I don't play games. At times, I request a little privacy, and if it seems reasonable, they do their best to accommodate me."

"Hmmm." I glanced backward at the car that was still following us at a safe distance. "And tonight, it was reasonable?"

"Sure." He nodded. "I hate to break it to you, Ky, but Maine is pretty remote. I haven't publicized my visit here, and no one's that interested, anyway. That's why they agreed."

"What about at the restaurant?" I had booked us a table for two. I had a mental image of Nicky's policeman squeezing between us as we tried to eat.

"He'll be at another table. When you sent me the name of where we're eating, I sent it to my security. They booked a table for him."

"Oh, okay." I managed a smile. "That works."

"Ky, I know being with me—dating me—it's not the kind of thing most people are used to. There are a lot of complicating factors. It's messy and maddening—and probably, I'm not at all worth the fuss."

"That's not what I was thinking at all." I shook my head. "I just—I wanted to know. I want to do the right thing. I don't want to embarrass you or get you in trouble."

"You couldn't embarrass me, Kyra, and you won't get me into trouble. I can manage that just fine on my own." He shot me a wry glance, and I had to laugh.

"You'll want to slow down and make a right here, into the parking lot. That's the restaurant, the building up on stilts there."

Nicky parked the car, and I noted that the black Ford compact pulled in several spaces away. When I snuck over my shoulder as we walked toward the entrance, I saw a stocky man trailing us at a respectful distance.

"Before long, you almost forget he's there." Nicky took my hand in his and squeezed it. "It sounds horribly rude, but eventually, security fades into the background. You just get on with life, you know?"

"I guess." I couldn't imagine a time when I'd forget there was someone shadowing my every move.

"When it's just the two of us—my policeman and me, I mean—we talk. I don't ignore him. But when I'm with someone else, I try to do just that."

We approached the podium, and I stepped forward. "Hi. We have reservations. It's under Kyra Duncan."

"Sure. Just a sec." The hostess skimmed down a computer screen until she found my name. When she glanced up at us, her professional smile firmly in place, her eyes widened just slightly, and I knew she'd recognized Nicky. For the space of a few moments, I could tell that she was teetering between maintaining her poise and giving into uncontrolled gushing.

"Could we possibly have an outside table, near the edge of the deck?" Nicky smiled and pointed to the far side of the expansive wooden platform. "If that's all right with you, Ky."

"Sure. It's a nice evening." I nodded and lifted my sweater. "Plus, I'm covered if it gets chilly once the sun's set."

I didn't know whether it was her own fortitude or the fact that Nicky and I were acting normal, but the hostess managed to keep herself in check. She picked up two menus and began threading her way between tables. My eyes met Nicky's as we followed her.

"Sometimes, it's helpful when I give people a little space to recover," he murmured. "My sister calls it reasonable deniability—they can convince themselves that I'm not really who they think."

Our table was perfect, and the hostess stepped away once she'd handed over the menus and promised that our server would stop by shortly.

We were both silent for a few seconds, perusing the appetizer offerings. Nicky leaned forward and spoke in a quiet voice.

"Tom is sitting behind you, about four tables back. I just wanted you to know, in case I look over your shoulder from time to time. I'm not staring at another woman." One eyebrow shot up, and his eyes were mischievous.

"Good to know." I inhaled deeply and played with the corner of my napkin. "Not that I could blame you if you were. Looking, I mean. At another woman."

He lost the playful expression and frowned. "What do you mean?"

I lifted one shoulder. "I might do okay dressing up now and then, Nicky, but I'm not the kind of woman people would associate with you. And even though I don't read all of the magazine articles about you or follow social media about your love life, I'm not totally ignorant. I know for a fact that I'm not remotely your type." I kept my eyes focused on the small candle flickering between us, unable to look up at his face. I was afraid I'd see confirmation there.

"Kyra." When I still didn't lift my gaze, Nicky reached across the table and touched my cheek. "Ky. Look at me. What you just said—that's utter nonsense. First of all, half the stories about me in the media are flat-out wrong, completely made up. I haven't even met some of the women whom I'm reported as dating seriously. Others I've only seen socially or professionally. You can't believe what you read. And it's not exactly fair to judge me on those lies."

"I know." I tried to take a deep breath again, but my chest was tight. "I'm not in the least bit insecure, Nicky. Like you said to me the other night—I am who I am. I like me. I'm smart, and I'm capable and I'm strong." I let myself meet his eyes. "But the thing is, I like you, too. So even the strong, confident part of me wants to be someone you'll find attractive. I'm not the kind of woman who changes for a man, even for a man who turns her inside out when he smiles. But I couldn't take being with someone who didn't understand who I am."

"I think I understand who you are." He ran his fingers down my jaw and neck, making me shiver. "At least, I'm beginning to. I think you're still my friend from before. That's the heart of Kyra. That's at your core. The other layers . . . I'm willing to unwrap them, slowly. Like a seed coming to life, becoming a plant. I want to spend time with you and figure that out, and I want you to know who I am, too. Just give us the time and space, will you? I know it won't be easy. I know I'm leaving tomorrow to fly back home, and long-distance relationships are a pain in the ass. I get that. But let's try." He took my hand, folding my fingers into his palm. "Please."

My eyes drifted shut, and I sighed. "I don't think I'm capable of telling you no."

Nicky's soft chuckle held just a hint of triumph. "That's an excellent place to begin."

"I have to compliment you on your choice of restaurant. My meal was delicious." Nicky leaned back in his chair, grinning at me.

"Gav outdid himself, didn't he?" I lifted my napkin and touched it to my chin. "He'll probably come out to say hello. He does it for everyone, so don't worry that he'll make a fuss over you."

"Thanks for keeping me humble, Ky." He craned his neck back, staring up at the black velvet sky. "Look at all those stars. It's amazing how many you can see out here."

"The lack of light pollution makes all the difference," I agreed. "And I'm glad you wanted to sit outside, although it is getting kind of cold now, even with my sweater."

"Are you shivering?" He stood up a little and dragged his chair around the table until it butted against mine. "Come here. I'll keep you warm." He slid one arm around my shoulders and tugged me against his body.

"Or I could wait for the coffee we just ordered." I looked around for the server. "That would help."

"Are you saying you'd rather drink coffee than allow me to help you stave off the cold?" Nicky shook his head. "I'm insulted. Insulted and hurt."

Giving in, I laughed and snuggled closer to him. He really did radiate an enormous amount of body heat. "Nah, on second thought, I think you're better than coffee."

"Of course, I am." He paused a beat. "Although, now that I think of it, coffee and I have a lot in common. We're both strong, hot and . . . and we have the potential to keep you up all night."

My pulse began to stutter, but ignoring it, I cocked my head teasingly. "Oh, really? Hmm. Then I might have to rethink this. Maybe you're not good for me. You know, even though it tastes so good, sometimes when I drink coffee, it makes my heart race."

Nicky drew me closer, until there wasn't a breath of space between our bodies. With two fingers, he cupped my chin as he murmured, "I bet I can make your heart race, too. And I taste even better than coffee." He lowered his face until his lips hovered just above me. "But I promise, I'm very, very good for you."

Before I could answer or protest, he was kissing me, his mouth firm and demanding on mine. My eyes closed, and without hesitation, I opened my lips and stroked my tongue against his.

In that moment, everything else in the world vanished. There wasn't distance or time or space. I was at once the same fourteen-year-old girl dazzled by her first kiss on a Florida beach, and I was me, in the present, in the arms of the same man who was once again weaving his spell over me. I was every age I would ever be, but it didn't matter, because I never wanted to leave him. I never wanted him to stop kissing me, touching me . . . I was drunk with the need surging to life inside of my body.

Everyone around us fell away in a single heartbeat. I didn't care who was sitting nearby, who might be watching or what they might think. There was only Nicky, only me, and only this undeniable heat between us.

When he drew away, it wasn't far. He pressed his forehead against me, his eyes open and staring deep into my soul. His breath brushed over my cheek, and I shivered again.

Nicky smiled. "I thought I was warming you up, but you're still shaking."

I swallowed hard. "Not because I'm cold this time."

"But you didn't punch me. I'm calling that a win."

At my elbow, I heard someone clearing his throat. "I've got your coffee right here. Your server was heading out, and when he told me he was taking it to that pretty girl who talks about dirt all the time, I knew it had to be that crazy Kyra Duncan."

I turned, grinning at the chef. "Gav! I was wondering when you'd get your ass out here to play the gracious host. It's about time."

He leaned down to hug me, his eyes sweeping quickly over Nicky. "So you brought a date tonight, huh?"

I lifted one hand. "I got tired of waiting for you to notice me, Gav. Plus, we all know you don't see anyone but your Solidad, so I didn't stand a chance."

"True. Sad but true!" He laughed. "Tell me now. Was your meal the best thing you've ever eaten? Was it the best thing you've ever put into your mouth?" He winked at me. "I'm talking edible food now, folks. Keep it out of the gutter."

"It was amazing." Nicky extended his hand, keeping his other arm around my shoulders. "I haven't had a meal like that in a very long time."

Gav pressed one hand to his heart. "I'm honored, then."

"Ky tells me that you source all of your food locally." Nicky shifted a bit. "I do a little bit of work with food sustainability. I'd really be interested in talking with you at some point."

Gav's eyebrows rose. "Ohhhhh, so that's how you know our Kyra here? I wondered. That makes sense now."

I scowled at him. "No, that's not how we know each other, Gav. We're old friends. We've known each other for a very long, long time. But thanks for that vote of confidence in me."

The chef's face went bright red. "That's not what I meant, Kyra. But I mean—him. He's . . ." Gav coughed a little. "Now to be honest, I wouldn't have known, but the hostess told me that you were here with—well, she thought, she was pretty sure that he's, um . . ." His eyes flickered to Nicky. "You know. A prince or whatever."

"And there's no way I'd be out on a date with someone who's a prince or whatever?" I knew Gav didn't mean to be insulting, but he was.

"Ky." Nicky spoke up, his voice mild. "I don't think he meant anything."

"Of course, I didn't." Gav laid a hand on my shoulder. "Kyra, the truth is, I don't know this guy, but he's probably not good enough for you. I don't care if he's a prince or a king or a duke. You're a great girl."

And now I felt like an idiot. I blew out a long breath. "I'm sorry, Gav. I didn't mean to jump on you. Can we start over?" I swiveled a little, pointing at Nicky. "Gav, this is my friend Nicholas. We've known each other since we were kids. Nicky, this is my friend Gav. He runs this joint and lets me ramble on about soil and sustainability."

The two men shook hands again, Nicky laughing. "I'd still like to pick your brain some time about your processes here. I'm going back to London tomorrow, but maybe next time I'm visiting?"

Gav nodded. "I think I can do that." He squeezed my shoulder and winked at me. "If Kyra here gives her okay, that is."

I stood up. "Actually, why don't you keep Nicky company for a minute now while I excuse myself to the ladies' room? I need to pull together the tattered shreds of my dignity." I picked up my purse and smiled at the two men as I made my way toward the door that led inside the restaurant.

I'd only gotten a few tables away when movement caught my eye. A woman whose seat was facing my table slid me a furtive, almost guilty glance before she pulled up her menu to hide her face. As I passed, I saw that her cell phone was screen up on the table in front of her.

Instinct kept me moving; I didn't break my stride, even as I wondered if she'd been taking pictures of Nicky. If she was, what could we do? We were in a public place. There weren't any laws about taking pictures of other people unless they were used for illegal purposes.

As I washed my hands and dried them, I reasoned with myself. Even if the lady I'd seen had taken photos, what was she going to do with them? Post them on social media? Sell them to the tabloids? Who would care about Prince Nicholas eating dinner with an old friend?

Still, a twinge of unease followed me back to our table. Gav had disappeared—I was sure he'd returned to the kitchen, as the restaurant was busy—and Nicky rose to pull out my chair for me.

Once I was seated, I told him about the woman and the phone.

Frowning, he withdrew his own cell from his pocket. "I'll let Tom know. He can probably do some discreet looking around and see if anyone is trying to film us. But you're right, Ky. If someone's taking pictures, there's really nothing we can do about it."

I rolled my eyes. "It must drive you crazy, never knowing if someone's snapping a photo when you least expect it. I hate having my picture taken in the best of times."

"Mostly, it's all right. I'm used to it, first of all. This is how my life has always been. They only really get interested in me if I'm . . ." He hesitated. "If my name has been linked with someone else."

"You mean, if you're dating someone," I corrected.

"Yes. But even then, if it's just an ordinary woman in

Britain, someone who's not famous in her own right, they leave me alone. It's the models and the musicians and foreign princesses whom the press loves. I have no idea why."

"A bigger story, I guess." I finished my coffee, running the tip of my tongue over my lips. "I'm finished. Are you ready to go? Suddenly, I don't feel so comfortable sitting here."

"Yes, I'm ready. And I took care of the check while you were in the restroom." Nicky waggled his eyebrows at me. "Paid for it with my own money, and you weren't even here to be impressed by it."

"Next time." I forced a smile, but I really was eager to leave, to be back in the relative privacy of the car.

Neither of us said much until we'd been driving for a little while. I gave Nicky directions for getting back to my house.

"Kyra." He sounded tentative, which was very unlike him. "Ky, I meant what I said before. I'd like to see you again. I don't know exactly when or how, but we can work that out. I know you're going to be busy with your exams at the end of the term, and then . . . are you staying here for the summer? Or will you be back at home?"

I shook my head. "Shelby and I are both staying in Maine. I'll probably visit my parents for a few weeks at some point, but I need to be here to monitor my project plots. Shelby's taking a few summer courses at Grant."

"Would you consider flying over to see me?" In the dark, he reached across to find my hand. "I know it's a long trip, but I'd have a little more time and freedom if you came to me. My schedule is booked for the next few months."

"I guess that's one of the drawbacks of being royal," I observed. "Spontaneity isn't easy."

"No, it's not. Every once in a while, I can manage it, but

I have commitments. I don't like to let anyone down, particularly my family." His thumb rubbed over my knuckles, sending shimmers of lust up my arm. "That's what most people don't get. What I do—it's not because of some ancient loyalty or a misguided sense of importance. It's what we are—who we are. My family understands that the privileges we have come with a price. Service is everything. If I can give back to the world even a small bit of what I've been given, I'm obligated to do that."

I was quiet for a few minutes, digesting all that. "It's kind of like Spiderman, huh? 'With great power comes great responsibility?'"

"Ha." Nicky huffed out a laugh. "Maybe so. You've discovered my super power, Ky. Now you can't tell anyone."

"Your secret's safe with me. Just call me Gwen." I stared out the window into the dark. "Joking aside, I understand what you mean. Handsome and Honey are passionate about their business, not just because of the lifestyle it's given our whole family, but because of what we can give back to our community. To the world. They're paying for my education so that I can be part of that, and even though they'd never force me into working for Honey Bee Juices, I'll do it because it's the right thing. It's part of that responsibility."

"Exactly." He turned the car into my driveway. Behind us, the Ford's headlights shone through the rear window before the vehicle swerved to the left.

"Tom's waiting here until I'm ready to leave," Nicky explained. "He's giving us privacy."

"Oh." I fidgeted in my seat. "That's very accommodating of him." When Nicky stopped the car and switched off the lights, I added, "Do you want to come in? Shelby's home, but

I'm sure she'd be, uh, accommodating, too."

After the briefest hesitation, he shook his head. "I *want* to, but I'm not going to. Not tonight. My flight leaves very early in the morning, and we have to drive back to Bangor tonight. As much as I'd like to meet your Shelby, it'll have to wait until next time."

"She'd probably have a heart attack if you came walking in with me." I giggled. "She knew I was going out tonight, but I didn't tell her about you. Not at all."

Nicky regarded me with surprise. "You never told her you knew me? About our epic first kiss? I'm hurt, Ky. I thought girls shared all those deep, dark secrets with their best friends."

"They do, and I did, but I never said who it was. I always referred to you as Nicky, the boy next-door in the summers. I never let it slip that your other grandmother is the head of the British Commonwealth."

"Hmm. I think I like the idea of being Nicky, the boy next door." He unbuckled his seat belt and turned to face me. "Come here, girl next door, and let me kiss you one more time—for now. Let me give you something to remember until the next time I can kiss you."

We didn't have much space to maneuver in the small front seat with the console between us, but I managed to get up on my knees and face Nicky, who tugged me forward until we were face-to-face. When he kissed me this time, it was with a new sense of urgency and a ton of restrained desire.

"If I wasn't getting on a flight tomorrow, I'd take you inside, and I'd do what I've wanted to do all night." He trailed his lips over my jaw and down my neck.

"What's that?" My voice sounded drugged and sluggish.

"I'd find out what you have on beneath that teasing skirt.

It's just short enough to make me think that if you bent down in the right way, I might get a tempting peek of what I want to see." He sucked gently at the hollow in my throat where my pulse thrummed erratically. "And of what I'm dying to touch."

"Would you?" I laughed softly. "If you weren't leaving tomorrow, I'd peel off this shirt of yours and lay beneath you, just to see the muscles in your arms when you brace yourself over me."

"Ughhhh." Nicky closed his eyes, banging his head into the back of the seat. "Damn the office that made my travel arrangements. I wish they'd built in a few more days. And a few more nights."

Framing Nicky's face in my two hands, I smiled into his gorgeous blue eyes. "Next time, right? This isn't all the time we have. There's going to be a next time."

He sighed deeply, his answering grin huge. "Yes. Yes, in fact, there will be. I'm going to make that a priority as soon as I'm home and settled. But hearing you say it—knowing you believe it—that's enough for now. That makes me very happy, Ky."

I ducked my head, shy now all of a sudden. "Believing it isn't easy—but I believe in you, Nicky. Don't make me sorry about that, okay?"

He gazed down at me, all humor gone now. "I won't. You can trust me, Kyra. I promise."

CHAPTER Eight

"RISE AND SHINE, SLEEPING BEAUTY."

Someone shook my foot, and still mostly asleep, I scowled and kicked at the hand, moaning words that were unintelligible even to me.

"Kyra, c'mon. Wake up. I'm making you waffles for breakfast, but we're out of milk. I need the car keys so that I can run to the store and get some."

Waffles. That was definitely the magic word. I opened one eye and tried to focus on Shelby. "In the front pocket of my purse, hanging on the hook in my closet."

"Thanks, sweetie. Be right back." She paused by my door. "You might get out of bed and set up the waffle iron for me. Maybe make some coffee."

I grunted. "'kay."

For a few minutes, I didn't move at all. I listened to Shelby's steps down the hall and through the kitchen. When I heard the back door open and then close, I finally rolled over and reached for my phone.

There was a text message notification, and a smile I couldn't hold back if I'd wanted spread over my face.

Good morning, beautiful. I hope you wake up as happy as I did this morning. On the plane already, and by the time you see this, I'll probably be getting ready to land in London. Talk to you later today.

I hugged my arms around my middle, giving a happy sigh that almost turned into a squeal. But it didn't, because even if Nicky was already across the Atlantic, I was too cool to squeal over a boy. Or a man. Yeah, Nicholas Windsor was most definitely a man.

Glancing at the clock, I tried to figure out the time difference and how long the flight between Bangor and London might be. The plane probably *was* preparing to land about now, as Nicky had predicted, or maybe it already had, and Nicky was on his way to his apartment. His apartment in the palace, which was something I couldn't think about too long, or it would totally freak me out.

The slamming of a door made me jump, and I sat straight up in bed, pulling the sheet nearly to my chin, my heart pounding. There was no way Shelby could be back already; the closest convenience store was ten minutes away on a good day. She probably hadn't locked the door, because we rarely did. Who the hell was coming into my house? A burglar? A serial murderer? Oh, that would be just my luck: here I'd finally connected with a nice guy, and now I was going to get my throat slit in my own bed.

Adrenaline surged into my bloodstream as a dozen scenarios flitting across my brain in the seconds before Shelby came stalking back into my bedroom. Her eyes were wide, and she didn't look happy. I wracked my brain, trying to figure out why she might be pissed at me.

She opened her mouth and started to speak, and then closed it again, as though the words just wouldn't come.

"What's wrong?" I scrambled out of bed and nearly

tripped as the sheets were wrapped around my knees.

"Kyra." Shelby managed to ground out my name. "Why the hell is there a bunch of photographers and reporters out in our front yard?"

Confusion and bewilderment replaced the panic I'd felt a few minutes before. "What?"

"Reporters, Kyra. I walked out the door, went around the house to the driveway, and they were waiting there. They all started yelling *your* name, taking pictures, and asking if it's true that you're dating Prince Nicholas." She tapped her foot on the floor, and her lips were pressed into a tight line. "Something you need to share with me, Kyra?"

"Shit." I sat back down on the edge of the mattress and covered my face with my hands. "Shit, shit, shit."

"Yeah, I think you're going to have to come up with something better than that." Shelby threw up her hands. "Is it true? Is the mystery guy you've been seeing lately really *Prince Fucking Nicholas*?"

"Um." I gnawed on the corner of my lip. "It's not exactly . . . I mean, it didn't start like that."

Shelby cocked her head and raised one eyebrow. I recognized that expression. It meant, *keep talking.*

"I didn't lie about who he was," I rushed to explain. "When I said I'd met someone I'd known when I was a kid, that was true. It *is* true."

"And . . ." She rolled her hand. "And you used to play with kids from the British royal family when you were little?"

"Well, yeah. It's complicated, but his grandmother on his mother's side was a friend of Honey's. She lived in the house next to us on the beach in Florida. So when he came to visit with them every summer, we used to play together. It wasn't a big deal."

"Mmmmhmmmm." Shelby clearly needed more.

I decided that in the interest of time and expediency, I'd leave out the whole first kiss deal. "So then he was at that dinner at Handsome and Honey's place last week, and we sort of . . . reconnected." I bit the side of my mouth to hold back the smile that threatened to take over my face at the memory of that first evening. "But nothing happened then. I wasn't holding out on you."

"Nothing happened *then.*" Shelby nodded. "Which tells me that something has happened *since*. Also—hello, you have dinner and start to hang out with a prince? Ky, I don't care that he's an old family friend. You don't hold that shit back from your best friend."

"You're right. I'm sorry. But I didn't know if it was going to be anything, and then . . . it was." I met her eyes. "Full disclosure time? He kissed me last night. And we had a super romantic dinner. And I think it might actually be something. But he's back in the UK now, so—"

As if on cue, my phone began to ring. Butterflies exploded in my stomach when I saw the caller ID on the screen, and I answered it quickly.

Before I could get out more than a hello, Nicky was speaking tersely into my ear. "Kyra, we have a situation."

"Yeah, I'm aware." I gave Shelby wide eyes.

"I just got off the plane in London, and I was mobbed by the press." He muttered something that I didn't quite catch, but I could imagine what it might be. "They were all yelling at me about you. Kyra, did you say anything to the media?"

I couldn't answer him for a moment. Hurt and a little pissed at his assumption, I hoped he could hear the annoyance in my tone. "Of course, I didn't. What do you think of me? I didn't even tell Shelby. She just found out what's going on when she tried to leave the house to buy milk and ran into a bunch of photographers in our front yard." I sniffed a little. "She needed milk to make me waffles, because she's such an awesome friend, and I hadn't even told *her*. So please don't insult me by assuming I'd blab to the press."

"Kyra." I heard the apology in his voice even before he spoke the words. "I'm sorry. That was a shitty thing for me to say. I was taken by surprise—like I told you last night, reporters don't take that much notice of me usually. I can come and go without them bothering me. I didn't have any warning this time. I guess I sort of went over the edge. I really am sorry."

"It's okay." I took a deep breath. "But how did this happen? And why do they care?"

"They have a picture of us," Nicky said grimly. "It's a little blurry and dark, but it's clear enough to see you and to recognize me."

"The lady with the phone?" I rubbed my forehead, where a headache was lurking. "I told you I thought she was taking pictures."

"Probably," Nicky agreed. "Not that there was anything we could've done at that point, even if my policeman had caught her in the act."

"But how did they figure out who I am?" I hadn't seen anyone I recognized at the restaurant. "Gav would never tell anyone. He's not that way."

"You made the reservation last night in your name," he reminded me. "It wouldn't take much investigation to find that information. And the hostess recognized me—she had your name on her computer. Not that difficult to come up with the right answer when you add two and two."

"Ack." I dropped back down onto the bed, closing my eyes. "What a mess. What do I tell them? How do I deal with this?"

Nicky sighed. "It's best just to be as pleasant as you can be. Don't talk to them, but don't run away. Smile and ignore their questions. If you have to say something, say 'No comment.'"

I wrinkled my nose. "Great. On the other hand, I could just stay in the house until they get bored and go away."

"You could do that, but then you and Shelby wouldn't get your waffles, would you?" There was a teasing note in his voice. "By the way, please do apologize to Shelby for me. Please tell her that it was totally my fault you kept her in the dark. And tell her . . ." He hesitated. "Tell her that I can't wait to meet her the next time I'm in the states."

I swallowed. "So . . . there's definitely going to be a next time? All this . . . the press . . . it doesn't scare you off?"

He laughed softly, and the intimacy of the sound thrilled my heart. "I think that's a question I should be asking you, not the other way around. It's going to take more than some idiots snapping pictures and yelling questions to frighten me." He hesitated. "What about you?"

"Puh." I blew out a breath. "Please. I don't scare that easily. Besides, they'll get bored and go away soon."

"Right." There was a voice in the background, speaking low. Nicky said something in reply, but it was too muffled for me to understand. "Sorry, but I need to go now. I've got a meeting, and I'm late. Talk to you tonight?"

"I'll be here."

"Okay. Bye, then."

I sat with the phone in my hand for a few more seconds. The mattress dipped as Shelby sat down next to me. Her arms were crossed over her chest, and her eyes were full of curiosity.

"Want to catch me up on a few things, Kyra?"

The rest of that day was surreal, like something that was happening to a different person. Only, it wasn't. It was happening to me.

Shelby had listened to my explanation in complete silence. When I'd finally run out of things to say, she'd just shaken her head.

"I get it. I understand why you didn't tell me. And I forgive you. But holy shit, Kyra. He's a prince. You're dating a prince. That's . . . it's kind of insane."

I'd dropped back onto my bed, screwing my eyes shut. "I know."

"By the way, whoever outed you didn't know you at all. The reporters were all shouting your name when I came out—they thought I was you—but they were pronouncing it wrong. They said *Keera*, not Kyra. I didn't correct them, because—well, because I was too stunned."

"That makes sense. If they got my name from someone at The Meadows, from the list of reservations—that wouldn't tell anyone how to say it, just how to spell it. At least I know it wasn't anyone close to me who spilled the beans."

"So what comes next?" Shelby had laid down on the bed, too, stretching alongside me. "Are you going to England? Do you have to get a bodyguard? How does this work?"

I'd lolled my head slowly back and forth. "I have no idea, Shelby. No idea at all."

As much as I'd wanted to hide in bed all day and hope that

the reporters got tired of waiting, I had promised to meet Ed at the garden before lunch, which meant I had to get up and put on some clothes, even if there weren't any waffles coming my way anymore. It was too late for us to make them now, and I was too rattled to enjoy them, even though Shelby had calmed down enough to offer to make the necessary the milk run.

She trailed me from my room to the closet to the bathroom as I got ready to leave, peppering me with leftover questions.

"Did he talk about his family?"

"Does he live in a palace?"

"Is he an amazing kisser?"

"Is that really what you're wearing?"

At the last one, I wheeled around, hands on my hips. "Since when do you critique my wardrobe choices for working in the garden? Yes, this is what I'm wearing. Jeans, my boots and a sweatshirt. Those are garden clothes. If I put on a dress and heels to get on my hands and knees to dig, Ed would have me committed. And he'd kick me off the project, which would make me furious since it's *my* idea in the first place."

"Fine, fine." Shelby held up her hands. "I'm just saying, whatever you walk out in right now is what they're going to take pictures of, and those pictures will show up everywhere—and that's going to be the first impression you give the world. Couldn't you skip the garden today and go visit H squared instead? You could put on a really cute dress, and I'd do your hair for you."

"No, I could not." Catching up my curly hair, I wrangled it into a band on the back of my head. "Because Honey would think I was crazy if I showed up at her house, all dressed up.

I can't stop living my life because there are a few people with cameras in our yard, Shelby. Besides, Nicky wouldn't want me to change anything about myself. He said so."

"I'm not suggesting you should. But there's a difference between changing who you are and presenting who you are in the best possible light. When you're first dating someone, you realize that if this person is your one and only, eventually he's going to see you without make up, with your hair a mess. He's going to see you on sick days and PMS days—and yeah, he's going to see the not-so-pretty. But you don't show him that on the very first date, or he'd go running into the hills, just like you would if he showed up unshaven in dirty boxers and a three-days' growth of beard. Putting your best foot forward isn't lying about who you are."

"I agree with you. Which was why, when Nicky was here, he saw me all dressed up, and he saw me in jeans. He saw me at our romantic dinner in my cute little dress, and he saw me at the garden, mucking up dirt. I don't have to impress him." I sat on the edge of my bed to tie my Converse.

"It's not Nicky I'm talking about here. It's the world, Kyra. It's his family. They're going to get their first look at you in these pictures."

I stood up, reaching for my sunglasses. "And that is why I'm wearing my sneakers and not trudging out in my garden boots, which are in the back of the car. If they follow me to the garden, they can see me in my boots." I paused as a new thought occurred to me. "I hope they don't follow me to the garden. I don't want people tromping all over my plants. That would suck."

"That's what worries you most, huh? Your plants? Aren't you the least bit spooked about what they're going to write about you? Aren't you at all nervous?"

"Shelby, relax. This isn't a big deal." I dangled the car keys from one finger. "Do you need to use the car? You can drop me off if you do."

She shook her head. "No. I'm here all day, studying for finals. Without milk or waffles, of course."

"Sorry. I'll try to remember to pick up the milk on the way home, and maybe we can have waffles for dinner. Okay?" I bent to kiss her cheek. "See you later, chick. Thanks for forgiving me and understanding about Nicky."

"Yeah, yeah, yeah." She waved her hand. "Go on. Go get mobbed by the press and let them photograph you in your dirty jeans."

I stuck out my tongue at her. "They're not dirty. They're well-loved."

"Whatever!" she yelled after me, so that I was laughing when I opened the door to step outside . . . and was immediately overwhelmed.

Once upon a time, I thought celebrities who wore sunglasses all the time were being ridiculous and putting on affectations. But now . . . now, suddenly, I got it. Because even with my sunglasses, and even though not all of the people taking pictures were using flashes—it was gray and cloudy outside—I was momentarily blinded on my own front stoop.

"Keera! Over here! Keera! Are you Keera? Keera! Are you dating Prince Nicholas? How did you meet? Are you in love with him, Keera? Are you moving to England? Are you planning to see him again? How long have you been together? Keera! Over here. Smile for us, love! Give us a smile!"

I wanted nothing more than to run back inside my house and slither under my bed. I forced myself to try to walk forward, keeping my head down until my eyes cleared and I could see where the hell I was walking. I was terrified that I'd stumble over a rock and land on my ass. Talk about first impressions.

"Keera! Are you in university? Do you have a job? Did you see the pictures of you with Prince Nicholas? What did you think?"

"Keera—"

"Actually, it's *Kyra*." I couldn't stand it one more moment. Hearing them yell my name—saying it wrong—was like nails on a chalkboard. "Kyra. If you're going to yell my name, could you at least pronounce it right? Thanks."

As if all the reporters thought with one brain, they fell silent when I spoke. I could still hear the click of the cameras, though. I managed to reach my car.

"Kyra, then." The voice was closer than I expected it to be, and I startled. "Kyra Duncan. I'm Sophie Kent. Would you like to give me a statement about your relationship with Prince Nicholas? Something that we can print—you know, your side of things. So that the world can hear your story. What it's like to be an American girl dating a British prince."

When I didn't answer, she went on. "If you don't say something, we'll just run the story based on what we're guessing and seeing. Conjecture. Give us something to print."

I opened my car door and turned to face the woman standing behind me. She was about my age, I guessed, holding a camera and a small recorder. I knew she was here because she had a job to do, but I didn't like the situation any better, even though I understood the why.

With a ghost of a smile, I shook my head.

"No comment."

Chapter Nine

TO MY RELIEF, THE REPORTERS DIDN'T FOLLOW ME TO THE garden. I drove with one eye on my rearview mirror, watching for anyone who might be trailing me. I even took the precaution of driving a circuitous route, but it didn't matter—when I pulled in, the parking lot was empty except for Ed's truck.

When I joined him at the control plot, he hardly spared me a glance before he launched into an update on the plants, the weeds, the bugs and the soil test results. For a solid fifteen minutes, I only had to make grunting noises of affirmation as he spoke. It seemed that Ed remained blissfully unaware of anything going on with me.

I spent two wonderful hours immersed in the soil and plants, forgetting anything that had to do with England, reporters or cute guys who kissed me until I forgot how to breathe. I'd left my phone in the car on purpose; being away from everything was a wonderful respite, and I needed it.

But nothing good lasts forever. After Ed and I walked to the parking area, he climbed into his truck and rattled away. I slid into the driver's seat of my car and checked my phone.

I had over fifty messages.

"Shit," I groaned, my voice reverberating in the emptiness of the car. For a dizzy moment, I considered driving far, far away, to some place where no one knew me or could find me. It was tempting, but it was also impossible—and running away was a coward's escape. I was no coward.

With a deep breath, I began scrolling through messages. The first five were from my mother. Apparently, Honey had filled her in on last week's spring-the-prince on Kyra dinner, but now that she'd seen photographic evidence, she was gushing and wanted ALL the details. The next six were from my sisters—four from Lisel and two from Bria—demanding an update and accusing me of being "the worst sister in the world" for not sharing my news with them. Then there were two from Honey, asking if I was all right and if I needed any help.

Bless my grandmother. It hadn't even occurred to me that I could hide out at my grandparents' house until all of this blew over. They had acres of land and security. I'd be safe there, and no one would bother me. It was definitely a thought to tuck in the back of my mind.

The rest of my messages were from old friends who hadn't contacted me in years, or acquaintances from both college and grad school. A few came from numbers I didn't recognize and asked pointedly personal questions that I deleted hastily.

Are you sleeping with Prince Nicholas?

How's the sex?

Were you a virgin when you met?

"Oh, my God." I dropped my phone on the passenger seat and closed my eyes, leaning my forehead on the steering wheel. "This is insane."

My phone buzzed with a new text—this time, it was Shelby.

Check out TMZ. You made their site—and their show.

"Great. Just great." I groaned again, but I swiped my fingers across the screen and did an internet search until I found the site in question.

Prince Nicholas finds love in the US!

Britain's Prince Nicholas, cousin of the heir to the throne, has often been known as the playboy of the royal family. But it seems now he's broadening his horizons and coming across the pond to find love.

This picture was sent to us by a vigilant reader in Coby, Maine—a small town south of Bangor. You can see the lover prince with his American girlfriend at a local restaurant here—and you'll need an oven mitt to pick up the HEAT of the kiss between these two.

Sources tell us that the woman in the photo is Kyra Duncan, 24, a student at Grant College. Other people at the restaurant with the pair say that they couldn't keep their hands off each other all evening—and that neither of them were shy about showing the sizzling attraction between them.

Although Prince Nicholas flew back to England today, we're betting it won't be long before these two hook up again.

Meanwhile, we reached out to Kyra to get her take on her royal boyfriend. She didn't have a comment for us. But clearly, she wasn't dressing for a date today.

Below those words was a picture of me from earlier, standing by my car as I opened my mouth to give my *no comment* answer. My mouth was opening, the camera had caught my head mid-turn, and I looked horrible.

"Holy shit." I dropped my head back to the steering wheel. "Holy fucking shit."

The phone buzzed again, but this time, I was afraid to look at it. When I did peep down at where it rested on my lap, the number on the caller ID was unfamiliar. I hit ignore. Five seconds later, it started again—different number, still unknown.

Picking up the phone, I placed it face-down on the seat next to me, started up my car and drove home.

I'd hoped that the hours I'd spent at the garden would have allowed time for the reporters to grow bored with waiting and leave. But when I turned into the driveway, there was still a knot of strangers holding cameras. True, that group was smaller than it had been—but they were still there.

I picked up my phone and shot Shelby a terse message.

I'm home. Make sure the door is unlocked, please.

The reporters who had lingered clearly were the more tenacious of the bunch, but apparently, they were also slightly less bold. No one crowded my car as I climbed out and made a dash for the back door, although the minute I'd left the safety of the driver's seat, they all began calling to me.

"Kyra! Are you going to see Prince Nicholas again soon?"

"Kyra! Over here. Do you think you're going to be the new American princess?"

Well, at least they had my name right this time.

I made it inside and closed the door behind me with a long sigh of relief. Shelby glanced up at me from the kitchen table, where she sat in front of her laptop.

"You okay?" Her voice was sympathetic.

"I guess so. It's crazy . . . and that's just the ones who are actually here, in this country. Shelby, you should see the messages on my phone. And hear the voicemails. People are nuts. And why? Because someone took a picture of me with a guy who happens to be part of a famous family in England?"

Shelby cocked an eyebrow at me. "I did a little investigating while you were gone. I saw the picture that set all this off. That wasn't just a friendly peck, Kyra. The kiss was hot. That's what people—the press—are responding to."

I pulled out the chair across from her. "I was an idiot. I didn't think anyone would care that much. We're not news. Not really."

"Hmmm." My friend shook her head. "Maybe not. But that doesn't always seem to matter. Like I said, I did some digging and some reading while you were at the garden—"

"Didn't you have finals you were supposed to be studying for?" I crossed my arms over my chest and gave her my best stare.

She had the good grace to look a tiny bit guilty. "Well, yes. And I will. Eventually. But this was important, too. We need to get ahead of this if we're going to figure out how to live with people camped outside our house for the foreseeable future."

"Eh." I waved my hand. "I don't think it's going to last, Shel. Once Nicky and I aren't seen together again, everyone will lose interest, and the reporters will leave. They'll have a new story to follow."

"You might be right," she conceded. "But it doesn't hurt to be prepared, right? So I read a bunch of articles about how other people who've been in this situation before you have coped."

I shot her a warning glare. "If the word *Kardashian* comes

out of your mouth, I'm leaving."

"No, not them." Shelby rolled her eyes. "Those are people who want the attention. I was talking about those who had to deal with the media because of dating a member of the royal family, since that's what's applicable to your situation. Some of it's changed over the years, because now we have the added pressure of everyone in the world carrying a phone that's also a camera, and there's the twist of social media, too. But a few elements stay the same."

"Lay it on me." I spread out my hands. "I'm all ears."

For the next twenty minutes, Shelby did just that, sharing with me the key points of what she'd read about the women—because they were all women, as it happened—who had been linked to members of the royal family in the past.

"It seems to me that the number one rule is not to talk to the press about anything real or important. Like, you could comment on the weather, or say something about what you're wearing or a TV show, but you shouldn't ever mention anything about the royal family or your feelings there. One of Prince Charles' girlfriends did that years ago, and she was cut off cold."

"I think that's common sense," I remarked. "No man wants to read that his girlfriend's been dishing about him in public."

"True." Shelby nodded. "You should try to avoid talking at all with the press, unless it's absolutely necessary, because they've been known to twist things in such a way to make it look like you said something you didn't. Also, you don't want anyone to think you love the attention, because then someone might think you're a Kardashian-type. At the same time, you can't go all Sean Penn on reporters and punch them. Basically, you're walking a tightrope between being polite and not being too excited about the media being here."

I sighed and laid my head on the table. "I'm going to screw this up, Shelby. You know I am. I'm not good at pretending to be someone I'm not."

"You are *not* going to screw anything up. You don't have to be someone else—it's like when you go to events with Honey and Handsome. You know how to mind your manners there, and you know what they expect of you. This is the same. Just don't act as though you were raised in a cave."

"I'll try my best." Turning my head, I rested my chin on my hand and regarded my friend. "This might all be a moot point, anyway. Nicky probably will take one look at these pictures from today and never call me again."

"I doubt it." Shelby grinned at me. "According to the media, he took aside a bunch of reporters today and told them to go easy on you. He asked them not to run you off before he had a chance to convince you that he's worth the bother."

Something deep in my heart melted a little—the part of my being that still hadn't quite accepted the fact that a man like Nicky might truly be interested in a woman like me.

"There. That look right there." Shelby pointed at me, her smile victorious. "That's an expression I've never seen on your face ever before. It tells me that this—that Nicky—is more important to you than you realize. That's why, even if the reporters are annoying and you don't like them camping outside our house, you're going to smile and be polite and pleasant. Because if they're part of the Nicky package, you have to learn to deal with them."

I shrugged. "Maybe you're right."

"Of course, I'm right. I just—" The doorbell rang,

interrupting whatever pearl of wisdom Shelby was about to impart. We both frowned at each other before she leaped to her feet.

"You stay here. If it's one of the reporters, I'll fend them off." She hustled toward our front door, calling over her shoulder. "Although they've been out there all day now and never knocked or got really close to the house."

I stayed in the kitchen, but I heard Shelby open the door and have a brief, quiet conversation. When she returned to the kitchen, she was carrying a huge bouquet of flowers and a small brown paper bag and wearing a broad smile.

"What's that?" I got up and reached for the flowers, but she held them away from me.

"Ah, ah, ah. Keep your hands off. They're my flowers." She held up the bag. "And this is my gallon of milk. Both were sent to me by a certain sexy prince, along with a sweet note apologizing for the surprise this morning." She sighed and clutched the bouquet to her chest. "Forget you. I think I'm in love."

"Nicky sent *you* flowers?" I grabbed the small card from her hand and read the note aloud. *"Dear Shelby, Please accept these flowers as my way of saying I'm sorry about the reporters camped outside your house this morning. Also, forgive both Kyra and me for keeping the secret—it truly wasn't her fault. The milk is a gift for both of you~I hope you'll consider making Ky her waffles, so she'll have to let me off the hook, too, and not blame me for her lack of breakfast. Looking forward to meeting you soon~Nicholas Windsor"*

Shelby opened the refrigerator to stow the milk before she found a vase for the flowers. "I'm telling you, Kyra. He's a keeper. I have a good feeling about this."

"Don't say things like that." I sat back down at the table. "I'm afraid to believe."

"You?" Shelby scoffed. "Since when have you been afraid of anything?"

"It's new. We're just beginning to get to know each other, and now people are yelling questions to me about whether I want to marry him." I stretched out my legs and toed off my Converse. "You know when you've just started dating a guy, and your family or your friends make a big deal about it?"

Shelby snorted and turned her back to me as she ran water in the glass vase. "I'm very familiar with that. Vivian used to sing the K-I-S-S-I-N-G song every time she found out I was even mildly interested in a boy. It was mortifying."

"Exactly." I shook my finger. "Now imagine that on a huge scale, with people you don't know and have never met—and they're all singing the K-I-S-S-I-N-G song. Only maybe the guy just wanted that one kiss. Or maybe he wants more, but he wants to take it slow. And now with the expectations of the world in full view, he feels pressured to either run away and leave you alone or to take things up a notch. I don't like it either way." I gnawed on the corner of my lip. "I really like Nicky, Shel. I want to have a chance to see where this might go. We have so much in common, and he makes me feel things . . ." I trailed off. "Let's just say there's no lack of attraction between us. And he makes me laugh, and when he looks at me, I feel pretty. I feel special. But at the same time, I'm comfortable with him. I can be myself. At least, so far. I'm trying to keep in mind that we haven't known each other that long."

"That's not true. You told me that you spent ten summer vacations with him."

"I did. But that was then. We knew each other for ten

years, and then we didn't know each other for ten years. In my head, I'm still trying to reconcile the Nicky from before with the Nicky from now. I had a crush on one, and I think I might really like the other."

Shelby opened a cabinet to take out the waffle iron. "Maybe you should try not to overthink this, Kyra. Let it happen. Take each day as it comes . . . and let's see where it goes." She smiled at me as she set a glass bowl on the counter. "For now, forget about the reporters and what may or may not happen. Just relax and be grateful, because thanks to the consideration and kindness of your prince crush, I'm about to make you the most kick-ass waffles you've ever eaten."

CHAPTER Ten

Nicky: *How were the waffles?*

Kyra: *They were, as Shelby promised, the most kickass waffles of all time. Thanks for supplying the milk.*

Nicky: *Happy to help. And now more importantly, how are you?*

Kyra: *Also kickass.*

Nicky: *Glad to hear it. I'm sorry again that I jumped to conclusions—and then jumped on you. I was taken by surprise, in that we didn't know press was there until I was already on my way off the plane. There was some kind of communication mix-up. And I felt horrible about you having to cope with all of that on your own.*

Kyra: *I survived. And they'll probably go away soon, right? When they don't see us together again right away and they figure out that I lead a painfully boring life.*

Nicky: *Maybe, but I've learned not to expect the media to do the expected. So be vigilant. If you need help—if they trespass or harass you—get the police involved. I can't do anything from here, which is even more maddening.*

Kyra: *Please don't worry. I really can take care of myself.*

Nicky: *I know you can. But maybe I'd like to be close by to help so you didn't have to deal with it all the time.*

Kyra: *I'd like that, too.*

Nicky: *I just saw a picture of you. You're beautiful.*
Kyra: *UGH, Nicky, I so am not, and any picture they took probably made me look like a doofus.*
Nicky: *There's that word again. You are not, nor do you look like, a doofus. You were in jeans and your boots. Looked like you were heading into the garden. How's it going, by the way? Your project at the garden, I mean.*
Kyra: *I was on my way in there when they started snapping. They've begun following me to the garden, but today, campus security came by and routed them out. And everything is moving along as we'd predicted. We're hitting some pest issues with the natural gardening, but Ed and I both think it's a short-term problem that should begin to respond to the co-planting soon.*
Nicky: *Excellent. I might have to invite you to one of our food sourcing symposiums. That would be one way to get you over to London.*
Kyra: *True. Another would be to simply invite me.*
Nicky: *If I knew I could actually spend time with you, I'd ask you over here in a second. But my schedule is so full right now that I'd barely see you between coming and going. But soon.*
Kyra: *I'm not complaining or hinting, Nicky. I was just saying that you don't have to come up with some elaborate reason to get me to England.*
Nicky: *Good to know. I could just think of a good way to ask, huh? Dear Ky, my lips miss yours. Bring them on over.*
Kyra: *That would do the trick.*

Kyra: *I had to call the campus police today. A woman came into one of my classes and sat in the back, and during the break, she came up and began asking me questions. And not about soil science, either.*
Nicky: *I'm sorry, Ky. Did they eject her?*
Kyra: *They didn't get the chance. She left before they got there. But it was embarrassing. People at school . . . they've started treating me differently. They don't always talk TO me, but they seem to think I've suddenly gone deaf, because they sure as hell talk ABOUT me.*
Nicky: *People are . . . incredibly thoughtless sometimes. But your true friends know you. They'll stick.*
Kyra: *Yeah, I guess. Shelby's the only one I trust right now. She fends off the reporters if they start getting pushy. And she doesn't ask me stupid questions, either. Shelby and my project partner Ed are the only two who still look at me the same way. With Ed, I think he honestly hasn't noticed anything weird going on. He's just really focused on the science.*
Nicky: *Is there anything I can do?*
Kyra: *Come over and hold me and stroke my hair and tell me it's going to be all right?*
Nicky: *I'm virtually stroking your hair right now. And it's going to be all right.*

Kyra: *I'm sorry about this, Nicky, but I'm going to have to say that you're wrong. That's all there is to it.*
Nicky: *I'm absolutely not wrong, Ky. Don't you think I know better than you do about this?*
Kyra: *Uh, no I don't in fact. Did you have a second major in Shakespeare? I did. I know that shit inside and out.*
Nicky: *Maybe so, but he wrote plays about my ancestors. That*

should give me more standing.

Kyra: *Well, it doesn't. I'm telling you, Juliet wasn't nearly as in love with Romeo as he was with her. She went along with it because he was so dramatic and insistent, and she thought he was an okay guy, but she wasn't gaga over him like he was over her.*

Nicky: *She killed herself for him, Ky. Twice, if you count the fake death.*

Kyra: *Yeah, well, she was a teenaged girl and she got caught up in the drama. But she didn't do it because she was crazy in love with him.*

Nicky: *Are you making a point here, Ky? Are you trying to say that you're just going along with me because I'm—wait, let me scroll up—oh here it is. Dramatic and insistent.*

Kyra: *No, of course not. I'm going along with you because I'm hot for your bod. Duh.*

Nicky: …

Kyra: *You still there? Sorry, I didn't mean to shock you.*

Nicky: *You didn't shock me, but you definitely made me very happy. Okay, I'm glad to know it's more than drama. Also, I'm hot for your bod, too.*

Kyra: *I'd suggest phone-making-out, but I know one of your relatives got caught doing that a while back, and it was a big thing, so I think it's better that we refrain.*

Nicky: *Sadly true on all counts. We'll have to wait for in person making out.*

Kyra: *You could always write me letters. Like I suggested before, ten years ago. And you never did.*

Nicky: *I feel the same way now. I'm not a good letter-writer.*

Kyra: *Yet you can text me the equivalent of an epic novel? How is that different?*

Nicky: *It is because it is. And because you're texting me back, giving*

me immediate gratification.
Kyra: *You're all about the gratification, are you?*
Nicky: *You know it, baby.*

Kyra: *Nicky, does your family hate me? When they see all the pictures, I mean?*
Nicky: *Of course, they don't. This isn't anything new to us, Ky. It's a way of life.*
Kyra: *Right, I get that, but I mean, do they see pics and say, Nicky, she's a dog. Find another girl.*
Nicky: *Uh, no. No one has said anything remotely like that. Alex said she remembers you well and that you've grown up to be even prettier than you were last time she saw you, and Daisy says she remembers that you were always very kind to her when we'd visit. So that's a winning situation.*
Kyra: *And your parents . . .?*
Nicky: *Rarely if ever express an opinion when it comes to my love life. They trust me to make the right decisions.*
Kyra: *Okay.*
Nicky: *Okay?*
Kyra: *I said yes. I just wish . . . I wish a lot of things. I wish I didn't take such terrible awkward pictures. I wish they wouldn't take pictures of me when I'm doing things like bending over to get something out of the car. And mostly, I wish we didn't have to be so far apart from each other.*
Nicky: *I wish that last one, too. Soon, Ky. I promise.*

CHAPTER Eleven

Romance or Hype?

Three weeks after those super HOT pics of Britain's Prince Nicholas with his new American girlfriend hit the internet, questions are swirling about what's happening now. Although press coverage of Maine girl Kyra Duncan has been non-stop, we haven't seen any repeat dates. Nicholas has been carrying on with his engagements on the far side of the pond.

Sources tell us that there are plans in the works for Kyra to make a quick trip to London, but who knows? Maybe this was just a fly-by royal hook-up, and these two aren't destined for a happily-ever-after.

I stood in the check-out line at the grocery store, my eyes glued to the carton of eggs in my basket. Whispers swirled around me; I should've been used to it by now, but I'd spent so much time over the past weeks hiding at home that being out now felt daring—and dangerous.

"She's not even that pretty. I mean, look at her. Look at the picture on that magazine. She's, like, plain."

"I don't even think she has make-up on. And the hair . . ."

The first girl giggled. "I read something on line that called her the American Cinderella. But she's more like the ugly step-sister."

My throat burned, and I was sure my face was bright red. This was why I didn't leave my bedroom unless it was absolutely necessary. Unfortunately, today it had been just that. Shelby was sick in bed, and today was Honey's birthday, which meant I had to bake her a cake. It was family tradition: on my grandmother's birthday, everyone gathered up here in Maine, and I made a German chocolate cake.

But we didn't have any eggs—both Shelby and I sucked at efficient weekly grocery shopping; we always ended up running out three or four times a week to pick up what we'd forgotten. Since there was no way I could ask my poor beleaguered and feverish friend to go to the grocery store . . . here I was.

"Do you think she even really met him? Or do you think it was, like, one of those things where they doctored the picture to make it look like they were together?"

"Maybe he was drunk. He saw her through beer goggles." They laughed again.

I was not the kind of woman who stood by while people talked about me. I was the type who championed the underdog and called out the mean girls who tried to make me feel bad about myself. But right now, my hands were tied. If I said anything—if I so much as acknowledged their cruelty—my reaction would be news. Someone would take a picture of the expression on my face, or someone else would leak my words to the press, and then I'd look like a cry-baby.

I'd spent nearly a month doing my damnedest not to look like an idiot, a weakling, a baby or a jerk. I'd smiled as the reporters and photographers had shouted my name and increasingly personal questions. I'd let Shelby show me the pictures that were appearing on line so that I could figure out what I was doing to get caught with unfortunate expressions on my face. I'd stood in front of the mirror and practiced keeping my face motionless.

It was a good skill to have right now, as I pretended to be both deaf and completely insensitive to what the girls around me were pseudo-whispering.

"You ought to be ashamed of yourselves." The voice I heard next wasn't whispering; it wasn't pretending to even try. I wanted to turn around and see who was talking now, but I didn't. I held it together a little longer.

The girls stopped giggling, and the voice behind them—behind me—went on, her tone biting and censorious, with a healthy dose of a strong Maine accent.

"You should be ashamed of yourselves. Standing here, talking about this woman—this woman who's been dealing with a bunch of ridiculous garbage from the press, just because she had the misfortune to be seen with some guy who's famous because of his family. But look at her. She's got class. She might not be like one of your plastic idols, with a fake tan, a fake nose and fake bosoms . . . she's real. And you—you two should be ashamed of yourselves."

The silence that surrounded all of us in the moment that followed was deafening. No one spoke. My heart was pounding, and my hands shook a little as I reached down to pick up the eggs and move them to the belt.

The cashier finished the transaction with the man in front of me. I felt eyes watching me still, but I forced myself to keep the vaguely pleasant expression on my face, the one that privately I thought made me look as though I had early onset dementia.

My eggs moved down the belt, and the cashier dragged

them over the scanner. The beep was loud in the continuing quiet, broken only when the check-out woman cleared her throat and gave me the total.

I had the money in my fist already, ready to pass over. It wasn't exact change, but it was close enough. I hoped no one noticed the way my fingers were trembling as I dropped it into her palm and began to walk away, trying not to move too fast. I didn't want anyone to think I was running away, even if I was.

"Miss! You forgot your change. And do you want me to bag that?" The cashier called after me, but I knew if I turned around, I'd have to meet her eyes, and then I'd inevitably end up glancing at the girls behind me in line and at the older woman who had taken up for me. I didn't want to do that. I didn't want to see any of them. I just wanted to be gone.

I didn't feel safe again until I was back in my car, on the road, speeding toward home. I followed our new protocol and pulled around to the back of the house, beyond where the reporters would go. It shortened the route to the back door and meant less time I was out in the open, with people shouting at me.

But it was a good day, because no one was waiting. Shelby and I had learned that the presence of the media ebbed and flowed like the tide. Sometimes, they drifted away, when other news was more important. Then something would happen—a new story would pop up, with unnamed sources that insinuated insider information about Nicky and me, and they'd all be back in full force.

"How was it?" Shelby was slumped at the table, her eyes glassy and her face pale. She was in her robe, and her blonde hair was a messy halo around her head.

"Fine." I didn't need to give my friend the ugly details, not when there wasn't a thing either of us could do about it. "I got the eggs. Are you okay if I start on the cake? I don't want the smell to make you feel worse."

"Yeah, it's all right. I'm not nauseated, it's just my throat and my chest. I'm not sleeping because of the cough." She leaned her cheek into her hand. "I think maybe it's just Maine. I need a dose of Florida to get better."

I began to pull out the ingredients I needed to make the cake. "Shel . . . you know, if you want to go home, go back to Florida for a while, it's okay. I know this whole mess has been stressful on you. I'm worried that it's making you sick. So you know, you could take a break. If you go home for a little while . . . you could get back to real life. No reporters, no cameras—just normal stuff."

She sighed. "I don't know, Ky. I want to be here for you—I don't want to abandon my best friend when she needs me. But maybe I could just take a week or so. My mom's been asking when I'm coming home, and Vivian wants me to visit before she gets too far along." Shelby's older sister was pregnant with her first child.

"Of course, she does." I opened the fridge and pulled out a bag of coconut. "You should do that."

"I didn't want to say anything, but now that things are getting quiet, maybe it would be a good time."

A pang of hurt hit my chest, but I worked hard not to let it show. Shelby wasn't wrong. Neither of us would be unhappy to see the end of the press attention, but I was keenly aware that if reporters went away, it was because they'd determined that I wasn't newsworthy anymore—that Nicky and I were not, in fact, a couple.

I myself was beginning to wonder about that. Nicky hadn't forgotten me—there was no question about that. He called me every day at least once, and we texted all the time. He often voiced his frustration over the distance between us. But we hadn't been able to work out a solution to that particular problem. His schedule was set up well in advance, which meant he couldn't simply pop over the Atlantic for an impromptu date. And since he hadn't asked me to visit him in London, I didn't feel comfortable making arrangements to fly over there. Not yet.

"I think it's a good idea." I began to measure cocoa into the bowl. "If you make the arrangements, I'll take you to the airport. Do you want to wait until you feel better?"

Shelby wrinkled her nose. "Will you hate me if I say I already made the arrangements? Mom called right after you left. I'm going to fly out on Monday."

"I could never hate you, Shelby." I managed a faint smile. "I don't blame you for wanting to get away. If I could, I would."

"Why can't you?" She stood up and came around the table to lean against the counter. "You could fly down to Florida with me. You could stay with me, at Vivian and Charlie's house. The change would be good for you."

"I couldn't do that to your family, but thanks." I cracked an egg into the bowl.

"Have you heard anything from Nicky?" Her voice was tentative. "Anything about . . . well, anything?"

I glanced at her. "Last night, he said this was getting ridiculous and that two reasonably intelligent people should be able to work out a way to see each other, even if they do live with an ocean between them. He's getting frustrated." I dried my hands on a towel. "He's not the only one."

"Hmmmm." The worried expression in Shelby's eyes was one I'd seen frequently of late.

"Don't *hmmmm* me. He's not ditching me, Shel. If it weren't for the whole press craziness, this time apart—it wouldn't be a terrible thing. We're getting to know each other better every day, because we talk and we text—without the pressures of being together physically."

"The pressures? Is that what you said? Or did you say without the pleasures?"

I rolled my eyes. "Both. Yes, I would love to live close enough that I could see Nicky every day. Close enough that we could go on real-people dates and actually kiss good-night. But it's also true that we're forced to talk about things that otherwise might get brushed under the carpet, if we were spending all our time making out."

"So it's like the old days? Nicky is courting you?" Shelby smiled and dabbed at her red nose with a crumpled tissue. "That's sweet."

"It is." I clicked the beater attachment onto the mixer. "But I'm not going to lie, Shel. I'm getting antsy. Restless. Being courted is wonderful, but it's not great for making me feel secure about . . . this thing between Nicky and me."

"Your relationship? Are you really scared to call it what it is?" Shelby tilted her head and regarded me curiously.

"I'm not scared," I defended myself. "I just don't want to get hurt."

"Pretty sure that's the definition of scared."

"No, it's the definition of smart and cautious." I knew I wasn't going to win this argument, but neither was I going down without a fight. "If Nicky decides one of these days that

I'm too much trouble, I'm the person who's going to be left to pick up the pieces."

"Do you feel like he might do that?"

Slowly, I shook my head. "No. I mean, I don't know. When we're talking and when I'm reading his texts, I don't think he would. But in the off-times, it's harder to hold onto that."

Shelby nodded, a small frown between her eyebrows. "God, Kyra, when did we get angsty? We used to be these fun girls who didn't care about any guys. We did what we wanted, and we laughed at those silly females who lived and died on whether or not their stupid boyfriends called. When did we become those silly females?"

I reached for a rubber scraper and flicked on the mixer. "Correction, Shel. *I* became one of those silly females. *You* are still fun and carefree. You're still . . . I don't know, Snow White having a blast with the seven dwarfs. I'm the ugly step-sister. The ugly, insecure and silly step-sister."

"Huh?" Shelby squinted. "Snow White didn't have any step-sisters. Also, I'm not sure I like your implication about me and seven guys."

"No, not Snow White's step-sister. Cinderella's." I peered into the mixer bowl and turned down the speed of the beaters. "I was in line at the grocery store, and these girls behind me recognized me. There was a tabloid in the rack alongside us, and—well, it doesn't matter. But one of them said I didn't look like Cinderella, I was more like one of her ugly step-sisters."

"That's bullshit." Shelby's outraged expression went a long way to soothing my wounded pride. "Who the hell wants to be Cinderella, anyway? She did the housework, hung out with mice and relied on a fairy godmother to get ahead in life. Plus, she wore glass shoes, which, yeah, they might be a fashion-forward choice, but they're dangerous as fuck. One wrong move and you've got shredded feet."

"Shredded feet," I snickered.

"I'm just saying . . . think about it. Don't be Cinderella, Ky. Cinderella flounders around and never takes charge of anything in her life. Even when the prince is there to make all the women in the house try on the glass slipper, old simpering Cinderella is locked up in the tower, wringing her hands, while the mice do all the hard work of bringing up the key. That's not you. As long as I've known you, you were the woman making things happen. So if you have to be the step-sister, fine. Be the step-sister. But be the best bitchin' damn step-sister you can be—no glass heels for you. The bitchin' step-sister wears . . ." She narrowed her eyes, considering.

"Converse," I completed her thought with a laugh. "It's what old Cinderella should've worn in the first place. She could've made a fast getaway."

"Abso-fucking-lutely."

"Kyra!" My mother swept me into a tight hug before I was inside my grandparents' house. I just barely avoided dropping the cake.

"Hey, Mama!" I leaned up to kiss her cheek. "Watch Honey's birthday cake. If it ends up on the floor, I'll have to explain to her why we're eating German chocolate from the tiles in the foyer."

"Oh, here, let me take that. I'll carry it to the kitchen.

Mrs. Muller and I are almost finished making dinner."

That was another non-negotiable when it came to Honey's birthday. This was a family meal, which meant it had to be cooked by family. Since her housekeeper fell under the family heading, Mrs. Muller was allowed to participate, but my mom was the chief chef of the day.

"Is that my princess?" My father jogged down the steps and scooped me up, spinning me around. "Look at you! You're smart and strong and beautiful."

It was the mantra my sisters and I had heard since birth. Our daddy, the son of two former hippies, was the most affirming, feminist-friendly man on the planet, and he never missed a chance to remind us that even though intelligence and strength were more important than physical beauty, we were without a doubt the most exquisite creatures in the world.

"Thank you, Daddy." I hugged him and patted his arm. "But if you don't mind, could you cool it on the princess, please? If anyone outside the family heard you, it would look bad. Like I have ambitions."

My father chuckled and tweaked my chin. "Aw, Kyra, it's only us here." He held my shoulders and stared down into my face, his brows drawn together. "Has it been that tough on you, peanut? Mom and I have been worried, but Honey and Handsome said you were doing all right. They said you were dealing with it."

"Of course, I am. Is there any choice?" I sighed and rolled my shoulders. "It's fine, Daddy. All the attention is starting to go away. So are the reporters. I'm not going to miss them."

"Hmm." My father studied me. "And what about Nicky? Is he going away, too?"

I wrinkled my nose. "He went away a month ago. I mean, he went back to the UK."

"But from what I hear, you're still in touch. Your sister said it's a hot and heavy romance."

"Which sister said that?" I balled my fists and rested them on my hips.

"Ah . . ." My dad's expression took on a vagueness that I knew was intentional. "I can't remember. It was just something I heard in passing. But the important thing, Ky, is that he's treating you right. Prince or no prince—I've known that boy since he was a tot, but that wouldn't stop me from straightening him out if he falls out of line."

"Understood, Daddy. I'll be sure to pass that on next time Nicky and I chat." I gave him one more quick side hug before meandering into the main part of the house, where Honey was holding court from her favorite wing-backed chair, with my sisters sitting on the sofa.

"Happy birthday, Honey." I bent to kiss her cheek.

"Kyra, you're here, finally." She made a show of looking around me. "Where's my cake? Don't tell me you forgot it."

"Mama took it into the kitchen already. Don't worry, Honey. It's delicious. Or at least the batter was."

"Wonderful. It wouldn't be my birthday without my Kyra cake."

Lisel gave a fake cough. "Teflon granddaughter."

Holding my hands behind my back, I subtly flipped her the bird.

"Honey, what did you do for a cake before Kyra born? Or before she was old enough to bake?" Bria inquired.

My grandmother lifted one elegant shoulder. "Oh, people bought me cake. But Kyra's been baking me my cake since she was eleven years old. And every year, it only gets better."

I looked at Lisel and Bria over my shoulder, raising my brows as I pointed to my chest. "Child prodigy, here."

Bria made a gagging noise, and I laughed as I turned around to hug her. "Oh, c'mere, brat. Look at you. When did you get to be the pretty one?" I hugged my baby sister tight. "I thought you were going to be the gangly one forever."

"I've always been the pretty one." Bria preened, but it was all show. Bree was gorgeous, but everyone knew that she was also crazy smart. She'd skipped two grades in elementary school, and although she was not yet eighteen, she had already finished two years of college.

"You're all beautiful, but more important, you're lovely, compassionate young women." Honey tucked her bare feet up under her in the chair. "I'm proud of all of my granddaughters."

I sat down on the sofa between Bria and Lisel, and as I listened to the good-natured sparring going on, some of the tension I hadn't realized I'd been carrying with me began to dissipate. It had always been this way with my family; they were my safe spot, my happy place. No one was talking to me about how awkward I looked in the pictures that had been popping up on websites and tabloids; none of them asked me if I'd been in touch with Nicky or was planning to see him soon.

"When are you coming back to Florida, Honey?" Bria leaned forward a little. "The beach house is so empty without you and Handsome there."

"We're flying back on Monday. I wanted to celebrate in Maine this year, since we hosted that symposium on organic growing."

"And because Kyra's up here," Lisel added. "You didn't want her to have to leave her precious plants."

"Hey." I kicked my sister's foot. "Don't be dissing my babies." Digging my phone out of the pocket of my shorts, I began to scroll through my photos. "Want to see some pictures? They're growing so fast."

Lisel laughed. "No, thanks. I see them on the emails you send out to all of us every single day. I think I'm good."

I smirked. "You're just jealous because I got the green thumb in the family."

"I'm not jealous of that. I got the fashion sense. We both make the world a prettier place . . . just in different ways."

"You're not wrong," I agreed. Lisel had just completed her degree in design and was planning to work in New York this fall. "I've missed you since I moved up here. Poor Shelby has to tell me what to wear."

"Or what *not* to wear," Bria put in. "And judging from some of the pictures I've seen on the internet lately, she's not doing her job."

There was a loaded silence in the room for a moment. I could tell by the expression on Bria's face that she hadn't meant what she'd said to be hurtful; it wasn't like her to be mean. I took a deep breath and stuck out my tongue.

"Bitch." The word held no heat at all; Bria knew that and grinned.

"Hey, you're representing all of us in a way. All I ask is that you try not to be photographed in jeans that are over four years old, okay? Have a little pride."

"Dinner's ready, everyone!" My mother called to us from the doorway to the kitchen. "Per Honey's request, we're eating on the patio. Grab your drinks, and let's go outside."

It was a perfect early summer day in Maine, and although the sunshine had been warm all day, the breeze that blew over the flagstone deck was cool and refreshing. I found a seat at the long wooden table, jostling for space between my father and Lisel. My mom and Mrs. Muller were the last to join us.

"Who miscounted?" From his position at the head of the table, Handsome frowned and gazed around at the place settings. "We seem to have one extra spot. Are we missing anyone?"

"It must be for Jeremiah," Bria joked, referencing her childhood imaginary friend. "Don't worry, Handsome, he doesn't eat much."

"But I do." The deep voice came from the open doorway behind me, and I spun in surprise, my mouth dropping open as Nicky strolled out. "Thanks for saving me a seat, Aunt Maggie. Happy birthday."

He paused briefly next to Honey's chair, wrapping her in a quick, warm hug. The room exploded in voices, most of them aimed my way.

"Did you know he was coming?" Lisel whispered, her eyes wide.

I shook my head. I felt a little dizzy, as though I'd dropped into an alternate universe of the unexpected. Nicky was heading toward me, his eyes smiling and watchful. When he reached my place, he leaned over to press a kiss to my cheek.

"Hi, Ky. Surprised?"

"Just slightly." I gripped my hands in my lap to keep them from shaking. "What—when did this happen? How long have you been here? How long can you stay?"

"Here." My father stood up and slid over to the empty chair. "Nicky, you can sit next to Kyra. Sounds like you have some catching up to do with my daughter."

"Thank you, sir." Nicky flashed my dad a grin before he pulled out the chair and sat down. "I think I'd better make it good."

"Let's start passing the food before it gets cold," my mother interrupted. "Nicky, you can do your explaining while we eat."

"I wasn't sure I was going to be able to pull it off—getting over here." Nicky helped himself to potato salad. "I had a gap in my schedule, but there was a chance I was going to have to take an engagement on behalf of my sister. While I was waiting to see how that ended up, your grandfather emailed and invited me to your grandmother's birthday dinner. I didn't tell you, Ky, because if it didn't work out, I didn't want to disappoint you." He slid a portion of barbecued ribs onto his plate. "I'm in Maine until Tuesday afternoon, then I have to fly back."

"And he's staying here, with us," Honey added. "It's more private than a hotel. The press can't come past the gates."

"Oooooh." Bria wagged her eyebrows. "Sounds romantic."

"Shut up, Bree." I glared her way, and Nicky laughed.

"Bria? Is that really you? Last time I saw you, I'm pretty sure you were begging me to give you a piggyback ride."

My sister giggled. "Sounds about right. And hey, you know, if you're game, I'd be more than happy to let you deliver on that ride now."

"No." I nudged at her foot under the table. "Behave yourself, Bria. Don't make Nicky sorry he came all this way for Honey's birthday dinner."

"Kyra, I hate to break it to you, sis, but I don't think he

flew across the ocean to say happy birthday to Honey." Lisel winked at me before shifting to respond to our grandfather, who was asking her a question.

"She's right, you know." Nicky reached for me under the table, taking one of my hands in his. "I didn't fly over for dinner. Or for Honey. Or even for birthday cake, which I saw as I came through the kitchen—and it looks amazing." He threaded his fingers through mine. "I came to see you. And only you."

A joy I hadn't felt in many weeks bubbled up in my chest, and I let myself look into Nicky's eyes. The steady promise and the warmth I saw there erased all of the stress and embarrassment of the past month.

I wanted to answer with some pithy quip, but all I could manage was a smile and two heartfelt words.

"I'm glad."

CHAPTER Twelve

"WHAT KIND OF FLOWER IS THAT?"

I craned my head to follow the direction Nicky was pointing, squinting against the bright sunlight flooding over us. We were lying on a quilt in the middle of my grandmother's flower garden, and I'd been drowsing, nearly dozing, before Nicky spoke.

"Oh. The yellow one?" I rolled over onto my stomach, propping myself on my elbows. "That's *Cypripedium parviflorum.* Variety makasin. More commonly known as lady's slipper. It's a type of orchid."

"Ah. And here all I was thinking was that it was pretty and it smelled nice. Now the science geek in me feels totally inadequate."

I snickered. "The science geek. You, my friend, are the furthest from a science geek that I can imagine."

"Hey! Are you calling me stupid?" Nicky scowled at me.

"Never." I leaned sideways to kiss his cheek, just because he was here next to me and I could do it. "You're very intelligent and knowledgeable about many things. Including many *science* things. But you're not a geek. You're a science . . ." I considered briefly. "A science hunk. How about that?"

"Is it a good thing?" He reached over to brush the curls away from my face.

"It is. A little dated, maybe . . . it's a word my mother uses a lot. She says when she first saw my dad at their freshman orientation in college, she wanted to talk to him because he was a real hunk."

"It must be a strictly US-based colloquialism. Is it short for something?"

"I think . . ." I cast up my eyes. "It's probably short for 'hunk of manly goodness'. How's that?"

"Depends. Did you just make it up this minute?" Nicky narrowed his gaze.

"I did." I grinned, and Nicky poked me in the ribs, sending me into peals of giggles. "But you should be flattered, because my invention was totally inspired by you, my sweet hunk of manly goodness. Oh, correction. My sweet *science* hunk of manly goodness."

"Hmm." He rested his chin in his hand. "Am I, then?"

"A sweet science hunk of manly goodness? Absolutely."

"No. Yours?"

My heart flutters, which had been almost constant since Nicky had surprised me two days before, went into overdrive. I dropped down and rolled to my back again, so that I could see his face more clearly.

"You are. If you want to be, that is." I traced the line of his jaw. "Do you?"

He stared at me, heat filling his eyes. "Yeah, I do." Shifting, he caught my hand and pressed his lips into the palm. "If you'll be my . . ." He twisted his mouth a bit in an exaggerated pose of deep consideration. "My sexy goddess of womanly virtue. How's that?"

I pretended to pout. "It doesn't say anything about my intelligence. And virtue makes it sounds like I'm jealously guarding my virginity, which—" I cleared my throat. "Well, not that you're asking, but that ship has sailed."

"True. Okay, let me think about it. How about this: my clever goddess of womanly sexiness."

I nodded. "I like that. But it's kind of a mouthful. It doesn't roll off the tongue the way my science hunk does."

"You're right. I'll just have to say you're my Ky, and you'll know that all the other stuff—the intelligence, the goddess, the sexiness—it's all implied in those two syllables."

Happiness so deep and rich that it almost choked me swept over my heart. These last few days with Nicky . . . I couldn't think of any time in my life that I'd been more content or more filled with hope. We hadn't done anything exciting, aside from afternoons swimming in the estate pool, walks in the orchards that surrounded the house and times like this, lounging in the garden. But it was enough, because we were together, and the world hadn't intruded.

At my grandparents' insistence, I'd been staying here at their home, too. It made sense; I didn't have to drive back and forth, and it gave Nicky and me more time together. Nicky had insisted that I put my phone away in a drawer and that we both stayed away from the television and any social media, so that nothing would disturb us. I didn't mind that at all, except that now and then, I wondered what the world was saying.

I'd asked Nicky if the media had realized he was flying over here. He'd given me an enigmatic shrug and replied, "They always know what's going on."

I didn't push him beyond that, mostly because I didn't want to know. I was going to Scarlett O'Hara this whole thing;

I'd think about it next week, once Nicky was gone again.

"I don't want to leave." As though he'd read my mind, he sighed the words, wrapping loose strands of my hair around one of his fingers.

"The garden, you mean?" I wasn't being obtuse; I knew what he was saying. But I still wanted to hear the words.

"This garden, yes. This house. But mostly, you." He stretched out his arms and lay flat, his cheek against the quilt. "I don't think I've felt this safe and normal since the last summer I spent in Florida, at Gram's."

"It's been a wonderful few days." I skimmed my hand up his arm. The light blue T-shirt he was wearing didn't do anything to disguise the hills and valleys of muscle that covered his shoulders and back. He was so tempting lying there next to me, his eyes closed and his dark blond hair mussed by the breeze.

We were alone here. Honey and Handsome had left for the airport early this morning, heading back to Florida, where they would enjoy the beach and chaperone Bria, who had a lifeguarding job there for the summer. Mrs. Muller had been by earlier today to make sure we had enough food and to close up the parts of the house that would remain unused until my grandparents returned for Thanksgiving.

But she'd left just after lunch. Nicky's policeman was staying in one of the small guesthouses, here in case we needed him but otherwise staying out of our way. There wasn't another soul around for miles, and everything was silent except for the trilling of the birds.

We'd been slightly cautious, just a little tentative since Nicky had been here. He'd kissed me good morning and good night, and he held my hand while we walked. We stopped under trees in the orchard for long, desire-drunk kisses. While we watched movies at night, Nicky wrapped one arm around me and held me close. But we hadn't gone any further. I never would have even considered sleeping in his room while Honey and Handsome were in the house. I didn't think they had delusions about my sex life, but I respected them both too much to push those boundaries.

But now . . . we were alone. The sun was hot on us, and I'd been dying by degrees to touch Nicky . . . to feel his hands on me. With fingers that were only a tiny bit hesitant, I ran my hand down his spine, stopping at the hem of his shirt. I paused for a beat and then slid underneath, smoothing my touch over warm, solid skin and muscle.

Nicky didn't move, but his breathing hitched slightly. I explored him, learning the scape of his body, thrilling to the feel of him.

"Ky." He breathed my name on a sigh. "My Ky."

"Hmmmm." Emboldened, I dropped my lips to the expanse of skin revealed between his pushed-up shirt and the waistband of his shorts. Closing my eyes, I pressed tiny kisses to his spine, to the valley on either side and then upward, nudging the cotton of his tee out of the way as I went.

"Kyra." Nicky groaned, turning over to his back and reaching for me at the same time. "God, that feels good."

"You taste good." I buried my face in his neck. "And mmmmmm, you smell good, too."

He pulled me up so that I was sprawled across his chest. "I want to taste you, too." His fingers combed through my hair at the back of my head as he gently forced my head down to kiss my lips.

Need surged within me, and I took control of the kiss,

angling my head to deepen our connection. I opened my mouth so that his tongue could find mine, stroking and exploring.

His other hand, the one that wasn't buried in my hair, feathered down my back to rest on my ass. Beneath me, I felt his desire for me, a hard ridge against my hip.

I wanted to sit up, undress both of us and slide onto him, inch by intoxicating inch. But something, some unlikely caution, held me back. I couldn't say why, but I wasn't ready to take that step, not when everything still felt unsettled. I was sure about Nicky. My feelings for him were strong and true, and I believed him when he said he wanted me, too.

But beyond that, nothing was certain—from when we'd see each other again to where either of us saw this going in the long-term. That was why I couldn't take that last step. Not yet.

Being smart and sensible, though, didn't mean that all pleasure was out of the question. Drawing up both of my legs, I bent my knees and pushed into a sitting position, straddling Nicky's hips.

He gazed up at me, his eyes hazy and hooded. His lips were slightly parted, and his chest rose and fell rapidly.

"God, Ky. You're beautiful. Breathtaking." His hands bracketed my hips, and the way he looked at me, the way he held me—I felt like what he said. Beautiful. Wanted.

Crossing my arms over my stomach, I grasped my shirt and stripped it off, tossing it to the side of the quilt. Nicky's eyes flared as he lifted his hands to palm my breasts over the thin lace of my bra. His thumbs brushed over my nipples, and I hissed in a breath as both rosy tips tightened at his touch.

"Kyra. I want to put my mouth on you." He sat up,

wrapping his arms around me, and I hummed a little as my center ground into him. His fingers lowered between us, curling over the edge of the bra's cup and pushing my boobs into prominence. Bending his head, he drew the nipple between his lips.

I dropped my head, arching my back to give him better access. The world spun around us, and everything vanished except Nicky and me and this exploding passion between us.

"Sir!"

I jerked back out of instinct, covering myself with both arms. Nicky immediately pulled me closer, protecting me from being seen. I ducked my head into his shoulder.

"What's the matter, Tom?" His voice was terse and strained.

"Sir, we have a little bit of a situation. It's come to my attention that someone—ah, we assume media presence—is within the vicinity and has rigged something so that they can see into the garden. I'm very sorry to interrupt, sir, but I think you might want to consider . . . moving inside."

"Fuck." Nicky ground out the word, and I felt his arms tense. "Do you know what they got? How long have they been there?"

"Not sure at the moment, sir. We're investigating and doing what we can to remove them, but as they are not on private property, there's a limit to what we can do."

"Of course." Nicky swallowed, and his hand smoothed over my hair. "Ky, can you reach your shirt to put it on?"

I nodded, my head rubbing against him. I wasn't ready to lift up my face yet.

"All right, then. Tom, we'll be inside in a moment."

"Of course, sir. Is there anything I can do to—"

"No, just some privacy, thanks." After we heard the snick of the door closing, Nicky added, "But apparently privacy is too fucking much to ask for."

I drew in a deep shaking breath. The mood of the afternoon was shattered, and suddenly, I didn't feel safe and happy anymore.

"I'm sorry, Ky." Nicky repeated the words for the fourth time since we'd come inside. He was slumped in Honey's favorite wing chair, his phone in his hands, as I lay on the sofa, watching him in silence.

"You didn't do this, Nicky. And there was no way you could've anticipated it. So please stop beating yourself up." I rested my chin on my bent arm. "You're many wonderful things, Nicholas Windsor, but omniscient is not one of them. I'm okay with that."

He turned eyes to me that were filled with a miserable mix of guilt and anger, though I knew neither were directed at me.

"The thing is, Ky, I did know . . . something. The other day when we snuck out to see your project plots—someone saw us, and the pictures were published. The reporters knew I was here. And I knew that they did. But I managed to convince myself that as long as we stayed on your grandparents' property, we'd be all right. I was reckless and stupid."

I pushed myself to sit up, frowning. "Why didn't you tell me? About the pictures, I mean?"

He pushed one hand through his hair, leaving it standing on end. "I didn't want to ruin our time together. I was going to tell you before I left, so that you wouldn't be blind-sided, but I didn't think there was any good reason to make you worry when we were still together here. I'm sorry. I was trying to do the right thing, but apparently, I'm incapable of figuring out what that is anymore."

"No." I shook my head. "You *did* do the right thing. I had a beautiful couple of days of relaxation, where I didn't think about the outside world at all. I needed that, Nicky. I needed the break, and you gave it to me. The truth is that I'm not an idiot. I knew, in the back of my mind, that it was probably pretty likely someone had figured out you were here. I chose not to think about it while we were alone together."

He smiled for the first time since Tom had interrupted us in the garden. "I guess that makes us both ostriches, doesn't it? Willing to bury our heads in the sand for the sake of a little peace."

"Well . . ." I uncurled my legs and rose from the sofa, advancing on Nicky where he sat. "If I'm going to be an ostrich, I can't think of anyone I'd like to be in the sand with other than you." Bracing my hands on either arm of the chair, I leaned over to brush a kiss over his lips.

"Funny, that's exactly how I feel about you." Nicky slid his arms around my middle and tugged me down to sit on his lap. "You know, here inside the house, no one can see anything. We could pick up where we left off, in the garden."

"We could. Where's Tom now?" I really wasn't psyched about the idea of getting interrupted yet again by Nicky's security detail.

"He went back to his little house. He's working on damage control and finding out what recourse we have to keep those photos from being published." Nicky skimmed his lips down the column of my throat, breathing deep. "God, Ky, you smell amazing. What's that scent? It's like springtime lives on your skin."

I smiled, combing my fingers though his hair. "It's hyacinth. Where I grew up, in the Brandywine valley outside of Philadelphia, hyacinth is the first flower of spring. Well, crocuses, too, but I liked hyacinth better. Their smell is just intoxicating. When I was younger, Honey and I had a competition to see who found the first bloomed hyacinth each year. When I turned sixteen, she commissioned a perfume to be made specifically for me from the scent of the flowers. She's had it made into lotion, body wash, shampoo . . . so I have it on me all the time."

"Hmmmm. So are hyacinth your favorite flower? I'm filing that away for future reference."

"They are." I arched my neck so that he could nuzzle the pulse at the base of my throat. "Purple and pink. But never cut ones—I only like them planted, in pots or in gardens. When you cut them for vases, they die faster. They're too beautiful to cut. I want to love them where they belong, in the soil."

"Ky." Nicky brushed my hair over my shoulder. "Sometimes I worry that maybe . . . that's what I'm doing to you. Like cutting flowers and putting them in water for the selfish need of enjoying them . . . am I making your life brutal by wanting to be with you? Am I ruining you because of how much you mean to me?"

I snaked my arms around his neck and held on tight. "No, you're not. Nicky, I love flowers and plants and all things green, as you know, but I'm not some delicate blossom. I'm strong. I wouldn't let you do anything that could hurt me—that would ruin me. I promise. And it's not selfish if it's what

I want, too."

His kiss was searing and possessive, the barely banked passion fueling my own need. "Tell me that we're not going to let all the obstacles tear us apart. Tell me that you trust me. Tell me that we're going to figure this out. Tell me that all of this—me and all of my baggage—isn't too much for you."

I leaned my forehead against him, my lips curving into a smile of promise. "I trust you. I believe in you. I believe in us. We're going to figure it out, and neither you nor your, uh, baggage is too much for me."

His arms wrapped around me, drawing me even closer, and for a moment, he sagged against me in relief, his breath tickling my neck.

"I don't want to lose you, Kyra."

"Then don't." I laid my hand alongside his cheek. "Kiss me, Nicky, and make me forget that anything else exists."

When his mouth sealed over mine, the world and all of its complications vanished. There was only the two of us.

CHAPTER Thirteen

Romantic Rendezvous Goes Viral!

Just when we thought things were cooling off between Britain's Prince Nicholas and his American love interest, Maine heiress Kyra Duncan, the two were spotted together near her home in New England. We found the lovebirds visiting a garden at the local college Kyra attends.

But wait! It gets better. Just in case you thought maybe the two were just friends—nope! Our cameras also caught the pair in a heated embrace outside of Kyra's grandparents' estate. These photos say it all, and what they say is TOO HOT FOR PRINT!

Sources say that things are sweeter than ever between the lovers. Should we start getting ready for a transatlantic royal wedding?

Stay tuned!

"Good morning, Kyra!" Sophie Kent, one of the reporters who had been a regular since the first day of coverage, called to me from her spot alongside my path to the car. "Off to the garden?"

I smiled, pausing as I did. I was learning, and one of the lessons I'd figured out was that they were going to take pictures, and when I stopped briefly, it made for a better photo. It was that fine line between accepting the inevitable and seeking attention.

"Yes, off to the garden," I echoed. "Lovely day, isn't it?"

"Very pretty." She stepped a little closer. "Any plans for the weekend?"

I forced my shoulders to relax and gave a little laugh. "Oh, yes, big weekend ahead. Lots of writing of reports and binge-watching TV. I'm a wild woman." Instantly, I regretted the last part of what I'd said. I had learned that some reporters liked nothing more than to take real quotations out of context and make it sound as though I'd said something completely different.

Before I could do anything else to get myself in trouble, I made a beeline for the car. My hand was on the door, about to open it, when Sophie spoke again.

"Just wondering because it's come to our attention that Prince Nicholas has a clear calendar this weekend, and there's buzz he's planning a trip to the states. Anything to add?"

I kept my head down and my eyes on the steering wheel as I opened the door and climbed into the car. "No comment."

Backing out of the driveway, I waved to the small knot of reporters there and headed to the college. Once I was a little bit down the road, I clicked on my bluetooth car speaker and called Shelby.

"Hey, it's the chick who's doing a strip tease for Prince Nicholas in her grandmother's garden." She giggled.

"Stop. I'm going to hang up on you." I rolled to a stop at an intersection. "You sound better. The flu finally let up?"

"Finally being the operative word. Mom says it was the Florida sunshine and healthy air that healed me. Vivian says it was the food she made me. Aunt Gail says it was the flu, and the flu runs its course. I think she's probably right."

"So Florida is where it's at, huh? Have you decided to go ahead and stay down there for the rest of the month?"

"If you're okay with it, yeah, I think I will. It's been a nice break, especially . . ." Her voice trailed off, but I knew what she had been about to say.

"Especially now that the reporters are back in full force, you mean. Yeah, you're not missing anything but stress and mess up here. So stay down in Florida as long as you can." I turned at the next light.

"You should come down, too. You could come stay with us, or you could visit your sister and your grandparents at the beach. It would be good for you."

"Funny you should say that." Slowing, I pulled into the parking lot of the project plots. "Because I was thinking that maybe if I was to be at Honey and Handsome's next week, you might mosey over and say hello."

"Mosey? Since when did I become a cowboy? But are you seriously coming down?" Shelby's voice took on an added lilt.

"It's not for public knowledge, but yeah. Nicky came up with this idea before he flew back to London last month, after Honey's birthday. His family still owns the house next door to my grandparents, and it's private—fenced, set back from the road, not viewable from the beach, which is private . . . we got spoiled with our little bit of time together in Maine, and now we want more."

"So . . . you're flying to Florida? When?" Shelby demanded.

"Friday. But I'm going to be sneaky about it. I had to enlist some help, in the form of my project partner, Ed. He's going to drive me from the garden down to the airport in Boston. I'm hoping I can get enough of a head start on the media that they won't have time to set up any ingenious new ways to violate our privacy in Florida. No rented bucket trucks or anything like that." We'd learned that several enterprising photographers had done just that—rented a bucket truck for the day and then parked it just far enough away that they weren't trespassing. The result had been the pictures of Nicky and me in the garden—and thanks to new high-powered lenses, not much had been left to the imagination.

"Look at you, being all Mata Hari." Shelby sounded impressed. "What did Ed have to say about the plan?"

I laughed. "I had to spend fifteen minutes explaining to him who Nicky is and why the media was so interested in us. Once I got him to understand that, he was more than happy to lend a hand. Or a car."

"Awesome. So you'll fly to Florida, go to your grandparents' house, and Nicky will be the boy-next-door once again. It's like going full circle. Back to the beginning. Think he'll kiss you on the beach?"

"Probably not on the beach, since we can't be sure of privacy there, but he damn well better kiss me in the house alongside the beach. Otherwise, I'm making a long trip for nothing." I pulled the keys out of the ignition and released my seatbelt, but I didn't leave the car quite yet. "And I'm not actually staying at Handsome and Honey's house. They're going to be in California, touring vineyards all weekend, and Bria's going to the Keys with Lisel and a bunch of their friends. As far as the press knows, I'm staying at my grandparents' house, but in reality . . ."

"You're shacking up with the prince. Scandalous, Ky. Just scandalous." Shelby giggled. "Does that mean you're sealing the deal this weekend? Giving over the goods? Going all the way?"

"None of your business," I replied loftily. "But in the interest of full disclosure to my best friend . . . I'm in a better place to go there now than I was before. I trust Nicky. He really . . . he's not messing with me. He's not playing around. It's not as though I'm just another girl to him. I seriously believe that."

Shelby sighed. "I really believe it, too. I haven't asked you this before, Ky, because I didn't want to be one more person putting pressure on you, but where do you see this going? Should I get my passport updated so that I can be at a wedding in the UK some time soon?"

I fiddled with the keys in my hand. "I think that's rushing things. In a perfect world, we'd take the time to get to know each other even better—maybe by living in the same time zone for a little while. I'm grateful for the time I have with Nicky, whenever it happens, but I'm also aware that it's not real life, you know? When we're together, we're not living in the actual world—we're in this set-apart place, so it's like a vacation romance. I want to know that we can make it work when we're both dealing with jobs and the daily stress of life."

"That sounds like it would require one of you to make a big move—and in this situation, I have a hunch it's not going to be Nicky relocating," Shelby observed. "His work, such as it is, can't be done over here."

"Don't think that hasn't occurred to me. I don't want to jump the gun and assume that something's going to happen when I'm not sure about it yet, but in the back of my mind, I've been playing with different scenarios. I know that Honey and Handsome would understand if I had to make some changes to our agreement—about me working for them after I finish my degree. But I don't want to ignore my commitments, either." I stretched backward to tuck the keys into my front pocket. "It'll all work out, somehow. But right now, I'm at the garden, and I need to get to work before Ed kicks me off my own project."

"Can't have that happen. You'll let me know when you're down here, right?"

I nodded, even though I knew she couldn't see me. "Nicky will have to fly back before I do, so I thought you could come over after that for a little beach time. You can bring Vivian if you want. We can hang out and have some fun."

"I'm all over that. Talk to you later, chick." She paused. "And Ky? For what it's worth, I think you're handling all of this beautifully. Try not to let it get to you—all the what ifs and hows. Just let it happen. Everything is going to work out. I have a feeling."

"Let's hope you're right." I reached for the door handle. "Because even though I'm trying to be smart and make the right choices . . . it's hard when my heart is involved. And I haven't said this even to myself yet, but Shel—I think I'm falling in love with Nicky."

"Of course you are, you dweeb," she laughed. "You've been halfway in love with him for months now. Anyone can see that. But don't sound so worried. Falling in love is a good thing. It's—all wondrous and romantic and shit. Embrace it. Let it happen. Because I'm pretty sure you're not alone. I think the prince is head-over-heels for you, too."

I thought about Shelby's words for the rest of the day. It made my stomach flutter to believe it, even in my own heart, but

I was pretty sure she was right—if I was in love with Nicky, he was feeling the same way, too, unless he was an incredible actor.

I couldn't understand why, because I was nothing special. I was confident enough to be secure and content in my own person, to know that I had something to offer the world at large, but on the other hand, Nicky could have any woman he might want. The idea that he would choose me—that he might love me—both exhilarated and terrified me.

Being alone at home to brood with my own thoughts didn't help. I missed Shelby's presence, her cheerful whistling and our constant back and forth of witty repartee. I also missed her input as I began to pack for my trip to Florida. It was painfully clear that I'd ignored my wardrobe for the past few years; the last time I'd bought a new bathing suit, it had been for spring break in my freshman year of college. I knew Nicky wouldn't expect me to be dressed to the nines when it was just the two of us, but then again . . . it was going to be just the two of us. I wanted to look sexy in whatever bathing suit I wore for lounging at the pool. I wanted some pretty new lingerie for our nights together.

I was smart enough to know that an impulsive shopping trip right now would be a disastrous idea. The press would scent a last-minute excursion to the mall in Bangor—which was the closest shopping center to me—like a shark scented blood, and they'd begin shadowing me all the time.

However . . . a little on-line shopping might be in order, I decided. I hated buying a bathing suit without trying it on, but I'd just have to make an educated guess and a leap of faith. I'd bring my old one in case my educated guess was a disaster.

An hour later, I had confirmations that several packages

would shortly be winging their way to my grandparents' home in Florida. I shot both Honey and Bria a quick text, letting them know that I'd ordered a few things and that they should *not* open the boxes when they arrived. I was fairly certain I could trust Honey, but Bria was another story.

On Thursday night, I noticed that the reporters who usually left once I cheerfully assured them that I was in for the evening lingered just a little longer. I knew they couldn't see into my bedroom, but just in case, I made sure all of the blinds were shut tight as I packed the last few necessities in my suitcase. And just to be on the safe side, I waited until the dark of midnight to sneak the bag into my car's trunk.

The next morning, I could have sworn every reporter watched me with an extra dose of suspicion. I was careful not to do anything out of the ordinary; I locked the front door, but I didn't give into my need to double check the locks and the lights. I didn't want it to appear that I wasn't going to be back home in a few hours.

"Good morning, Kyra," Sophie greeted me. "Prince Nicholas was seen at the airport in London last night, boarding a flight to the US. Will you be seeing him while he's here?"

I'd made it a practice not to lie to the press. I avoided, I gave them the standard and innocuous *no comment,* and I ignored, but I never told an outright fib. I had to tread carefully here. If I pretended that I hadn't heard the question or evaded it too pointedly, they'd know something was up.

"Is the prince landing in the northeast? I don't think he's going to be in Maine on this trip." I summoned up what I hoped was a regretful and brave smile. "Sorry."

"Kyra, are you heading to meet the prince?" Another reporter was bolder than the rest and asked the question directly.

I pointed to my car. "I'm heading to the garden, as usual. And if I'm late, my project partner isn't going to be happy with me." I waved. "I'm sure I'll see you later. Have a good day."

Apparently, my attempts at diversion weren't wholly successful, because more than a few of the photographers jumped into their cars to trail me. I forced myself to drive at the speed limit and to take my normal route, although just before my usual turn, I took a right onto the campus, crossing over the boundary that kept the reporters from following me. Just about a mile within was a student parking lot that mostly deserted now, as very few students were on campus during the summer term. I spotted Ed's light blue pickup truck and pulled alongside of it, jumping out as quickly as I could. Opening the trunk of my car, I tossed my suitcase into the bed of the truck and covered it with the worn blanket back there.

A few minutes later, I was at the spot where I'd lost my press tail, glad to see that they were still lingering there, waiting for me. I grinned and waved as I turned back to the main road that led to the garden.

The journalists weren't allowed to go any further than the parking lot there, but it didn't stop them from yelling out my name when I got out of the car.

"Kyra! Where'd you go? Were you trying to shake us?"

I laughed and shrugged. "Had to drop off something on campus. Remember, I *am* a student. Spending my days dodging all of you isn't my real job."

They chuckled good-naturedly, shaking their heads, but I noticed that they didn't leave. Instead, all three cars parked near mine. Yeah, they definitely had decided something was off today. I crossed my fingers that my plan would let me successfully elude them—for a little while, at least.

When I crossed past the tree line into the garden, Ed was standing at the end of a row holding a shovel. He greeted me with his normal grunt.

"How are the tomatoes looking in the experimental plot?" I asked him. "I sprayed neem oil on the control plants yesterday. The aphids were getting bad on them."

"So far, so good. We have more blossoms on the experimental ones, but the control plants are bigger. I guess we'll see." He glanced over his shoulder and lowered his voice, as though he expected to see spies in the trees. "Did you drop your bag?"

"Yeah, it's in the back of your truck." I twisted the hem of my T-shirt between my fingers. "Some of the reporters followed me all the way here. I think they're planning to wait for me to leave the garden."

One side of Ed's mouth twisted a little. "Guess they'll be waiting a while, then. We should probably get moving if you're going to get to Boston on time for your flight. My truck is dependable, but she doesn't exactly fly down the highway."

I extended my hand. "Lead the way."

I rarely used the path that led from campus to the college gardens, since I was almost always coming from home when I worked on the plots. But Ed seemed to know where he was going. We were both silent until we emerged from the wooded area onto the black top.

"I don't see anyone." He peered around. "The coast is clear."

"Yeah, they're not supposed to come onto campus, but it's not like there's an armed guard watching out for them to sneak in. Better safe than sorry."

Ed opened the passenger door for me before he climbed in on his side and started up the engine. I knew I was probably being ridiculous, but I scrunched down in the seat and curled up in as tight a ball as I could, hiding my face in my arms as he drove slowly through the college and exited at the far end, away from the gardens.

"Do you really think they're going to try to follow you all the way to Boston?" Ed sounded skeptical. "Why do they even care? I mean, I know you explained to me, and I've seen the pictures now. But I still don't get it."

"Well, they're just—" I stopped abruptly. "Wait a minute. You saw pictures? Which ones? Where?"

He cleared his throat. "Well, ah, I had to tell my girlfriend what we were doing today. She won't say anything to anyone, don't worry, but I couldn't just drive two hours to Boston with another woman without letting her know what was going on."

I nodded. "Sure. I understand that."

"Well, so, I told her, and she already knew about you and the prince. She showed me stuff from the internet."

"Ohhhh." I buried my face in my hands. "This is mortifying."

"Why?" The truck picked up speed as we left the small town behind us and hit the mostly empty backroads. "You didn't do anything wrong. Even the pictures with the two of you outside—you didn't know some idiot with a camera and a bucket truck would be spying on you. I wouldn't want anyone snapping pics in my backyard. Sometimes, my girlfriend and I go swimming down at the pond near our house, and, ah, we don't always wear swim suits."

Ewww. I didn't need to know this. "I appreciate your

understanding, Ed. And yes, you're right. We didn't have any idea there were photographers nearby, but what I'm learning is that when you're dating a prince, you have to assume someone is watching at all times. That's why I came up with this idea for getting to Boston. I know you probably think I'm being dramatic about it, but if flying down to Florida from a different airport gets the press off my back for even a little while—well, it will be worth it."

"If you say so." He cast me a sideways glance. "This prince—he's a good guy? He's not one of these rich men who doesn't know his head from his ass?"

"He's a very good guy," I assured Ed. "The best. And he loves to talk about plants and growing food sustainably—you'd like him. If he wasn't absolutely amazing, I wouldn't go to this much trouble to see him." I was quiet for a few seconds. "The prince part—the part of him that's famous—that's the part I put up with because at his heart, he's so much more than that. He's sweet and funny and kind and really smart—and he treats me like a princess, even when I'm just me. Just Kyra."

Ed gave a little cough. "I know I've only known you since we both started this graduate program, but I happen to think just Kyra is a pretty great girl. So he's got to be something special to deserve you."

I sniffed, moved by Ed's unexpected sentiment. "Well, I think you're amazing, too, Ed. I didn't know you had a girlfriend. Is she anyone I know?"

He smiled broadly and shook his head. "Nah, I doubt it. She's not at the college. Her name is Jessie. We've been together since we were in high school, and she's a waitress in town. But we're the real deal. We're getting married next year, after I finish my master's degree."

"That's wonderful. I'd like to meet her some time."

He nodded. "Maybe when you get back, some time."

The drive to Boston was blessedly uneventful. Every now and then, I got brave and checked my phone to see if there was anything about Nicky or me, but nothing popped up.

Just before we reached the airport, a text message notification buzzed, and with trepidation, I swiped to see what it was.

A beach picture filled the screen, the empty stretch of sand and sun-dappled ocean waves making me smile.

Paradise awaits. The only thing missing is you. Get here soon.

"That must be him, huh?" Ed smirked. "The look in your eye . . . that's the real thing, all right."

"He's already in Florida, waiting for me."

"Well, then, I guess it's good that we're here." Ed eased the truck to the curb in front of the departing flights sign for my airline. He shifted into neutral. "I'll just jump out and get your bag."

I laid my hand on his arm. "No, stay here. It'll be faster if I can just get it and head right to check in. I'm hoping to get to the gate before anyone realizes I'm here." I leaned over to give my friend an impulsive if slightly awkward hug. "Thanks so much, Ed. I couldn't have done this without you. I really appreciate it. Oh—" I fumbled in the pocket of my jeans. "I have gas money for you right here."

"Don't worry about it." He held up his hand. "It was my pleasure. I'm glad I could help."

I hesitated. I knew Ed had to be barely scraping by as a grad student at Grant. "But, Ed . . ."

"Tell you what." He patted my arm. "When we finish our

project next year and get the highest grade in our class, you can take Jessie and me to dinner to celebrate, okay?"

I smiled. "It's a deal. I'm going to hold you to that."

"Now get going before that policeman comes down here and rattles my cage for stopping too long."

I hopped out of the truck and reached into the bed to retrieve my bag. Keeping my head down, I hustled into the airport, more eager than ever to reach Florida—and Nicky.

CHAPTER Fourteen

"I'M PRETTY SURE THIS IS HEAVEN."

With a smile, I opened my eyes and turned my head to look at Nicky, who was stretched out beside me in the hot bubbling water of the Jacuzzi. Droplets of water clung to the olive burnished skin of his chest and shoulders, and I had to fight the temptation to lick them away.

I'd been here at the beach for all of three hours. Miraculously, I'd managed to keep a low profile and evade the press, thanks to Ed's help and the efficiency of the car service I'd arranged to pick me up at the airport in Daytona.

Nicky had greeted me with a searing kiss, a bone-crushing hug and food that he'd had delivered. As we'd eaten, the sun had sunk low in the sky, sending pink and golden rays over the protected patio.

Since it had been too late for the beach, Nicky had suggested that a soak in the hot tub would be perfect after we'd both spent a long time traveling down here. I'd hesitated only a fraction of a second; the wine I'd consumed with dinner had lowered my inhibitions enough that I wasn't going to let bathing suit anxiety stop me from relaxing with Nicky.

"Ah, Ky . . ." Nicky had cleared his throat. "I put your

bag—and the packages you'd had sent to your grandparents' house—upstairs in my room. If that's not okay . . ."

I'd closed the distance between us, wrapping my arms around him and pressing my body close to his. "It's okay, Nicky. It's *very* much okay."

His answering smile had been huge and beautiful.

To my relief, the bathing suit I'd ordered had fit me perfectly, and whether it was wine goggles or simply the fact that I was feeling positive about myself, I thought it looked pretty damn good.

Now, as I regarded the tempting specimen of masculinity next to me, I gave a small sigh. "It *does* feel like heaven. Is it the hot water, the wine or the extreme privacy, do you think?"

Nicky reached beneath the water and found my hand, twining our fingers together. "None of the above. It's you, Ky. You being here with me . . . that's what makes it heaven. You make it perfect."

I let my eyes drift closed again and maneuvered myself a little closer to him. "Funny, I was thinking the same thing about you. When I'm with you, Nicky . . . everything else fades away. It all becomes background noise, and all I see—all I know—is you."

He tugged me closer, grasping my knees and swinging them over his hard, muscled thighs. "All I want is you. It's crazy, you know? But when I'm back at home, with everything that's familiar and part of my life, it doesn't make sense anymore. I only feel peaceful and whole when we're together."

His arms wrapped around me until my breasts were crushed into his chest and my face was close to his. His blue eyes bore deep into me, searching for some answer that he must have found there. His gaze blazed with heat, and his lowered his mouth to cover mine.

"I love you, Kyra. I want to show you how much."

And then his lips consumed me, his tongue delving into my mouth, finding mine and parrying with it in an enticing dance. My arms twined behind his neck, anchoring me to him, holding us together nearly as close as we could be.

One of his hands wandered down to cover my breast, with only the soaked cloth of my bathing suit separating us. I arched my back and twisted until I could move one leg to his side, effectively straddling his body, lining up my aching center with the hard ridge of his desire. When I ground into him, Nicky groaned and brought his other hand down to grip my ass.

"Show me, Nicky." I breathed the words against his lips. "Show me how much. Show me everything. I want to feel all of you—over me and against me and inside me."

As though he'd only been waiting for my permission, Nicky stood up, water streaming from both of our bodies. Wheeling around, he lifted me to the side of the Jacuzzi and stood between my knees. He framed my face in his hands and kissed me as my hands gripped his back.

His fingers dropped to curl around the cup of my bikini top, and his fingers found the rosy tip of my nipple, pinching lightly. I moaned into his mouth, pressing myself against his hand.

"Need to taste you." He groped around to my back and unhooked the bathing suit top. "I want to see all of you, Ky. I want to touch you everywhere with my tongue and kiss every inch of your skin."

I wriggled my arms to shake loose of the bikini top straps. "Start here."

I didn't need to tell him twice. Nicky cupped one breast in his hand and drew the turgid point into his mouth, sucking hard until I gasped and writhed. He moved his lips to the other side and slid his fingers down lower, until they teased the waistband of my bathing suit bottoms.

"You're so beautiful, Kyra." He kissed the center of my chest and down my torso, making me shiver when his tongue teased my stomach. Pausing at my navel, he blew softly and moved even lower.

"Nicky." I heard the naked and raw desire in my own voice.

"Lay back, Ky." He rose up over me and managed to find a towel to lay on the wood behind me. "Lay back and let me make you feel good."

I lowered myself onto my elbows, my eyes never leaving Nicky as he hooked his hands into the sides of my bikini and eased them down my legs. The tips of his fingers drew tantalizing lines on my inner thighs, teasing higher and higher until I couldn't stand it another minute. Moaning, I dropped my head back between my shoulder blades.

"Be patient, sweetheart." I heard strained laughter in Nicky's murmured voice. "Good things come to those who wait."

"I'm hoping *come* is the operative word here." I shifted, trying to force his touch to where I needed it so badly.

"Mmmmmmm. Remember what I told you. I want to touch you everywhere with my tongue . . ." He dipped his head down between my legs. "And that's what I intend to do."

His mouth covered my core, and sensation assaulted me from every direction. I closed my eyes and gave myself over to the onslaught of pleasure, until all I could do was call out his name, over and over, as he brought me to the pinnacle of pleasure and plunged with me over the edge.

I was still trying to recover my breath, trying to keep from spinning out of control into sweet oblivion, when he stood up over me.

"Ky, you are incredible." He feathered soft kisses on my throat. "Let me take you upstairs and love you."

I managed a smile. "I thought that was what you just did."

"Oh, darling, that was only the beginning. I have plans . . . plans for us. Let me show you."

The only thing I could do was nod. It was apparently enough, because without waiting another moment, Nicky scooped me into his arms and carried me into the house.

The bedroom Nicky had chosen for us to share was the same one he'd occupied when he'd visited his grandmother here as a child and teenager. Perched on the end of the bed, wrapped in an enormous thick towel, I gazed around, smiling reminiscently.

"When we were little, we played in here on rainy days. Do you remember?" I twisted to see Nicky, where he stood drying off with his own towel.

"I do. We built entire cities with Legos, and we had epic games of Parcheesi."

"And then, one summer, Honey and your grandmother said I couldn't go into your bedroom and you couldn't come into mine. We had to stay out on the beach or by the pools or in the living room downstairs. I didn't get it back then."

Nicky approached me, his eyes fastened on me, dropping

his towel as he came near. "I did. It was the year I was fourteen and you were twelve. You were still mostly a little girl, but I'd gotten tall that year, and my voice had begun to change. I wasn't looking at girls the same way. My grandmother told me that it was no longer proper for us to be alone in our bedrooms together."

"The next year . . . I noticed how broad your chest had become." I turned and laid my palms flat against that same chest, which was even wider now. "I wanted you to notice me more. I wanted you to see me like a girl, not just a kid you always played with."

"And I didn't want to do that, because it was too much. When I pretended you were just Ky, the same kid, I was all right. But when I found myself looking at your ass in a bathing suit or the way you tucked your hair back behind your ear . . . then I knew I was in trouble."

"Still, nothing changed that year." I ran my hands down Nicky's arms, thrilling at their strength and hardness and at the way his jaw tightened at my touch.

"Not that year," he agreed. "But the next summer . . . you had grown up even more. You were filling out a bathing suit . . . and I couldn't look at you too closely without embarrassing myself." His fingers wandered down to nudge my towel out of the way until it dropped behind me onto the mattress. With exquisite tenderness, he bent to kiss the top of one breast.

"And all I knew was that you made my heart pound . . . that I wanted you to really see me, and if you didn't kiss me, I was probably going to die." I combed my fingers through his hair. "Do you know that ten years later, I still feel that same way."

"Don't die, Ky." He slid his hand around my neck, forcing me to look up at him, and lowered his mouth to mine. "All you ever have to do is ask. Kissing you is one of my favorite things to do in all the world."

"Mmmmmm." I swiped my tongue over his bottom lip, sucking it into my mouth. "Just one of them?"

"Yes. Just one of them, but it leads to my other favorite things." He eased me back onto the bed and then straightening, he took off his swim trunks, robbing me of every last breath at the sight of him. "At least, I hope it does. I hope it leads there."

"Oh, I'm sure of it." I stretched my hand to curl my fingers about his length. "Look at you, Nicky. You're . . . incredible. Every inch of your body is perfect."

His cheeks flushed, and his lips parted as his breath came more quickly. "Hardly perfect."

"Perfect for me," I insisted. "You're better than any dream I ever had. And you even surpass the fantasies I had for a solid six months after you kissed me the first time."

"You fantasized about me?" He smiled and reached down to touch my cheek with one finger. "Tell me about it."

"Well, I was only fourteen, so they were pretty tame, as fantasies go. Mostly, they involved you kissing me more and taking off your shirt. I wasn't to a place yet where I could deal with anything below the waist. But I wondered what it would be like to touch your chest . . . to feel you pressed against me. And I'm telling you, now that I know, that it's even hotter than I dreamed."

"Hmmmm." He closed his eyes and sucked in a breath as my fingers explored him. "Will you think less of me if I admit my dreams about you were decidedly less innocent?"

I laughed softly. "Back then, or more recently?"

"Both. When we were teenagers, I used to daydream about being with you in the ocean and untying your bathing suit top. I'd gone to a school where the boys spent a great deal of time talking about girls and boasting about things they'd seen and done—most of them made-up stories, I think—so I had a good template for what I wanted to do with you. I thought you'd wrap your legs around my waist and then . . . well, you can figure out what we did."

"In the ocean, Nicky . . ." I shook my head, but I couldn't fight the grin that crept over my face. "Just so you know, having sex in the ocean is *not* one of my fantasies. I had a friend in college who thought that would be romantic, and she ended up with a raging, horrible infection—in a place no one wants that kind of thing. No, thank you."

"Duly noted. No nookie in the sea." He leaned over me, nibbling down my neck. "But then, we don't need the ocean, do we? We have a perfectly good bed right here."

"Seems like it would be a shame to waste it," I agreed. "Didn't you ever have dreams about the two of us here? In your bed? We could make that one come true."

"We could." Nicky stood up and lifted me into his arms again, the towel falling away altogether, leaving both of us nude. Carrying me around to the pillows, he laid me down carefully before stretching alongside my body. "And you know what? This is perfectly right, that we're making love for the first time here, in this bed. I've never been with anyone else here. This is where I dreamed of you all those years ago . . . and this is where we really begin."

I rolled to my side and touched my lips to his. "This is where I want to love you, Nicky. Let me show you how much."

Sliding one leg over both of his thighs, I ranged my body over him, smiling when his eyes went molten with need. He gripped my hips, his fingers kneading into my ass.

"How did you know?" he whispered as I lowered my mouth to kiss his lips. "This was exactly what I used to imagine you'd do. You were always so strong and so sure, Ky. I knew you'd be the same here as you were everywhere else."

"Too strong and sure?" I paused. I didn't want Nicky to feel that I was taking control if he wanted to be in charge.

"Never." He lifted his hands to cup my breasts. "It's part of your charm and your beauty, Kyra—being confident. Knowing who you are. It's what draws me to you." He pinched both nipples between his fingers, sending trills of sharp want down my body. "Take your pleasure. Make yourself feel good."

"What brings me pleasure is sharing it with you." I wrapped my hand around his jutting erection, moving up and down, watching his face to see the need there. "I want you to feel my love in every touch."

"Mmmmmmm." Nicky thrust himself into my fingers. "I always do, Ky. Every time you touch me. Every time you look at me."

Running my free hand over his chest, I hummed a little in satisfaction. My heart was pounding in anticipation and desire, but my mind was clear enough to remember to be smart. "Do you have condoms? I have some in my bag, just in case, but—"

His smile was slightly distracted. "In the drawer. I put them in there, not assuming, but hoping."

"No judgement here. Convenience is everything right now." I crawled to the side, rolling my eyes when Nicky took the opportunity to give my backside a swat. I found the brand-new package of condoms right where Nicky had said, and I pulled out a handful. Optimism never hurt anyone.

Tearing open one square packet, I settled myself over him again, positioning the rubber over him and rolling it on. Nicky watched me, and once I'd covered him, he took my hands in each of his, our fingers knitting together.

"Ky . . ." He murmured. "My Ky."

"Always," I replied. Rising up on my knees, I hovered for a moment. "I love you, Nicky. I always have." Before he could respond, I sank down onto him, hissing in a breath at the feeling of fullness, of being linked to him not just in this moment but for all time. There was a sense of marvelous inevitability, as though we'd always been fated to find each other and to be together like this.

We were both still for a beat, our eyes locked. And then I lifted my hips, finding a rhythm that overtook us both, building into an intensity that sent me spiraling once again into an endless current of bliss.

"Kyra." Pushing himself up with one arm, Nicky hooked the other one around my waist, holding me to him as I ground down, so that when his muscles all tensed into one hard, long thrust, I was as close to him as I could be.

His chest rose and fell rapidly, and he pulled me down to sprawl over him, our hearts thudding against each other. I felt his hand tangle in my hair, skimming down my back, and his lips brushed my forehead.

"Ky."

I smiled, my lips curving against the skin of his chest. "Hmmmm?"

"Twenty-six-year old me just had every expectation

blown completely out of the water. Sixteen-year old me thanks you for fulfilling every dream or fantasy I ever had." He rolled over, caging me in with his arms, grinning down. His forehead touched mine, and he kissed me deeply, with heart-rending intention.

"And all of me . . . loves you so much."

Chapter Fifteen

"I totally disagree with you." I dug in my heels, both literally and figuratively, tunneling a double trench in the sand in front of me.

"Kyra, love, you can't disagree with me when I'm presenting you with facts. Indisputable, non-debatable facts." Nicky used one finger to drag my sunglasses down so he could see my eyes as he spoke in his I'll-be-patient-if-it-kills-me voice. It took everything I had not to stick out my tongue at him.

"They are *not* facts. It's your opinion, and I'm allowed to think you're completely wrong." I pushed my sunglasses back up my nose. "When you are."

"Uh huh. Well, let's not debate the facts, then. Let's talk about results. Refresh my memory, sweetheart. Who won the sand castle contest?"

I scowled. "That's not relevant to this discussion."

"How is it not relevant? I believe it's actually the whole point. The contest was based on the structure of the sand castle. And the judges—"

"Were totally biased. Obviously." I sniffed and crossed my arms over my chest.

"Wait a second—now you're claiming that I won because

of who I am? The judges gave me an unfair advantage because of my family?" Nicky sounded slightly outraged, and I had the good grace to feel slightly guilty.

"Well . . . maybe. But maybe not. Probably not." I was positive the judges back then had given the first prize to Nicky because they all knew he was a prince. But I wasn't going to push this issue, because I also knew how hard it must be for him, never being sure whether or not he had earned something on his own merit. "I still think mine was the superior design."

"Yours was definitely prettier." Nicky brushed the hair out of my face, winding a curl around his finger. "Your design choices made for a more attractive sand castle. I'll concede to that."

"But that didn't win me any prizes. *I* didn't get the ribbon or the ten-dollar gift certificate to the five and dime store." Yeah, it was petty, but even a decade later, the loss stung. Mostly because Nicky and I had been meant to enter the contest together that year, but our argument over strength versus visual appeal had ended that plan.

"I'm sorry, Ky." He murmured the apology against my neck, just below the lobe of my ear. "I'm sorry that we didn't enter together. I'm sorry that you didn't win. Would you like me to see if I can find the ribbon so I can give it to you? And I could take you down to the five and dime and let you pick out whatever you want."

"Hmph." I tried not to shiver from pleasure, since now Nicky was nuzzling the crook where my neck met my shoulder. "You're humoring me. I'm not going to fall for it."

"I'm not humoring you. I'm trying to make it up to you. I was a selfish, mean kid, and I should make it better."

"You weren't selfish or mean." I tilted my head to give him better access. "You just thought you were right. And that you knew better than me."

"Hmmmm." The tip of his tongue darted out to touch my skin. "Do you forgive me, Ky?"

"I'll think about it." I sighed, smiling and letting my eyes close. "Do you know how good it feels when you touch me?"

"I know how good it feels when *you* touch *me*." Nicky drew me closer to his side. "I can't believe the sun is setting already. And I can't believe I have to leave you tomorrow."

"Why does the time when we're together fly by, and the time when we're apart drag on forever?" I snuggled against him.

"If I had the answer to that, I'd solve it. I'd slow down time for our days together, and I'd put it on fast forward whenever we had to be away from each other." He kissed my cheek and ran his nose along my jaw, sniffing. "You smell like hyacinth growing on the beach."

I laughed. "They don't grow on the beach. Too much sand."

"Now *you* need to humor *me*. I'm saying you smell good. It's a mix of your perfume with the sand and salt." Nicky slid our fingers together and lifted our linked hands to his lips. "When can we be together again? It helps if we know how long we have to make it until next time."

"I don't know." I shrugged. "My next semester begins in three weeks."

"And my schedule is insanely booked for the next two months. I'm traveling—but in the wrong direction. I'm going to be in Asia and in Europe. No North American trips planned for the foreseeable future." He sounded as glum about that as

I felt hearing it.

"It's all right, isn't it?" I turned my head to look into his eyes. "We can make this work even if we have to be apart for a bit. We'll just . . . we'll video chat, a lot. We'll text and call, like we have been." I nudged him in the ribs. "You could write me letters."

"Good God, Ky, when will you get over the letter writing deal?" He grinned at me, his expression softening the words. "And don't try to use Shakespeare again. It won't work."

"Fine. But the other stuff will. Won't it?" I was more anxious than I wanted to express.

"It will." He stared out into the ocean. "We just have to trust that it will. We have to be patient." He turned to glance at me. "Like with your plants, with the experimental plot. You let things happen naturally. No manipulation. We'll wait until the time is right, and something will happen to give us a chance to see each other again."

"That sounds incredibly passive. It sounds like we're just going to sit back and let fate take control. Nicky, I'm not very good at that. I'm more of the jump in and take-charge kind of woman."

He snickered. "Color me surprised. Remember, I've known you for a long time, Ky."

I tightened my grip on his hand. "I'm well aware of that. One of the things I love about you is that you know me. And I do understand what you're saying, that we can't force things. But I wish we had at least an idea about when we might be on the same continent again."

"That sounds like a fair and reasonable request." Nicky narrowed his eyes. "Do you have any kind of holidays in the fall? A break in your school schedule?"

"Yes. In late October or early November, we have a week off. And then another week for Thanksgiving." That sounded like a very long time away.

"You'll want to spend Thanksgiving with your family, won't you?"

"In a perfect world, sure. You could come, too. You could enjoy the wonders of a Duncan family Thanksgiving in Maine. It's lots of fun—we'll eat turkey and pies and watch Christmas movies and tell stories about each other. Oh, and we watch football. American football, not what you call football. It's very intense, but it's also wonderful."

"Sweetheart, I'd love to spend the holiday with you and your family, but remember, we don't celebrate it in the UK. I'll have a full schedule that week."

"Well, then, I guess we'll need to aim for the earlier break." I liked that idea better, anyway. Sooner was definitely preferable than later.

"All right, then. When I get back home tomorrow, I'll check and see if I can move some things around for that time. Send me the exact dates. We'll figure it out."

"It's still a very long time from now." I sniffled, knowing full well that I sounded petulant. "Two and a half months."

"It is." Nicky nudged my chin up and touched his lips to mine. "Too long. But maybe something will happen between now and then. Something good. That's our compromise, Ky. We'll plan for the next time, but we'll also stay open to the possibilities of sooner."

"Possibilities, huh?"

He ran a finger down my cheek. "Yes. You and me, Ky, we're all about the possibilities. Hold onto that, and I will, too."

"You're moping again, aren't you?" Shelby nudged me with her toes. "I can tell. You get all quiet and introspective. I can practically feel you falling apart."

"I'm not falling apart." I crossed my arms over my chest. "I'm just . . . thinking. That's allowed."

"No, it isn't." She shook her head. "We're sitting on the beach. On this beautiful private beach, on this gorgeous sunny day, and we're two totally hot chicks. In a couple of weeks, we're going to start our last year of grad school, but for now, we're on a little vacation, and so that means we have an obligation to think about nothing serious. We are morally and practically obliged to be frivolous and crazy and have fun. The only thing we have to consider are which umbrella drinks we want next."

"Uh huh. All right." I adjusted the wide straw hat I was wearing. It was ostensibly to protect my face from the sun, but really, both Shelby and I knew the hat was to hide me from the photographers who were probably lurking nearby.

In the three days since Nicky had gone back home to England, I'd tried to focus on relaxing and having fun, just as Shelby said. She'd shown up forty-five minutes after he'd left, and I knew her goal was to cheer me up, to keep me from being sad now that the man I loved was an ocean away.

I was trying to be a member of team fun and frolic, but it was hard. All I wanted to do was curl up in my bed and sleep. I wanted to close my eyes and pretend that Nicky's arms were still around me. I wanted to relive every moment we'd spent together. I didn't want reality—stupid, painful, hard reality. I wanted fantasy and pretend. I wanted to bask in the world where Nicky and I lived together—the place of possibilities, as he'd called it.

But because Shelby, assisted by my sister Bria, was trying so hard to keep me smiling, I played along. I laid out here on the beach every morning, lounged in the pool in the afternoon and spent the evenings watching mindless chick flicks and eating junk food.

And although I'd intentionally avoided checking on what the media was saying about me, I'd snuck in a few peeks here and there. I'd read the stories about how I'd evaded reporters in order to get down here to Florida undetected. I'd seen the fuzzy pictures of Nicky and me on the beach, walking hand-in-hand. We had made the decision not to let them bully us into hiding, realizing that it was likely photographers would be able to snap pictures from the public portions of the beach.

"We can't let them dictate how we live, Ky," Nicky had reminded me. "Once we do that, we run the risk of becoming virtual prisoners. Let them take their photos. We won't do anything outrageous . . . and if they happen to catch us holding hands or kissing, I don't give a damn."

"Speaking of drinks, here comes your sister with our next round." Shelby waved to Bria. "Perfect timing! I hope you went heavy on the rum."

Bria set down the tray on the small table between our lounge chairs. "I don't understand why I'm allowed to bring you drinks, but I can't have any myself." She scowled at me. "I didn't sign up to be a glorified cocktail waitress."

"But you do it so well." Shelby patted her arm. "Listen, kid, I feel your pain. I'm a little sister, too. The thing is, we can't have you drinking out here where someone could take a picture. We'd all get busted. So while I know it's hard, just remember that you're serving the common good by helping out Kyra and me."

"I think you're both full of shit." Bria perched on the end of my lounge chair. "Who's to say that I'm not drinking water or juice? Or a virgin sex on the beach? The reporters can't tell."

"First of all, by its very name, a virgin sex on the beach is an oxymoron. You can't be a virgin and have sex on the beach." Shelby took a long sip of her drink. "Clearly."

My sister smirked. "Well, there was this one time on the beach when I—"

"I don't want to hear it! I don't want to know!" I clapped my hands over my ears. "Stop right there."

"Second," Shelby went on as though she hadn't been interrupted. "You're right that the photographers couldn't prove you were an under-age drinker, but with the media, it's all about perception. It's not always the truth—it's how they choose to make it look."

"You're right about that." Bria nodded. "For instance, some of those pictures of Kyra they've published make her look like a slob. She's not. But it's how she's standing in the moment they snap the photo or the angle they take it from."

"Exactly." Shelby lifted her drink in salute to my sister's observation. "Which brings up a good point. Kyra, I think it's time to revisit how we handle the press attention. Now that we know this isn't going away any time soon, we should be proactive."

"What exactly does that mean?" Personally, I preferred my own ignore or evade methods. They worked well and didn't stress me out.

"It means that you should be more aware of how you're

being portrayed and try to take control. Remember, the reporters might be stalking you, but ultimately, you make the big choices in how they see you."

"Right." Bria lay down alongside my legs, look at me upside down. "Maybe think about dressing a little nicer when you know the press is going to be there. We could go shopping before you fly back to Maine and get you some cute outfits."

"And we can work on your expressions, how you are carrying yourself," Shelby added. "I've been doing some research. If you look at pictures of the royal family, they all seem to have this look they wear on their faces . . . it's kind of bland, but it shows up better in photographs. Try to keep your mouth shut because they also seem to capture you with it open."

"What do you think about her hair?" Bria cocked her head. "Maybe if she cut it just a few inches—"

"Stop." I struggled to sit up straight in the lounge chair. "Stop it now. I'm not cutting my hair. I'm not changing how I dress. I thought you two were supposed to be helping me relax. Instead you're stressing me the hell out. So just stop talking. I don't want to think about reporters, photographers or how I show up in pictures. I'm sitting on a beach, and I'm drinking away my sorrows because my boyfriend is several thousands of miles away and I don't know when I'm going to see him again. We're not strategizing or making me over. Got it?"

Shelby and Bria gazed at me with wide eyes, silent, evidently shocked my outburst. They exchanged glances that made me feel like I was five years old, throwing a temper tantrum in front of my parents.

"Okay, Ky." Bria sat up and patted my knee. "No makeovers. No serious talk."

"Right," Shelby echoed. "Here. Finish your drink, and then we can go inside and watch some . . . I don't know, what do you want to binge tonight? *Grey's Anatomy*?"

I shook my head. "Too much angst. Something lighter. How about a superhero movie? Something with a hot guy and some snark in it."

"*Guardians of the Galaxy*." Bria nodded decisively. "It's got snark to spare, and Chris Pratt is pretty."

"Sold." I drained my drink, closing my eyes as the rum hit my stomach. "Let's go up to the house, get some food and have another round of drinks. Tonight, we're not talking about reality. We're not even thinking about it."

"Got it." Shelby stood up and offered me her hand. "The only decision I'll ask you to make is whether I should order pizza or wings."

"Both," I decided. "No choices. Just fun and escapism, for at least one more night." Tugging down my hat some more, I followed Shelby and Bria up the wooden pathway to my grandparents' house.

And if I noticed the glint of sunlight off the camera lens fifty yards away, I chose to ignore it. Let them take their pictures. Today, I didn't care.

CHAPTER Sixteen

Is Nicholas Moving On?

It's been well over a month since we've seen Prince Nicholas with American heiress Kyra Duncan, making royal watchers wonder if things have cooled between the couple. Was this simply a summer romance that's run its course?

And adding fuel to this theory is the fact Nicholas was seen out on the town last night with ex-girlfriend Lady Sylla Gates. The two apparently crossed paths at a birthday party for their mutual friend, Daniel Evanson, and they were getting cozy on the dance floor, according to several onlookers.

The prince and Lady Sylla were linked on and off for a few years during their time at university. At the time, sources close to both of them said that the prince wasn't ready to settle down yet, while Lady Sylla wanted a commitment. Could the timing for these two exes finally be right?

Meanwhile, back in the states, Kyra Duncan offered no comment when asked for her reaction to pictures of Nicholas and Sylla. She's begun the last year of her graduate program, which may explain why she doesn't have time for royal romance . . . even with the irresistible Prince Nicholas.

"If they're so convinced that you and Nicky aren't together

anymore, why are the reporters still hanging around?" Shelby glared out the window of our kitchen.

"Because for every story like the one about Nicky and this Sylla, there's another one claiming that we're meeting in secret or planning to. They don't trust me anymore—not after the trip to Florida." I sighed, glancing at my friend over the top of my computer screen. "Come here and tell me what you think of this one."

Shelby dropped the edge of the curtain and came to stand behind me, studying the images of different hairstyles on my laptop. "They're all pretty, Kyra. I think they'd all look good on you." She leaned down and tapped one picture. "That one's my favorite."

I frowned. "Could I pull that off? Or will I look ridiculous?"

"Of course, you wouldn't look ridiculous. You're beautiful, Ky." She took hold of my hair and twisted it up. "It's just cutting it a few inches in the back and styling it a little in the front. It won't change you."

"Hmmmm." I tilted my head. "I don't know. What if everyone thinks I'm doing it because of all the fuss about Nicky and his ex-girlfriend? They'll write that I'm changing how I look to try to get him back."

"Which is wrong, because you don't need to get him back—you still have him." Shelby pulled at the chair across the table from me and sat down. "You said he told you that the whole Lady Sylla thing was something the press blew up, right?"

I nodded. "I know it is. Nicky wouldn't do that to me. Plus, he called me after he'd gotten home from that birthday party for his friend Daniel, and he was definitely alone—or he's a much better actor than any of us might suspect." My cheeks warmed, remembering the night in question.

"I take it from the way your face just went red that you two had some long-distance fun that night?" Shelby raised one eyebrow. "Kyra. I'm shocked. I'm appalled. I'm—"

"Jealous?" I suggested.

"Damn right, I am. Not of Nicky, per se, but you really are a lucky girl. He adores you. So I'm relieved that you're not letting the stupid tabloid stories upset you."

"It's not easy," I admitted. "Not because of Nicky and me—what they write doesn't threaten who we are—but because of what other people think. Some girl yelled out to me the other day while I was walking across campus, asking how I felt that my boyfriend was cheating on me. Even those who don't say anything are thinking it, I know. Or I suspect. There was a group working on the section of the garden near our experimental plot last week. They kept looking over at me while I was working. I didn't hear what they said, but all of sudden, Ed threw down his rake and went over there to give them a piece of his mind. He was pissed."

"Awww, it's sweet that he's such a good friend."

I smiled. "He really is. And his girlfriend Jessie is pretty great, too. We all had lunch the other day, and when I thanked her for being okay with Ed driving me to Boston back in August, she said the only thanks she wanted was an invitation to my wedding when I married Nicky." I shook my head. "She didn't seem to believe me when I said there was no wedding on the horizon."

"Well, not yet." Shelby shrugged. "But if things keep going the way they are, don't you think that's where you two will end up?"

"I don't know." I closed my computer. "We never talk about that. We talk about each other, and we talk about how we feel, and we talk about important stuff. But we never make plans for the future—not beyond when we're going to see each other again—which, incidentally, is in seventeen days and six hours and twelve minutes."

"Not that you're counting or anything," Shelby remarked dryly. "But this time, you're going to London. This isn't just a romantic fling visit. This one is serious. You're going to be in his town with him. You might meet his family. Scratch that, you'll almost definitely meet at least some of his family."

"Technically, I've met some of Nicky's family before. I'm staying with his sister Alexandra and her husband Jake. And I knew Daisy—well, Princess Margaret—when she was little, too."

"Those are sisters. I'm talking parents. Did you know Nicky's mom and dad back when you were kids?" Shelby folded one leg under her on the chair and leaned her chin into her hand.

"No, I didn't. Back in those days, Nicky, Alex and Daisy always flew over to Florida with their security team and some woman—I guess, now that I think of it, she was probably Daisy's nanny. I didn't pay much attention back then."

"Then it would be a pretty big deal for you to meet them now."

"You're probably right, but I'm not going to meet them on this trip, so I don't need to think about it. They're going to be in Poland while I'm there, on an official trip." I had been relieved when Nicky had shared that tidbit in the same conversation that he had suggested that I plan to stay with his sister Alex.

"You could always get a hotel room, I suppose, but if you stay at KP with Alex and Jake, we'll have more privacy and more freedom. They have plenty of room in their apartment, and Alex already said she'd love to have you. Daisy offered, too, but I'm going to recommend we ignore that—she's a notorious slob, that one."

I was slightly nervous about the idea of being a houseguest of Nicky's older sister, but that anxiety was definitely eased by the knowledge that I wouldn't be expected to spend with any other family members.

"You know, these things—royal romances—they don't usually move at the same rate that regular relationships do. I don't know if it's the pressure of the media, or just that they tend to move faster, but aside from a few notable exceptions, royals get married fast, once they find the person they want."

"Probably it just seems that way, because by the time the press finds out, it's already underway." I had no idea, but it seemed as likely as anything else. "I mean, look at Nicky and me. We actually have known each other for twenty years. Even if we got married next month—which is not going to happen, just in case you were wondering—it wouldn't really be a whirlwind relationship. I think the fast weddings happened more often years ago, when people frowned on couples living together before they got married."

"You might be right." Shelby regarded me. "Is that what you'd like to do? Live with Nicky first?"

"I'd like to live in the same time zone for a while. I can't imagine telling the world that we're going to get married before we've done that, at least. But I'm not sure I'm even there yet. I love Nicky. I know I do. And I trust that he loves me. It's the rest of it that I'm not sure about."

Shelby frowned. "The press attention? I think it would ease once you got married."

"Maybe. But Shel, I don't know." I stared down at the wooden table between us. "I feel like . . . I'm going to have to make a choice if this is going to work in the long term. I'm going to have to change. I won't be able to stay who I am."

"Nobody ever does, Ky." She reached across to cover my hand. "Nobody stays the same. You and I, we've been spoiled because we went right from college to grad school, and life's been pretty sweet. But next year, when we graduate, everything is going to change—and you can't stay that same person who spends hours mucking around in the dirt with plants. You're going to be working for Honey Bee Juices, and like it or not, Honey and Handsome are going to expect you to put on grown-up clothes every now and then and work in an office. I'm going to have to find a job somewhere, too—and it won't be fun and games. We're going to have to grow up, Ky."

"I know that." I rolled my eyes. "I'm fully aware that everything changes. But what if I have to become someone else entirely? What if the trade-off for loving Nicky is losing myself? I know I always say I don't read the articles or look at the pictures, but I do. I see the stories about Nicky's family. I know what's expected of people who are part of the royal family. I don't want to become one of those women who only thinks about what she's going to wear to the next dinner, but I also don't want to embarrass Nicky. I want him to have a wife he can be proud of—I want him to be proud of me. I'm not sure both of those things can happen."

"Maybe it's not that extreme. You could compromise, you know? Nicky's not a main royal. There are, like, eleven or twelve people between him and the throne, so the world doesn't have the same expectations for him that they do the others. The only reason he gets as much attention from the press as he does now is because he's such a hottie. And people love a royal hottie."

I smirked reluctantly. "You're not wrong. He really is smokin', isn't he?"

"He is. And that smokin' hottie is crazy in love with you, Kyra. He didn't fall for someone shallow or vapid. I don't think he's going to ask you to suddenly become someone you're not. So maybe you just need to trust in him a little more."

"You might be right." I reached back to lift the length of my hair from the back of my neck. "And maybe it wouldn't hurt to improve a few things about myself. I'd probably want to get my hair cut before I graduated anyway. Why not do it now? It's just hair. It'll grow again."

"Exactly." Shelby stood up and reached for her phone. "Can I call the stylist who does my hair? We could get you in at the end of this week."

I nodded. "Let's do it."

"... and I think we've finally come up with some policies that will allow more restaurants and groceries to donate the food they might otherwise throw away. There's a new group forming that will oversee the safety of the food and work out a good way for it to be repackaged for those who need it most. It's just a start, but it's a step in the right direction."

"It sounds like a good move." I lay on my bed, the phone

pressed to my ear as Nicky told me about his day.

"Yeah, it is." He paused. "You've been quiet. Are you all right?"

"Sure." I tried to force a lightness I wasn't feeling into my voice. "Why wouldn't I be?"

"I don't know." He sighed. "If you're going to make me guess, I can come up with a whole list of possibilities, including this ridiculous story about Sylla and me that won't seem to die, or the fact that we haven't been together in over two months and you're starting to wonder if I'm worth all the bother, or that you're going to be coming to see me in a few weeks and you're silently freaking out about that. Am I close to being on target?"

"Noooo . . ." I stretched out the syllable. "But then again, maybe a little. Not the part about you and, uh, 'the lovely Lady Sylla'. I mean, I don't love hearing about how the two of you met when you were sixteen and began a relationship that both of you always knew was meant to be. That's not fun and games for me."

"Then why are you reading the stories?" Nicky sounded frustrated. "I keep telling you, don't look at that garbage."

"I don't!" I shot back. "I almost never do, unless I come upon it by surprise. But the reporters who are here, still lurking outside my house, don't mind sharing the details with me. I understand that they're trying to get a reaction. I get that. I work hard not to give them anything." I rolled to my side and stared at the wall. "Do you know I spent thirty minutes yesterday practicing my bland face? The one that gives nothing away but doesn't make me look like an idiot in pictures? *That* was time well-spent."

"Ky, don't worry about it so hard. Don't let it get to you.

You know me. You know I don't give a shit about Sylla, and frankly, she could care less about me. She's involved with someone else, and I'm happy for her. We really were friends more than anything else back in school. So think about that when the press yells their crap. Remember that for me, there's only you. Always."

"I believe you." I screwed my eyes shut and willed the tears of self-pity not to come. They rarely listened, and tonight was no exception. One large tear plopped onto the sheet below me.

"Why do you sound so forlorn about believing me?" Nicky murmured, tenderness infusing his words. "God, Ky, I just want to be there with you. I want to wrap my arms around you and remind you why everything that's happening now is going to be worth it in the end."

"Is it?" I wiped at my face and sat up, hugging my knees to my chest. "I know *you're* worth everything, Nicky. I don't have any doubts about that. But where is this going? Where are we going to end up? I don't know how much longer this—how we're living now—is sustainable for me. I feel like I'm always on edge and about to shatter."

"I agree with you. I don't think this can go on the way it is forever, either. But the good news is that it doesn't have to. We only need to get through these next few months, and then everything will be different. Better."

"Will it?" I sounded pathetic even to my own ears, and I hated that.

"I didn't plan to have this conversation over the phone, Ky. I thought that was one reason you were coming to London, so we could talk about this. Make plans for the future."

"Really? I didn't know that was on our agenda. I thought

this was just a chance for us to see each other. To be together." I sounded like a bitch. A desperate, whiny bitch, and I hated it. "I'm sorry, Nicky. I'm not being very clear tonight. It's been a long day. A hell of a week. I'm just . . . struggling."

"I know." He spoke softly. "I would do anything to change our situation, so that you don't have to struggle, or if you did, so we'd be in it together. That's what I want to talk about when you're here. I don't want to live an ocean away from you forever, Ky. I love you. I want us be together. We only have to get through a little longer."

I nodded, which was silly, because he couldn't see me, but it made *me* feel better. "I can do it if I know there's light at the end of the tunnel. I can keep soldiering through if I know there's a reason for me to be brave and keep a stiff upper-lip."

"I happen to like your lips the way they are. No stiff upper lips or lower lips for me. Just Kyra lips. Preferably pressed against mine, or open underneath mine, or wrapped around—"

"If you go down that path, buddy, this phone call is going to take on a whole different tone." I interrupted him. "You know I love our phone sex, but tonight, I'm not sure I could pull it off."

"I don't want you to pull it off. Frankly, I'd prefer you didn't." His teasing made me smile, and suddenly, I felt much lighter. Nicky had that effect on me.

"Nicky, you make me happy." I had to say it. The words practically burst out of me. "You wonder if I'll decide you're not worth all the stress and baggage that comes along with you, but the truth is, I worry about the same thing. I'm not easy. If you wanted easy, you should've fallen in love with a woman from your own country who knows how to dress, how to be polite and how to pose for photographers. You should've fallen in love with Cinderella. But instead, you wacky boy, you fell for the anti-Cinderella."

"Is that who you are, sweetheart?" He laughed. "Actually, I love it. It's very you. Very Kyra. And in case you hadn't figured it out, I love the anti-Cinderella. I think she's fun and exciting and the perfect woman for me. Cinderella—she'd be boring. Plus, glass slippers wouldn't suit you."

I closed my eyes and snuggled down against my pillow, feeling the tension fall away. "I love you, Nicky. So much." Clearing my throat, I added, "And, um, maybe now I *am* in the mood for a little bit of long-distance nookie. If you were interested, I mean."

"Ky, when it comes to you, I'm always interested." His voice lowered. "And I happen to know that any kind of sex is a terrific stress reliever. We'd be wrong *not* to do it under these circumstances."

"If we must, we must." I giggled. "Should I close my eyes and think of England?"

"Only if England is what makes you hot and looks like me, baby."

I gave a little hum of anticipation. "Nicky? I can't wait to be in London with you."

"Neither can I. Now, tell me what you're wearing . . . and let me help you get rid of some of that tension."

By the time I fell asleep forty minutes later, the phone on the pillow next to my head, I was very relaxed.

CHAPTER Seventeen

GROWING UP, I'D TRAVELED QUITE A BIT WITH MY grandparents, but only within the borders of the USA. Honey and Handsome had no objection to international travel, but they were adamant that their grandchildren had to explore and know their own country before venturing out to the wider world. That was why all of us—three generations of Duncans—had spent weeks in their custom RV on road trips, driving to national parks and sites of historical importance during summers and school breaks.

My parents had offered me a trip to Europe for my high school graduation gift, but I'd asked for help buying a car instead, and they'd readily agreed. It wasn't that I didn't want to travel more, but a vehicle felt like a more practical choice.

This was why, when my plane touched down at Heathrow on a gray November day, it was the first time I'd set foot on a continent that was not my own. Now that I considered it, Great Britain wasn't a continent at all—it was an island, so technically, I was still a European virgin.

I was also jittery. I hadn't been able to sleep the night before my trip, so I'd consumed so much coffee on the way to the airport and during the flight that I'd lost count of how many cups I'd drunk. The caffeine buzz made it tough for me to focus on the task at hand—which was getting from the plane to the driver who was meeting me just beyond customs and security. Nicky had texted me a picture of the man, because clearly he couldn't hold up a sign with my name—that would've been gimme to the press, who were already in a frenzy about this trip.

We hadn't been able to cloak my flight this time, and someone on his side of the Atlantic had let it leak that I was going to be a visitor at Kensington Palace. The media presence at my house had quadrupled since that story had broken, and I cringed as they yelled their obnoxious questions at me every day.

"Are we getting a ring, Kyra? Is this trip an important one?"

"Will you confront Prince Nicholas about the Lady Sylla rumors, Kyra? Is that why you're going over?"

"Is a meeting with Her Majesty on the schedule, Kyra? Are you going over to be approved?"

I'd thought I'd reached a place with the reporters where I could ignore their more incendiary questions and simply play along where I was able to give bland, innocuous answers. But they'd stepped up their game now, and I found myself nauseated each morning before I left the house, putting off my exit until the last possible moment.

And then the day before I'd left, I'd lost my cool altogether. The question yelled had been one I'd heard all week, but for some reason, it had pushed me over the edge.

"Will you just mind your own goddamn business?" I'd exploded, turning with my hands on my hips. "Please, just go away and leave me alone. Just . . . go."

For one solid moment, they'd all gone silent, probably

shocked that I'd yelled. And then, like cockroaches, they'd surged forward, coming back even stronger. I'd fled to the relative safety of my car, and after class, I'd snuck to Honey and Handsome's house, where I could find a little peace and quiet. Shelby had been kind enough to drive my already packed suitcase to me at my grandparents' home, and I'd left from there the next morning. It felt like I'd chickened out, but at this point, I didn't much care.

The flight had been calm and uneventful, even though I'd caught more than one person casting speculative glances my way. On the way to customs, I tried to blend in with the crowd, convincing myself that over here, the press wasn't going to care about me. Not when they had real celebrities and the royal family . . . I meant nothing here in the UK.

That delusion was shattered the moment I stepped beyond security. I was suddenly surrounded by people and cameras, and for the first time, a wave of flashes went off within inches in my face. Up until now, reporters and photographers had only harassed me outside, but here in the airport, they had all to use the flash. I hadn't expected it, and I was so blinded that I was afraid to move.

"Kyra! Kyra! Over here, love! Kyra!"

I could hear my own name and a few other random words that rose above the cacophony. *Engagement. Prince. Queen. Family. Move in.*

Panic paralyzed me. I wanted to cover my face and my ears, to curl up into a ball and hide, but I could only imagine that if I did that, they'd trample me and tear me to bits. I was terrified.

"Here, get out of the way. Move, move. Stay back. Stay back, now." A warm hand gripped my arm, and I glanced up into the face of the man connected to it, recognizing him as the driver Nicky had sent for me. He smiled and patted my hand. "Don't worry, miss. I have you now. Let me show you to the car."

Numbly, I let him lead me forward until we reached a steel gray sedan with dark windows. He opened the door to the backseat and handed me in, and as I sat, my carry-on bag, slung over my shoulder, bumped against my hip.

"Oh!" I stopped him from closing the door. "My luggage. I have to get my luggage."

"I've got it handled, miss. Do you have the claim tickets?" He smiled reassuringly.

"Right here. There are two of them, and they're both green. They match. About so big." I held out my hands to demonstrate the size, but my new friend only nodded.

"Got it. No worries. You just settle down in here, and don't open the door for anyone, all right? Even if they knock on the window—and they will. Just sit tight. There's bottled water in the center compartment if you'd like some. I'll just grab your bags and then we'll be on our way."

He slammed the door, and I slumped back against the cool leather seats, trying to calm my racing heart. Adrenaline surged through my veins. That had been . . . frightening. Up until today, I'd had a mixed bag of feelings about the press, but most of those feelings were benign annoyance. I didn't like them following me, and I didn't like that they took unflattering pictures of me, and I hated that they complicated my life and Shelby's, too. Still, I'd understood that the reporters had a job to do, even if I found it distasteful. I'd even made friends with a few, especially with Sophie Kent, who was one of the most consistently present members of the media. She was always polite, even when she asked intrusive questions.

But I'd never been afraid of them. I'd never feared for my safety when I navigated through them between my front door and my car. It had felt like a sort of game between good-natured competitors . . . until today. Today, I'd felt as though those reporters in the airport would've cheerfully ripped me to pieces, if it meant they got an exclusive scoop. I cringed, thinking of what the resulting pictures were likely to be. So much for all of my practiced smiles with my head held high.

Even now, as the driver had warned, I could hear them just outside the car, knocking on the windows and pounding the roof. I concentrated on some deep breaths and on the idea that in just a little bit, I'd be with Nicky.

The popping of the trunk at the back of the car made me jump, but when I peered out, I saw it was only the driver loading my suitcases. He was speaking to the reporters, too; he wasn't being loud or threatening, but the strength in his voice apparently did the trick, since they all began to back away.

He climbed into the driver's seat and closed the door, turning his head to smile at me. "All right then, miss—we're all set. Are you ready? Feeling okay back there?"

I cleared my throat. "Yes, thanks. I—don't know what I would've done if you hadn't come along when you did. They just surrounded me, and I couldn't move."

"Pack of vultures," he remarked cheerfully. "Just doing their jobs, I guess, but they can get out of hand if you're not stern with them from the start. But don't worry, you won't have to deal with them once we're inside KP." He glanced in his mirror and slowly eased away from the curb. "By the way, I'm Harold. I'll be driving you while you're here in London. I hope you had a pleasant flight."

"It's nice to meet you, Harold. I'm Kyra." I rested my head against the back of the seat. "The flight was fine. And now that I'm in the car, I'm all right. Thanks again for saving me."

"Part of the job. Sit back now and enjoy the ride. The prince tells me this is your first time in England?"

"It is." I gazed out the window, eager to see anything that might remind me how far away from home I was. Mostly, I realized, things looked the same, aside from the fact that many of the cars were different and drove on the opposite side of the road. "How long is the trip from the airport to Kensington Palace? Will we pass anything special?"

Harold considered. "Hmm. It's about thirty minutes, give or take, and it's mostly just roads between here and there. But you'll have plenty of time to see some of the city while you're here, I'm sure."

"Oh, of course." I willed myself to relax, fighting off a mix of travel exhaustion, caffeine-induced nerves and post-terror recovery. Outside the tinted window, a new world was flying by, and I wanted to take it all in, but maybe it wouldn't hurt to close my eyes for just a moment . . .

Harold coughed loudly, rousing me from my dozing as the car slowed. We were underneath a portico, and when I craned my head to look around, I saw high walls and lots of green.

"Welcome to Kensington Palace, miss. If you're ready, I'll show you inside. I understand you're the guest of Princess Alexandra?"

"Yes." My voice still sounded groggy, and I hummed a bit

to clear it. "Thanks, Harold."

He jumped from the car and came around to open my door for me. I eased out carefully; my foot had gone to sleep along with the rest of me, and I didn't want to make my grand entrance by stumbling over the threshold.

Harold took my carry-on from me. "I'll take your bags go up to your room through the back entrance. Let me get this door for you." He stood back and gestured for me to go ahead of him up the four white steps that led to a simple black door.

At the top of the stairs, I paused, my stomach suddenly doing flips. I didn't know if Alexandra and her husband were inside waiting, or what I was expected to do or how I should act. Part of me wanted to turn around and beg Harold to tell me how to behave, but I knew that would be the wrong move. From here on out, I had to do my best to figure all of this out for myself.

I squared my shoulders, ran the tip of my tongue over my lips, and gave the driver a slight nod of my head. He smiled in what I took to be an encouraging manner and leaned forward to open the door for me.

Fixing on my face an expression that I hope said confident and yet pleasant and friendly, I stepped forward. For a moment, I blinked in the transition from the sunlight outside to the dim foyer, which appeared to be blessedly empty. Maybe no one was home yet. Maybe I'd be able to get my bearings before I had to be charming and make a good impression.

"What did you do to your hair?"

I lurched to the side, my head turning in the direction of his voice, and there he was, standing in the doorway, the sun backlighting him. He was wearing a pair of faded jeans, and his hands were tucked into the front pockets so that his shoulders hunched slightly. His eyes were fastened on me, and in them I saw the same steadfast love I'd been missing since he'd left me in Florida.

"Nicky." And then I was in his arms and he was holding me so tight that I could hardly breathe, but it didn't matter, because I was here and so was Nicky. His hands gripped my ass, and my hands linked together behind his neck.

"I can't believe you're really here." He covered my face with kisses, and then drew back a little, frowning. "Ky, why are you crying?"

"Am I?" I didn't know I had been, but a sob racked my body. "I just—I missed you so much, Nicky. I couldn't wait to be here, and then the reporters at the airport—I was so scared. They were all around me, and I couldn't move. I couldn't see to walk forward. If it hadn't been for the driver you sent for me—Harold—well, he was wonderful."

"I'm sorry that was your welcome to London, sweetheart. If I could've been there to kiss you the minute you stepped off the plane, you know I would've been. But that would've been even more of a mess."

I nodded. "I know. I was fine. But now, I'm even more fine because I'm here with you."

"You are indeed very fine." He mock-leered, making me giggle even though salty tears were still running down my cheeks. With a slight grunt, he hoisted me up so that my legs wrapped around his waist and took advantage of this improvement in position to kiss me hard, his mouth open over mine.

"Nicky?" I managed to ease just far enough away to murmur his name. "Isn't this your sister's apartment?"

"Mmmmmhmmm." He captured me again, lightly biting my lower lip.

"Is she . . . she's not here, is she?"

"Oh, yes, she's just here in the sitting room behind me."

With a small screech, I madly attempted to wriggle away from him. "Are you out of your mind?" I hissed.

"No." He laughed, his hands molding more possessively over my backside. "I was only joking, Ky. Alex and Jake aren't here. Jake's at work, and Alex is at a meeting. We're alone, and we'll be alone for at least three or four hours." He kissed the tip of my nose. "So I'm going to take you upstairs to the guest room my sister had made up for you, and I'm going to lay you down on the wide bed . . . and I'm going to make very sure that you don't have even one doubt about how happy I am that you're here."

I hung onto Nicky's shoulders as he turned around and began walking up the staircase just beyond the doorway on the other side of the foyer.

"My bags are—oh, shit, Nicky. Harold. He said he was taking my luggage upstairs. Is he here? You know, the driver you sent for me?"

Nicky gave a short huff of laughter. "Harold isn't exactly a driver, love, although he does drive. I sent him for you because he's part of my security team. He's one of my policemen—actually, he's one I trust the most." He reached the top of the steps and walked a short distance to an open door. "I wanted him to collect you, because you are precious to me, and I needed to be sure you got to me safely."

New tears filled my eyes. "That's the sweetest thing you've ever said to me."

He smiled and used his arm to click on the light in the bedroom we'd just entered. "I meant it. And now that we're here—" He kicked the door closed. "Alone. And together, finally. I'm going to spend the next few hours showing you in great detail exactly how happy I am that you flew over an ocean to come to me and trying to convince you that you should never, ever leave me."

I kicked off my shoes and pressed my body into his, nuzzling his neck. "I might be a hard sell, you know. I'm very stubborn."

Nicky chuckled and dropped me onto the soft mattress. "Oh, my Ky . . . I know. But that's all right. I'm fairly sure I'm up to the task."

And he was.

Chapter Eighteen

Being in London was . . . a whirlwind of adventure and new experiences. I woke up every morning in the beautiful bedroom Alex had kindly lent me, pinching myself to prove that this was real. I was in *England*, in the land of Shakespeare and the Beatles and Benedict Cumberbatch. I was staying at Kensington Palace, a place I'd only ever read about. Queen Victoria had been born here. History practically littered this place.

Alexandra and her husband, Jake, had welcomed me warmly, urging me to consider their apartment my home away from home. Nicky lived only a short distance away, in a small cottage around the corner; I visited him there frequently, even though I was sleeping in his sister's home.

"Why didn't you ask me to stay here?" I wondered one evening, as we sat by his fireplace. Nicky's arm enveloped me, and our legs were twined together. It was warm and romantic, and I was blissfully happy.

He hesitated. "Well, I was going to do that, but then I thought . . . I didn't want to make anyone uncomfortable with impropriety. I am very fond of your grandparents, and if your grandfather was unhappy with me because he thought

I'd done something to damage your reputation, I'd feel horrible. Alex offered her home, and it just seemed to make sense. You're close enough to me that we can see each other whenever we want, and I can still look your grandfather in the eye."

I twisted a little to smirk at him. "Isn't that a tad hypocritical, considering you just spent the last fifteen minutes with your head between my legs, making me scream? I appreciate your concern for me, Nicky, but I don't think Honey and Handsome are worried about my virtue."

Nicky snorted. "Maybe not, but I still don't think they'd want to know the details about what we do when we're alone. Trust me, I'm not sharing that with anyone, either. It's our business."

I rolled over so that my breasts were crushed into the hard planes of his chest. "You're so right. Let's get down to business again, shall we?"

He rolled his eyes at my bad pun, but then he kissed me until I was breathless, and what happened next was just one more thing we would not be sharing with my grandparents.

I didn't spend all of my time in bed with Nicky, even though that was an appealing idea. He managed to get us some private tours of places I was dying to see—the Tower of London, for instance, and Westminster Abby—and he even took me with him to a couple of meetings with Waste Not, where he asked me to explain some of what I'd learned about food sustainability and better farming practices.

As we chatted with Carol, one of the organizers, at the end of a meeting, she glanced at me speculatively and spoke to Nicky.

"Sir, perhaps your friend would like to join us at the luncheon meeting at the end of the week? The one we're having to raise awareness of better agriculture practices, with members of the government attending? I think she might have some interesting points to add to the discussion. And you know we need all the help we can get."

Nicky glanced at me, the corners of his mouth tipping up. "What do you think, Kyra? Care to be dragged into the fray with the rest of us? There are a couple of MPs who are stubborn about changes of any kind, including in farming and food sourcing. You could be my secret weapon."

I shrugged. "As long as I'm here, I'm happy to help. And you know that getting me to talk about farming and sustainability is never a problem—it's getting me to shut up that's the trick."

Carol laughed, her eyes sparkling with surprised humor. "All right, then. I'll add your name to our list." She cast Nicky a sidelong gaze. "I'm thinking we should seat her next to Sir Martin Barrett."

"That would be . . . devious." Nicky cocked one eyebrow. "And perhaps not fair to Sir Martin. He wouldn't know what hit him after Kyra."

"Hey!" I swatted him on the arm. "That's not nice. I know how to behave, and I never browbeat anyone into thinking the same way I do."

"Of course, you don't, darling." He winked at me. "You simply show them the error of their thinking until they come around."

"Then you're exactly who we need." Carol nodded. "Trust the prince to bring us the right person for the job."

Nicky slid his arm around me. "Her passion is just one reason to love Kyra. She has a whole slew of other wonderful qualities."

I glowed with his praise, and for the first time, I began to see the possibilities in our situation. I'd been fretting for months, sure that I'd be a detriment to Nicky, unable to recognize any way in which we might make the future work. But if there really was a place for me in his work—a place that complemented my own strengths—maybe there was hope for us, after all.

"I hope that's all right." Nicky squeezed my hand as we left the office building. "I know this is meant to be your vacation. I don't want to put you to work if you only wanted to relax."

"I don't mind at all." I leaned closer to him, bumping my shoulder into his arm. "I like feeling useful."

"Do you, now?" He drew up short just inside the doors that led out of the lobby. On the sidewalk beyond the tinted glass of the floor-to-ceiling windows, a crowd of reporters and photographers were waiting to ambush us. They'd been the only difficulty this week, though Nicky told me stoutly to ignore them. He certainly seemed able to do it; he never held back from touching me or failed to hold my hand when we were in public. I was both pleased that he wasn't trying to hide our relationship and worried that they'd only ramp up their harassment once they had solid proof that we were together.

"Do I like being useful to you? Of course, I do." I tilted my face up to his, smiling brightly. "I want you to like having me around. It sure beats the alternative."

"I do like having you here. Even when we're just sitting together, watching television . . . you make me feel peaceful. And when I have to go out, the idea of coming home to you—I've never felt that way about anyone before." Nicky traced my cheekbone with the tip of his finger. "But I don't want to be selfish with you, either. I would keep you here with me always, if I could."

I bit my lower lip. "What if you could? Wouldn't that be a good thing?"

"For me, yes. For you . . . sometimes I'm not sure." Something was warring within him, some struggle that he wasn't sharing with me. Before I could ask him about it, Nicky bent his head to kiss me, his mouth possessive and wanting. "Let me take you home now, Ky. I want to be alone with you, and I don't want to wait another minute more than absolutely necessary."

My heart pounded with anticipated pleasure. "Then let's not. Wait, I mean. Let's go home."

Without another word, Nicky tugged my hand, leading me through the doors. Harold waited by the car, and he climbed into the backseat as Nicky helped me into the front seat. I'd learned in the past few days that Nicky, like most members of his family, preferred to drive himself whenever he could, even though there was always a policeman present in the car, too. Harold was so quiet and unobtrusive that I sometimes forgot he was even with us.

"Kyra! Look over here, love! Your highness, will there be an announcement coming soon, then? Do you have anything to tell us?"

Nicky gave the press his standard brief smile and wave before he slid behind the wheel. As he pulled away from the curb, he reached across to give my hand a squeeze.

"Are you feeling particularly brave?"

My forehead knitted together. "That's a scary question. Why?"

He chuckled. "I'm going to cook for us tonight. Do you

trust me?"

I shifted in my seat until I faced him as fully as I could with my seatbelt still latched. "Haven't I proven that I do? I trust you with everything, Nicky. Everything I am and everything I want to be." I paused a beat. "But what are you making us for dinner?"

He wagged his eyebrows and smiled wickedly. "My specialty of the house. Roast chicken stuffed with fragrant rice, a side of creamed spinach that my mother taught me how to make, and for dessert . . ." He lifted my hand to his lips and kissed the back of my fingers. "Melted chocolate."

"Melted chocolate?" I frowned. "Just melted chocolate? How is that dessert?"

The glance he slid me was as molten as the chocolate he was describing. "You drizzle it over . . . whatever it is you want most to put in your mouth."

"Oh." A flush started on my neck and crept up over my cheeks. "How did you know that was my favorite way to end a meal?"

Nicky's only response was an evil smirk, and I groaned.

"How fast can you get us home? Suddenly, I'm ravenous."

"You've been holding out on me." I sank back in my chair and smiled at Nicky.

"Oh, have I been? How's that?" He turned from where he stood in front of the kitchen sink, his smile warming me.

"I didn't know you could cook. That chicken was incredible. If I'd known your hidden talent, I would've insisted that you feed me every night this week." I paused, thinking. "Also back in Florida. Think about how much delivery food we ate then."

"Ah, but don't you think we would've gotten tired of chicken?" He dried his hands on a tea towel, leaning against the counter's edge as he grinned. "Because while I can do that very well, sadly it's the only recipe where I can actually claim some success. Other than this, I burn boiling water."

"Well . . ." I stood up, rolling my shoulders. "If you can only do one thing well, that's a good one." I wandered around the granite island. "Your kitchen is really beautiful. Did you design it?"

Nicky laughed. "No. This cottage was renovated by my great-aunt years ago. Then my cousin moved in after university, and she had the kitchen redone. She has a degree in culinary arts, and she loves to cook. Right after the kitchen was finished, she got engaged and moved to an estate in the north. About that time, I was ready for my own place, so I moved in." He lifted one shoulder. "I don't use the kitchen as well as my cousin did. And I haven't made that chicken since Alex and Jake came back from their honeymoon."

"You cooked for your sister and her new husband? Aw, that's sweet." I tilted my head, my eyes steady on Nicky.

"Not only Alex and Jake but Daisy, too. We had a sibling dinner to celebrate. So it wasn't just sweet, it was downright brave." He smirked. "You haven't seen my youngest sister in a long time. She's a wild one."

"Does she live here? In Kensington Palace?"

Nicky shook his head. "No, she has a flat in the city. She doesn't want the constraints of living in a royal residence, she says. Daisy exists to complicate things. She drives her policemen absolutely insane. But she can be just as sweet and kind as she is crazy. That's the only saving grace about her."

"That, and she's gorgeous." I'd seen Princess Daisy's photos on line, and I knew Nicky's baby sister had grown up into a beautiful young woman.

"She's all right." Nicky tossed the dish towel down onto the counter. "But enough about my family. It's not too cold tonight. Want to take a walk in the gardens? It's very clear. We could pretend to look at the stars."

"Why would we pretend?" I crossed my arms over my chest.

"Because." He grasped my elbow and tugged at me to him. "We'll be too busy looking at each other to pay attention to anything else."

"Hmmmm." I pretended to think about the idea. "I think I can get behind that idea. Let me grab my sweater, just in case."

"Don't you trust me to keep you warm?"

"I do. But if I wear my sweater, you can concentrate on kissing me instead of keeping me from shivering. That sounds like much more fun to me."

We walked along the silent pathway with our hands linked. Every now and then, Nicky pointed out apartments and who lived in them, simply because he knew that I was interested, or he told me amusing stories from his childhood that had taken place within these walls. I drank it in, absorbing what he shared, wondering if it was possible that someday, this might be my home, too. I let myself dare to dream that I could be one of the mothers pushing prams up and down between the shrubs or chasing toddlers along the walks and warning them to stay away from the fountains.

We turned and walked down a few steps into the sunken

garden. It was dull and mostly dead this time of year, but Nicky described the splashes of color that decorated the plants during the spring.

"I couldn't name all the flowers, but I know you could." He raised our joined hands to his lips and kissed my fingers. Turning me so that my back pressed against his front, he pointed down the long pool to the far end. "See that archway? When Alex and I were small, she convinced me that if I ran through it fast enough, I could get to Wonderland. You know, where Alice and company live? I pretended that I didn't believe her, but when she went inside, I tried it, over and over, until I tripped and fell on a loose slate. Cut open my head and had to have stitches."

"Poor baby." I arched my neck to see him. "Do you have a scar?"

"Yeah, but it's in my hairline, so it doesn't mar my rugged good looks." He winked at me. "Still throbs from time to time, or so I tell Alex when I'm trying to make her feel guilty over something."

"Show me." I pivoted slowly in his arms. "Where's your scar?"

Nicky touched his forehead, feeling along his hair until he found it. "Right here." He guided my fingers there, too, and I brushed over the tiny ridge.

"Lean down," I murmured. "Let me kiss it better."

He smiled at me, a hint of amused indulgence in his eyes. I held his face between my hands and feathered my lips over the spot where he'd been hurt.

"There," I breathed. "All better."

"Hmmm." Nicky moved his head a fraction of an inch. "I think I hurt my lips that day, too, now that I think of it. You should probably kiss them better."

"Should I?" I angled my mouth over his and pressed my lips there, moaning softly when Nicky coaxed me to open to him. The tip of his tongue traced a circle on the sensitive skin just inside my mouth, making me sigh in pleasure.

"Ky." He combed his fingers through my hair. "My Ky. Do you have any idea how much I love you?"

"Nearly as much as I love you?" I laughed softly. "Which is enough to walk in barren gardens with you at night in November."

"True." He wrapped his arms around me and held me close. "But here we are in the moonlight, under the stars, and there is no place in the world I'd rather be at this moment. If I could, I'd freeze us here forever."

"Freeze might be the key word," I remarked.

From somewhere nearby, music suddenly filled the air. I glanced at Nicky questioningly.

"Probably one of the non-family apartments. The units that are open to the public for rental are just around the corner. Maybe someone's having a party." He touched my nose. "Probably annoying for their neighbors, but for us, it's serendipity."

"Oh, really? How so?" I leaned back in his arms to gaze into his face.

"Because I want to dance with you, Ky. That's something we've never done." He sidestepped us until we stood on the grass, and then he linked his hands on my lower back before he began to sway.

"This reminds me of junior high school." I rested my cheek against his chest, thrilling to the steady beat of his heart. "We had a vice principal who was a stickler about boys and girls keeping at least four inches of space between our bodies as we danced."

"Ah." Nicky's fingers drew teasing circles on my back. "And did you behave?"

"Always." I grinned up at him. "Actually, I didn't dance with boys often—and when I did, it was always because we were friends. No one was chasing me."

"Then they were all little fools." He dipped his head to kiss me. "If I'd been there, I would have requested every dance. And I wouldn't have followed the four-inch rule, either."

"We would've been in trouble, then," I observed. "And maybe you wouldn't have asked me back then. I wasn't a very girly-girl. Even in those days, I liked playing in the dirt more than I liked dressing up."

"Ky, sweetheart, that doesn't matter to me now and it wouldn't have mattered to me then. When will you understand that you are perfect?" He tucked a curl of my hair behind my ear.

"Hardly," I whispered. "I'm so flawed in so many ways, Nicky."

"To me, you are perfect." He brushed a kiss onto my forehead. "For me, you are perfect. And that's all that matters."

I sighed and snuggled against him again, closing my eyes as we continued to move slowly to the distant music. "What did I ever do to deserve you?"

I felt the rumble of his grunt deep in his chest. "Don't ask that. It tempts fate. Just . . . believe. Feel my heart beat and know for sure that it only belongs to you, forever."

And there in that perfect night, I trusted and believed in everything that could be.

CHAPTER Nineteen

A Royal Romance Disaster?

This week, all the buzz in London has been about American sweetheart Kyra Duncan, the latest love of Prince Nicholas, who's been in town for a visit. The couple hasn't been shy about displays of public affection as they've cavorted together across the city.

Most of the news and photos have been glowing tributes from those who love love and anticipate another transatlantic match for us all to coo over. However, despite that, there's a strong and growing voice of dissent who aren't so happy about Duncan or the possibility that she could be the next new member of the royal family.

"She's just . . . crass," one onlooker complained after catching sight of the couple this week. "She was wearing jeans and gym shoes, and she looked slovenly. That's not what a princess should look like."

One source tells us that Prince Nicholas took his girlfriend along to a meeting of the foundation Waste Not, where she was not shy in sharing her viewpoints and opinions on hunger and farming practices.

"She practically shut down the prince," says our source. "Here it was his meeting, his work, and she kept interrupting, correcting him, even. It was uncomfortable for everyone there."

Whether or not this kind of behavior will be tolerated by the prince and the rest of his family remains to be seen. According to palace insiders, Kyra is scheduled to return to her home in the states in two days, which will apparently be a relief to some who are not enjoying her visit in Britain.

I read the piece twice, my throat burning with humiliation. I hadn't meant to look at it; Shelby had sent me a link to a picture of Nicky and me that she'd loved, and the scathing article had been headlined on the same page, just above the photo.

It was a shame, because the picture of the two of us really was a good one. I might have had a smile on my face now, like I had in the photograph, if I hadn't been idiotic enough to read the story.

"Nicky." I glanced up from my phone, frowning. "The other day, when I was at the meeting with you, at Waste Not—did I overstep? Was I rude? Did I talk over you?"

"What? No. Of course, you didn't." He shook his head, his eyes fastened on the road in front of us. We were on our way to the luncheon Carol had suggested I attend, and until a moment ago, I'd been blissfully happy.

Last night, Alex had helped me choose a perfect dress and heels to wear, since the event was a professional one. She'd even made some suggestions about how I should wear my hair, and both of us had reminisced over one summer in Florida, when she'd taught me how to do French braids. I'd forgotten about that until she'd brought it up.

This morning, I'd felt as pretty and as perfect as I could. I'd greeted Nicky with a kiss when he'd come to collect me, and the expression of open admiration in his eyes had been the cherry on top of a lovely week together. I had begun to feel that maybe I really might be able to pull this off. Maybe I could be the kind of woman, the kind of partner, who Nicky needed. Maybe happily-ever-after really was possible.

And if I hadn't clicked on the link for the picture as we drove to the hotel where the luncheon was being held, I'd still have been living in that state of contented ignorance.

"Why would you even ask that?" Nicky spied the phone in my hand. "Oh, God, Ky. What did you read?"

I clicked the off switch and slid it into my bag. "I didn't do it on purpose. Shelby said she'd seen this picture of us and it was super cute. I wanted to see, too. But I guess between the time she sent me the link and now, they've updated that site with a story. And it's not a very nice one. As a matter of fact, it's horrible."

Nicky sighed. "You can't read that shit, sweetheart. People are going to talk. And as wonderful as you are, the sad truth is that there are always going to be people who don't like us. And there are also downright unpleasant people who only want to make everyone miserable. Don't let them get to you."

"But Nicky—this is about your work. I don't want to mess up anything." I twisted the edge of my coat sleeve between my fingers. "Maybe I shouldn't have come today. I don't want anyone to think I'm pushy."

"You're not. And besides, I asked you to come. So did Carol. We want you there, Kyra. We value your input. You're not coming as arm candy—you have something important to contribute."

I fidgeted a bit in my seat. "What if people think I'm being overbearing?"

"They won't. But if anyone does—" Nicky cast a steely glance my way. "Fuck them. They don't know me, and they don't know you."

I didn't have time to debate the point with him, because we were pulling up in front of the hotel. I sat still in my seat and waited for Nicky to open the car door for me, taking his hand as he helped me out.

"Smile, love," he murmured. "Don't let them see you're rattled. They smell blood, this bunch. They'll go for the kill if they think you're vulnerable."

I lifted my chin, met his eyes and forced my lips to curve, hoping it didn't appear more like a grimace than a genuinely pleasant expression.

Nicky held my hand tightly as we hurried to the door. Once inside, I sucked in a deep breath, grateful for the relative quiet.

"Sir, we're right this way." Carol, dressed in a bright blue suit, met us a few steps inside. "Ms. Duncan, thank you for being here, too. We're so pleased that you could join us." She leveled her gaze at me, and I knew that she'd read the article as well. I could see it in her eyes.

"I hope I can be helpful," I mumbled.

"I'm sure you will be, and we appreciate you taking the time on your holiday." She spoke with a certain intention, and I realized she was trying to show me support. I appreciated the effort, even if I still wasn't certain I should be here.

Nicky and I were both seated at a round banquet table, along with six other men and women. I noticed that some people gazed at me with open curiosity, while others tended to avert their eyes.

Straightening my spine, I summoned up any inner fortitude I had left and channeled the Kyra who knew how to charm businesspeople on behalf of my grandparents. How different could this be, really? People were people. If I was polite and pleasant, what could they complain about?

The first fifteen minutes were spent exchanging pleasantries and commenting on important topics like the weather and other meaningless niceties. I did my best to nod and smile, but I didn't have much to add. I was beginning to feel like a bobble head doll, only there to affirm what others were saying.

Then a woman leaned forward, pointing her fork at Nicky. "Sir, I saw your interview about the new policies in restaurants and groceries. I understand that you are looking for any ways in which to alleviate the hunger situation, but don't you think that's going to put at risk the very population you're trying to protect?"

Nicky lifted his napkin to his lips, pausing before he responded. "Mrs. Gummer, do you know how much food—how much good, viable, imminently edible food—is discarded in this country, because of policies that are ostensibly designed to protect people? You've seen the numbers—I know you have, because I've sent them to your office myself. It's disgraceful. And the idea that it's dangerous to stop food waste is at best a lazy response—and at worst, it's intentionally negligent."

Mrs. Gummer's thin cheeks flushed. "Sir, with all due respect, I'm not sure you're in the best position to speak about hunger. When have you or any of your family ever gone without anything you wanted?"

I sucked in a silent breath, waiting for Nicky to lose his cool. But he only smiled.

"I don't think that's germane to the topic at hand, but of course, you're right. I don't have to worry about where my next meal comes from. I could toss out enough unused food on any given day to feed a village and never feel the lack. But simply because something doesn't directly affect me doesn't give me the right to ignore its existence. In the mid-twentieth century, when Hitler was practicing genocide, the majority of people in Great Britain were unaffected. But we still cared, didn't we? We still sent soldiers there to liberate the camps, didn't we?"

"Are you likening what the Nazis did to our own government's policies, sir?" A man with a thick moustache lifted his eyebrows. "That's rather outrageous, don't you think?"

"People are dying." Nicky shrugged. "The power to alleviate suffering lies within the hands of the government. It's not such a leap when you look at it that way."

An older lady with long white hair inclined her head toward me. "Sir, perhaps we're making your guest uncomfortable with this subject. She's been very quiet."

Nicky shook his head. "Kyra knows as much about hunger, food sustainability and farming as I do, if not much more. She'll be happy to tell you her angle on the topic."

I opened my mouth to speak, but the lump in my throat kept me from saying anything. All I could see were the words from that article I'd read.

Uncomfortable for everyone there . . .

"Ky." Nicky prompted. "Why don't you share a little about other options we have to addressing the hunger problem? Tell everyone about what you've been studying." His eyes encouraged me, and even though I still didn't want to speak, I knew I couldn't disappoint him, either.

"I, ah." I cleared my throat. "I study sustainable farming practices. We're working on how to improve techniques so that farms can produce better, more wholesome food without a devastating impact on the earth."

"Are you now?" The same gentleman with the moustache tittered. "I find that amusing. My family has been in agriculture for generations. I doubt you could have taught my father or grandfather anything about being more efficient farmers." He hmmphed. "That's the problem with universities these days. They think they're discovering new topics and wisdom, but really, it's just old rubbish repackaged."

I drew myself up to sit straighter. The derision in this man's tone burned away the worry and regret I'd been clinging to, the fear that had been keeping me silent so far. Inclining my head, I echoed his earlier words.

"Are you likening the education system to Waste Not's proposed food repurposing, sir? If you are, then bravo. I can see you really get it. You understand that something doesn't have to be new to be valuable and useful."

His face froze. "Young lady—"

But I wasn't finished. "You're not entirely wrong that some of the things I'm studying in school aren't altogether recent discoveries. In fact, some of what I'm exploring is nearly a hundred years old. And others are ancient ways that our more recent ancestors stopped using when they were convinced that better living through chemistry was the way to go. But what we've learned is that in trying to make our food stronger and more resilient, we're killing the earth and poisoning her people."

Mrs. Gummer made a rude noise under her breath, but Mr. Moustache—I still couldn't remember his name—regarded me with interest. My eyes flickered to Nicky, wondering if I'd gone too far, but he was sitting back in his chair, his arms crossed, his face alight with pride and encouragement.

But at the tables around us, I noticed more than one

person listening to the interchange, and several had out telephones and were madly tapping away. I swallowed hard and worked to keep my voice even.

"I'm sorry. I didn't meant to be . . . pedantic. As Prince Nicholas mentioned, I'm studying agriculture, and maybe I get a little too passionate about it."

Around the table, people shifted in their seats, possibly in relief at the idea of dropping a sensitive topic. As the conversation went in another direction, I didn't look at Nicky. Instead, I focused on the embroidery of the tablecloth and the bland smile I was determined to keep on my face.

"Thank you for allowing me to be here." I'd repeated the same phrase four times in the past five minutes, as people stopped to speak to me. The luncheon was ending, but nearly everyone was milling about the room, chatting. Nicky had excused himself to speak with Carol and her assistant, leaving me feeling alone and awkward. I had sensed in the rigid, formal way he'd spoken as he'd moved away that he was frustrated with me, but I was at a loss as to what else I could have done.

He didn't seem to understand the position I was in right now. If I spoke my mind and was open about my thoughts, I ran the risk of alienating people not only from me but from him and his work. I had to be subtler. I had to be diplomatic. And if that meant stifling my own strong opinions . . . well, that was the price I'd pay for being who he needed me to be.

"Ah, the lady who has so much to say about farming techniques." An older man who I'd seen sitting at a nearby table approached me, his expression inscrutable. "I've been wanting to speak with you."

I stretched another fake smile across my face. "Hello. I'm Kyra." I extended my hand before it occurred to me that maybe he was some of kind of aristocracy and I was committing a faux pas.

But he didn't even blink as he gripped my hand and gave it a brief shake. "Martin Barrett, Ms. Duncan. A pleasure."

I frowned. That name was familiar. "Are you . . . *Sir* Martin?"

He laughed. "Does my reputation precede me?"

"Ah." I shook my head. "I remember Nicky—uh, the prince—mentioning a few people who would be here at the luncheon."

"Well, only believe a quarter of what he said about me." Sir Martin lowered his voice and leaned closer to me, as though confiding a secret. "He doesn't agree with me much these days, but I've known Nicholas since he was born. I went to school with his grandfather."

"That's nice." I sounded insipid, but I didn't know what else to say.

"We don't see eye to eye on some of his new ideas about farming and food supply," Sir Martin went on. "I think science and technology have only helped us in finding new ways of growing and preserving food. This movement for more naturalism and less processing—well, it's ridiculous. Mankind is meant to move forward. Genetically modifying our food is the next step in making it better. I fall in with the Americans in that way, but I'm fighting a battle here in Britain against the naturalists. And Nicholas is among those leading the charge."

"Of course he is." I tossed up my hands. "And he's right. In the states, we're battling against GMOs and other types of artificial food manipulation. In fact, being hands-off and non-interventionalist is the basis for my graduate thesis."

"Non-interventionalist?" He snorted. "I believe I'd call that anti-science."

"Not at all. It's simply a new way of looking at things—or maybe more accurately, a rediscovered way of living with the land instead of trying to control the land."

A glint of interest shone in the older man's eye. "I pride myself on having an open mind, Ms. Duncan. Tell me why I should reconsider my position. Convince me."

I took a deep breath and glanced around us. No one was really paying any attention to what I was saying, and I knew that Nicky and Carol had been particularly intent on changing Sir Martin's mind. If there was a way I could help without making it a big deal, maybe that would make Nicky happy.

I spent the next ten minutes explaining to my new friend what I did in Maine, the soil projects we were working on and the idea of natural farming. If he'd shown any sign of disinterest, I would've quickly cut it short, but he didn't. Instead, he asked intelligent, pertinent questions that led me to believe he was fascinated with the subject at hand.

"Sorry to interrupt." Nicky slid up next to me, his hand a light touch on my arm.

"Nicholas." Sir Martin inclined his head. "Your young lady has been educating me on some of the finer points of new farming techniques. She's quite amazing and very passionate about her topic. And frankly, she's an incredible young woman."

"Oh, no, not really." I shook my head. I didn't want Nicky to think I'd been over here talking about myself. "It's not that big a deal. Sir Martin was kind enough to let me share about what I'm studying. He's been very patient, listening to me rattle on."

"I'm sure he has been." Nicky's smile didn't reach his eyes, and the uneasiness I'd felt all morning stirred again in my gut. "Unfortunately, Sir Martin, I need to steal Kyra away just now."

"Of course, of course." The older man beamed down at me. "We'll talk again soon, I hope. I'd like to hear more about your work."

"Thank you, Sir Martin. I'm looking forward to it." With one last nod of my head, I allowed Nicky to steer me through the crowd of people who were also preparing to depart. I maintained the bland and benign expression that I'd begun to see as my mask.

"Are you ready to go now?" Nicky's voice was even and distant at my ear, and his hand rested on the center of my back, between my shoulder blades. "The car's waiting."

I frowned, glancing back over my shoulder. "What's the matter?"

His eyes were flat. "Nothing at all."

"Yes, there is," I insisted, stopping in my tracks and turning to face him. "What did I do wrong? Did someone say something?"

At last something akin to interest flared on his face. "Something wrong? How could you have said something wrong, when you barely expressed any opinion at all? You were perfect, Kyra. Which was what you wanted, wasn't it? To make everyone else in the world happy, no matter what it took."

A few people standing near us turned their heads, avid curiosity in their eyes. I felt my cheeks flush, and I reached out to grip his wrist. "Nicky, I wasn't saying—"

He shook off my hand. "We are not doing this here."

Through clenched teeth, I ground out, "I'm not the one who started anything here."

Without answering me, Nicholas turned around and began stalking toward the exit, leaving me to follow, painfully aware of the stares and the whispers all around me. I straightened my back, lifted my chin and made a point of moving with as much grace as I could muster. Which, let's face it, wasn't a whole lot, given who I was and the heels I had on, but I did my best.

Nicky waited just outside the door, staring straight ahead. He opened the passenger side door of the car for me, and I slid in, saying not a word. Out of the corner of my eye, I saw Harold in the back seat, studiously not looking at us. The man's eyes were darting here and there, ever vigilant, but I knew he was trying to give us at least the illusion of privacy.

Not that it mattered an iota. His jaw still clenched, Nicholas pulled away from the curb and drove through the streets, never so much as glancing my way. I stared through the windshield, hoping that I appeared to be calm on the outside when I was anything but inside.

The minute we were inside the Kensington Palace walls, Nicholas headed for his own cottage. Slowing to stop by the door, he lifted his gaze to the rearview mirror.

"Harold, I'm going to leave you here while I take Kyra to my sister's place. I'll be back within a few moments."

The policeman nodded. "Of course, sir. Good afternoon, miss."

I managed a semblance of a smile. "Thanks, Harold."

No sooner had he closed the car door that Nicholas

was off again, peeling around the corner to Alex and Jake's apartment.

"Nicky, I don't know what your problem is. I don't know what I did to set you off, but—" The beginning of a sob rose in my throat, and I swallowed it back. "But I don't like being treated this way."

"You didn't do anything. What on earth could you have done?" He turned in his seat to face me, but his eyes were focused somewhere beyond me. Whatever it was that had shaken him up, he'd regained his composure now—or at least he was putting on a good show of it. He was full-on Prince Nicholas mode, without a hint of my Nicky in sight. Something inside me shriveled up, and I felt an urgent, compelling need to get away as fast as I could. I didn't know how to deal with him this way. He was unfamiliar.

"All right, then." I reached for the door handle, fumbling to open it before I mortified myself with tears or screaming. It was a toss-up as to which might happen first. "I'd better go inside. I need to pack before I leave tomorrow."

"Probably a good idea." Nicholas shifted to face the front again and gripped the steering wheel.

"That's it, then? Am I going to see you tonight? Or tomorrow, before I leave?"

He shook his head. "I need a little space, Kyra. I have to . . . I just need some space." He exhaled through his nose. "Safe travels. We'll talk soon."

I paused in the midst of swinging my legs out of the car, but I didn't look at him. "Will we? Or is this it? Because if this is the last time I'd going to see you, I'd like to say something. I'd like to say . . . thank you for these last few months. It's been like living in a different world. Not always a good one, but different, and I think it changed me. I'd also like to say fuck you, Nicky, because you made me fall in love with you. You made me want to make plans for the future, to believe that we were going to spend the rest of our lives together. I wasn't going to tell you that, not now, not this soon, but if this is the last time we're going to be together, I want you to know it. I want you to know that every time you touched me, kissed me, looked at me like I was the only woman in the world—every time you loved me—it meant something to me. I thought it did to you, too, but I've been wrong before."

"Kyra." He sounded tired, but I heard frustration in his voice, too.

"No, I don't want you to say anything. I don't need your pity or whatever lines you throw at women when you're done with them. I was stupid enough to think it could be different with us. I thought we were friends who were more. I don't know what I did to make you change your mind. All I can think is that when I came here, I disappointed you. Is that it? Were all my quirks adorable in the states, but annoying here in England? That's the only thing I can think of that I did wrong. I'm sorry I outstayed my welcome and made you sorry that you invited me here."

"Kyra, none of that is true. *None* of it. You're not a disappointment—how could you ever be that? But one of us has to be—" He stopped. "Kyra, don't you see? You're trying to be what you're not. What I love about you—what I have always loved about you—is your strength and your confidence. That's why it's killing me to see you give that away. To see you change who you are and how you are. We sat at that luncheon today, and I saw you downplay your intelligence and accomplishments. I heard the way you back-peddled with Sir Martin, when I joined you. For the love of God, Kyra, you changed your hair."

I frowned. "I was trying to be—sometimes you have to make concessions. You have to bend when you're a part of a couple, and I know that—I'm not exactly royal family material as I am."

"That's why." Nicky closed his eyes. "That's it, right there. What does it matter that you're not royal family material, which of course is your opinion, not mine? Have I ever made you feel that you had to change to be with me? If I did—God, Ky, the idea that I did anything to make you believe you weren't enough—that's why we need to . . . take a step back. We need to reconsider. Because, Kyra, I don't want to live without you, but I will be damned if loving you means I have to destroy who you are."

"And you're the only one who has any say in this decision?" My lip was beginning to quiver, but I held it together.

"Obviously, because if I can't trust you to stand up for yourself enough to stay true to who you are, I can't expect you to make a hard choice like this for the both of us." He almost snarled the last words, and I couldn't take another minute of sitting there, feeling him rip us apart.

I managed to scramble out of the car and slam the door before I could hear him say anything else. Gripping my handbag tightly to me, I focused on putting one foot in front of the other until I got inside the apartment, at which point I broke into a run, dashing up the stairs to the guest bedroom I'd been occupying.

No one was home just now. I remembered that Alexandra had an overnight engagement in Scotland, and Jake had gone along with her. Her secretary was somewhere in the apartment, probably, but he wouldn't bother me.

I stripped off my dress and kicked away my heels, pulling on yoga pants, a T-shirt and a hoodie before I slid my feet into slip-ons. Right now, I needed clothes that offered comfort and mobility. Clothes for a fleeing woman, I thought to myself, my breath hitching just slightly.

But I wasn't going to cry now. There wasn't time for that. Now was the time for swift and immediate action.

My hands were only shaking a little as I yanked open drawers, and I called that a minor victory. Dumping all of my clothes onto the quilt that covered the bed, I strode to the closet and pulled out my suitcases. There wasn't time to fold everything neatly, so I stuffed it all into the bags as quickly as I could.

Darting into the bathroom, I grabbed all of my toiletries and makeup, dropping it into the bag and tugging the zipper closed. I slid my phone out of my pocket and skimmed my fingers across the screen until I spotted the email confirmation of my trip for tomorrow. With a few touches, I found room on another, earlier flight and confirmed that I'd be on it. The only problem was going to be getting to the airport. I couldn't exactly call a cab to pick me up from the center of Kensington Palace.

For a few moments, I stood in the middle of the room, stymied. And then I remembered the expression Nicholas had worn sitting next to me in the car, and I knew I had to do whatever I could to get away as soon as I could. My bags had wheels, and I was strong. I wasn't some lightweight who couldn't manage her own shit.

Without too much issue, I steered my luggage into the hallway and closed the bedroom door behind me. A pang of regret sliced through my chest, but I ignored it. Later I'd think about this and let myself wallow a little. But for now, I needed to get moving.

No one bothered me as I bumped down the steps, across the foyer and exited through the front door. I knew there was a better than good chance that some security camera was watching me, but I didn't care. Not unless they were going to chase me down and toss me into a dungeon at the Tower.

I did my best to walk sedately along the sidewalk that ran the interior perimeter of the Palace complex, trying to look as though I knew exactly what I was doing and wandered around dragging my suitcases every day. I was so intent on playing it cool that I jumped a mile when I heard a voice just behind me.

"Excuse me, miss." It was Harold, and he was leaning out the window of a small, non-descript white car, one hand resting on the wheel. "Can I help you get somewhere?"

I wanted to say no, that I was fine and could take care of myself, but the still-functioning part of my brain intuited that perhaps Harold's offer was actually his kind way of telling me that I was breaking some kind of rule.

Pausing, I frowned at him. "I need to go to the airport."

Surely Harold was aware of my original travel plans; I was positive Nicky had arranged for someone, probably Harold himself, to pick me up and drive me to the airport tomorrow. But the policeman didn't even blink when I made my announcement.

"Of course, miss." He jumped out and reached for my suitcases. "I'll get you there in a jiffy."

Within seconds, my bags were in the trunk, and I was in the passenger seat. The car ambled along the narrow way until we reached the gates, which opened as if by magic as

Harold turned out into the city.

We were both silent. I almost opened my mouth several times to explain why I was leaving today, and why I hadn't called to ask for help, but in the end, I decided it didn't matter. I wondered if Harold had played this role before, coming to the aid of women whom Nicholas no longer wanted. Maybe I was just the latest in a long line of discarded girlfriends. No explanations were needed.

He only spoke to ask me about my airline, and once we'd arrived at the terminal at Heathrow, he jumped out to help me with my bags.

"Thank you, Harold." I tried to muster up as much dignity as I could. "It's been a pleasure to know you."

"The honor's been mine, miss." He hesitated, as though he was about to say something else, but instead, he only shook his head and extended a hand to me. "I hope you have a safe and uneventful journey home. And I also hope that we meet again soon."

I wanted to bark out a sardonic laugh that said *unlikely*, but that would've been unfair to a man who had shown me only kindness. Instead, I nodded and made my way to the ticketing desk.

It wasn't until I was standing in line, waiting my turn to check my bag, that I began to think about the press. Clearly, no one had expected me to be at the airport today, because there wasn't a camera or a reporter in sight. However, mindful of the thousands of cell phones around me, I made a concerted effort to keep a bland expression on my face. The last thing I needed was a picture of me looking weepy and forlorn to hit the tabloids.

The ticket agent did a quick double-take when she saw

my name on the print-out, but she recovered and was professional. It wasn't until I'd gone through security and customs and reached the gate that someone approached me.

"Excuse me." The voice was soft and tentative. "Are you Kyra? I mean, the one who—you know. Prince Nicholas' girlfriend?"

She was perhaps fourteen years old, and her eyes shone with admiration and perhaps a touch of envy—not of Nicholas and me, I thought, but of the romance of it all. I imagined she was the sort of girl who wanted happy endings and fairy tales.

I evaded the question as I'd learned to do. "I'm Kyra. It's nice to meet you." I offered her my hand. "Are you traveling to the United States today, too?"

She shook her head. "Just coming back with my mum, and I saw you and told her it was you, but she didn't believe me. We're just back from Florida."

I smiled. "I'll bet you had a wonderful time. It's beautiful down there this time of year. Much nicer than where I live, where there's probably snow on the ground."

The girl laughed. "It was very warm, but the beach was lovely." From a few feet away, an older woman I assumed was her mother called out, and she glanced over her shoulder. "I guess I should go, but—could I possibly get a picture? With you, I mean? I wouldn't give it to anyone, just show my friends, I promise."

It was on the tip of my tongue to refuse, as I'd gotten in the habit of doing, but then it occurred to me that I was no longer bound to try to please Nicholas and his family.

I nodded, warning her, "I probably look a wreck just now, from getting ready to travel. So I really would appreciate it if you don't send this to anyone else. It would be embarrassing."

"I won't, I swear." She lifted her phone, tilted her head close to mine, and snapped the photo. "Oh, thank you so much. You're so nice, and just like a normal girl."

I smiled. "That's all I am. Normal."

"Can I ask you just one thing before I go?" She bit her lip and gazed up at me through thick lashes. "Is it just . . . wonderful? Being in love, I mean? It looks amazing, and so romantic and lovely."

My heart ached, not only for myself but for this girl who still had years ahead to discover what love and romance and relationships were really like. I wanted to warn her to be careful and to guard her heart and not to trust it—to go forward with a clear head and open eyes. I wanted to tell her to avoid plunging headfirst in love with a man who seemed to feel the same way about her.

But I knew my words would've fallen on deaf ears. She was young, and until she experienced love for herself, she wouldn't believe me even if I told her.

"Of course, it is," I answered her at last. "Just as lovely and romantic as you think."

Her eyes lit up. "I knew it. I just knew it. Thank you so much. Oh, and for the picture, too. For talking to me. You're so nice."

She flitted away to join her mother, and I watched her go, melancholy stealing over me. For a brief moment in time, I'd learned what it was like to have the admiration of people who didn't know me, for reasons I couldn't fathom. While I wasn't going to miss the media attention or worrying about every little thing I said or did, I realized that on some level, it was a privilege to be an unwitting role model. It wasn't something

I'd sought out, but under other circumstances, maybe I could have used the position to do some good.

The gate agent announced that my flight was boarding, and with a sigh, I hitched my handbag more securely over my shoulder and joined the line of waiting passengers. I glanced over my shoulder for one last look. My adventure in royalty was ending, and I was all right with that. I'd never chosen to walk that path.

It was the end of the love story that was breaking my heart. I had a feeling that getting over Nicky was going to take a very long time.

The Lloyd Post

Editor's note: The following piece was written by one of our staff reporters, Sophie Kent, who's spent a good part of the last year covering the romance between Prince Nicholas and American Kyra Duncan. Her opinion piece first appeared on her own blog, but she is graciously allowing us to share it here, too.

A break-up is hard. Ending a relationship with the person who has been your significant other, no matter how long or short a time that has been, is painful. Most, if not all, of us can relate.

Now imagine that your heartache is played out on the world's stage, for everyone to see. Imagine reporters asking you daily about the one person whose name you never want to hear again. Imagine photographers taking pictures of you, even when you feel miserable. Imagine being unable to forget or ignore, because there are stories about your pain in newspapers and online.

If you can imagine all of that, you know a bit about what Kyra

Duncan has been going through over the past week.

I met Ms. Duncan in April, when a story broke that she'd been spotted and photographed kissing a man who happens to be a member of Britain's royal family. From the start, this woman has been gracious, kind and patient with all of us members of the press who have taken up residence on her front lawn, following her everywhere and making her life enormously complicated.

When she returned from England this week, it was clear to me that something had changed. As a woman, I recognized the signs and symptoms of heartache in a fellow sufferer. At that point, she had every right to tell the lot of us to get the hell off her property. She would have been excused if she had been rude, nasty or unpleasant to us. She had nothing more to lose; if her relationship with the prince truly is over, as it seems to be, she doesn't need to behave out of respect for the royal family anymore.

And yet she has. She has carried on with being polite and kind. She hasn't said anything about anyone, nor has she hidden herself at home. She has shown incredible dignity under trying circumstances.

I don't know anything about the true nature of her affair with the prince. Perhaps they were very good friends whose love turned romantic for a season. Perhaps this was merely a fling. Or maybe it was something real and true that has been derailed by the complexities of twenty-first century life as a prince.

Regardless, I can't help being sad that it appears that Ms. Duncan won't be joining the family after all. Her class and unabashed sense of self could only add another dimension to what its members wryly call The Firm.

I, for one, think they are missing out. And if Prince Nicholas is reading this, I recommend copious amounts of flowers, boxes of chocolates and an enormous outpouring of apology for whatever you did. You let a good one get away.

CHAPTER Twenty

February

"KYRA?" SHELBY KNOCKED ON MY BEDROOM DOOR AND leaned her head inside. "I'm heading into town to pick up some milk and bread. We're supposed to get fourteen inches of snow tonight. Do you need anything while I'm out?"

I glanced up at her from my computer, frowning as my concentration broke. "Um . . . no. Thanks. I'm good."

"Okay." She lingered, her expression sober. "I thought I'd get us a six-pack and a couple of bottles of wine, too. Just in case we get snowed in, we might as well have some provisions, right?"

"Uh huh. Sure. Sounds good." I scrolled back to review what I'd just written, making sure I was hitting the points that I needed to cover. Thesis writing wasn't something I enjoyed. I wasn't sure anyone did.

"Want me to stop by the library and see if there's anything you might want to read? I mean, you know, in case we lose power and can't watch movies or work on the computer." Shelby leaned against the doorjamb, watching me.

I drew in a slow, calming breath. I knew my friend meant

well. She was worried about me—hell, she'd been worried about me for three months. She wasn't the only one, either. But the truth was that there wasn't a damn thing anyone could do, and all I really wanted was for them to leave me alone.

"If it makes you happy, Shel, sure. Stop at the library. But I doubt we're going to lose power. And my priority has got to be this paper. I want it done so that Ed and I can review it together in a couple of weeks. It has to be ready to submit to both the college and to Honey Bee's advisory board, too."

"I know all this, Kyra. But you're burying yourself in it." She raised one eyebrow, daring me to argue with her.

"Yep, I am." I wasn't going to fight what was clearly the truth.

"You're using it as an excuse to hide."

I snorted. "Hiding is one thing I haven't had to do in a while, Shel. If there's been one improvement in my life since . . . November, then that's it. You've got to admit, it's nice that we don't have to dodge anyone when we leave our house anymore."

"Yeah, I guess so." She hesitated. "If I thought you were coping with this, I wouldn't push you. I'd just let you deal with it. But since you got home from England last fall, you've just acted like nothing happened. Like your entire time with Nicky was something you want to forget."

"Well, duh." I rolled my eyes. "Who wouldn't want to forget it? It was an unholy mess. It was a momentary insanity. Forgive me that I don't want to wallow in the memories and deconstruct the whole thing."

"But it's not healthy. It's downright unhealthy, in fact. You have to face it and let yourself feel the pain so you can move on."

It was the same old song I'd been ignoring for months, but today I was over it. "I am moving on, in case you haven't noticed. I'm moving on with school and with science and with my future. I'm trying to move on with this thesis, if you would just leave me the fuck alone and let me do it." I ground out the last few words, feeling only a passing guilt when Shelby flinched.

"Fine." She threw up her hands. "Whatever, Kyra. You do what you feel is right for you. But don't be surprised when you wake up one day and realize that you've pushed everyone away from you in your effort to pretend that everything's fine."

She slammed my bedroom door, and then a few minutes later, she repeated the sentiment as she left the house. I heard the car start up and the spray of gravel hitting the undercarriage when she pulled out of the driveway.

The ensuing silence in the house was both a blessing and a curse. I could get back to my writing now, which was what I'd wanted, but what Shelby had said had rattled me more than I'd let on. It was too quiet for me to focus now, and with a frustrated groan, I closed the computer and dropped back against my pillows.

Shelby was wrong. I wasn't ignoring my pain. I was living with it—living in it—every single minute of every day. It never left, and it rarely let up. Memories and pain were my constant companions and my new best friends . . . ones I didn't want to let go, because if I did, it meant I was giving up my last fragile tie to Nicky. And I couldn't let anyone know how much I hurt, because doing so would've invited pity, along with a constant rehashing of what had gone wrong.

The hell of it was, I still didn't understand the answer to

that question. I remembered with crystal clarity what Nicky had said that last day, but somehow, it still didn't make sense. How could he be angry at me for trying to be good enough for him? How could he blame me for doing my best to be the kind of woman he needed?

Privately, I'd expected to hear from him after I'd returned to the states. I'd checked my phone obsessively in those early days, certain that he'd text me or call so that we could work this out. After all, we loved each other. With a little distance, I'd believed that at first. Nicky just had to realize that I was right, and that in making changes to myself, I was showing him how much I cared. I was proving that I was willing to be who he needed.

But my phone stayed achingly silent. There was no text from Nicky. Oh, there were plenty from other people—from reporters who'd wanted a comment on why I'd cut short my trip to come home or who had gotten a tip from someone at the Waste Not luncheon that Nicky and I had been arguing. Those messages I had deleted without a second thought. I didn't owe anyone an explanation, and I sure as hell wasn't going to tell my side of the story to a journalist.

For two weeks after my trip, the reporters hung around. They were suspicious, apparently, wondering if Nicky and I were staging this separation to throw them off the trail. Having to listen to their probing, prying questions every day as I left the house had been a real treat.

But oddly enough, it had been even harder when they'd slowly begun to drift away, when each day, there were fewer of them there. Finally, on Thanksgiving, there was only one left—Sophie Kent, the only reporter who from the start had been the most pleasant and professional.

She was leaning against my car when I came outside, her arms crossed. She stared at me, unsmiling, but there was a glimmer of compassion in her eyes.

"Off to eat turkey?" she inquired, kicking at a small pile of snow on the ground.

I stopped a few feet away. "Yeah. Well, it's the day for it." I tucked my fingers into the back pockets of my jeans. "How about you?"

She shrugged. "Probably. The hotel serves an entire meal, apparently, so I'll eat there . . . before I get on an airplane tomorrow morning."

"Hmmm." I shifted my weight and slid sunglasses over my eyes to hide the flare of pain this news brought me. "Well . . . have a good trip back." I cleared my throat. "Why are you here today? When everyone else has left, I mean?"

"Not really sure," she admitted. "I could have left this morning. But I guess I wanted to say goodbye."

"That was nice." I took a deep breath. "I appreciate it. Of all the people who've been camped out in my yard for the last seven months, you were one of my favorites."

"Oh, please." She snorted. "I was totally your favorite."

"You were the only one who acted like a real person to me—who treated me like a real person. That made you a favorite." I held out my hand. "Thanks, Sophie. It's been a pleasure."

"Same here." She pushed off my car and then hesitated. "Kyra . . . I just want to say that you really are a decent person. I've done reporting on lots of different people, both those who were supposedly linked to the royal family and those who are part of it. Most of the people who want to be royal are desperate and determined. They might not show it, but we can sense it. But not you. You've been kind to all of us who've spent time complicating your life, and you've shown tremendous grace under pressure. Don't think we didn't see that."

I bobbed my head, unable to speak around the lump in my throat.

"Well, that's all I wanted to say. I'll leave you alone now. Happy Thanksgiving to you, Kyra."

"Thank you," I managed to squeak out. Sophie sketched a wave my way and headed out to her car.

And that had been that. It had been the true end of my royal romance, and it was wildly anticlimactic.

I sighed and closed my eyes, wishing for the relief of sleep. But it didn't come, probably because I was sleeping a good fourteen hours a night. I was too well rested to need a nap in the middle of the day.

My life sucked, and I couldn't even manage a fucking nap.

Kicking at the throw pillow by my foot, I sat up and stared out the window. Tiny flurries had begun to fall, validating Shelby's prediction. I wondered what the weather was like down in Florida, where Honey and Handsome were enjoying the non-Maine winter. I wondered if my sisters were enjoying their post-holiday ski trip in Aspen.

And I wondered what Nicky was doing.

Just before Christmas, I'd gotten a call from a number I hadn't recognized, and when I'd answered, a reporter had politely asked me for a comment on the new relationship between Prince Nicholas and the French model Serene.

For a long moment, I'd stood holding the phone, staring at the floor, before I'd said slowly and softly, "No comment." And then I'd hung up.

So maybe Nicky and the model were together doing

something fantastic right now. Maybe they were curled up in front of the adorable fireplace in Nicky's cottage. Maybe they were talking with the staff at Waste Not, and Serene the model was actually saying the right things.

I hoped so, because I wasn't angry at Nicky anymore. I'd gone through the phase where I'd wanted him to be miserable, but that was over. I'd gone through the nights where I'd cried into my pillow until I was numb. I'd hidden that from Shelby, because I didn't want her sympathy.

And now I was simply back to baseline normal, just getting through everything. Get up, go to school, come home, do homework and housework as needed, go to sleep, wake up and do it all over again. I'd keep doing it until one day maybe something would happen to make me want to change.

The snow was picking up, and I frowned, hoping that Shelby would be home soon. Neither of us was the world's best at driving in the snow, but my friend, having been born and raised in Florida, was even less competent at it than I was. I began to envision her in a ditch or crashed into a tree, and panic made my stomach clench.

I didn't want to call to check on her in case she was still driving and shouldn't be distracted by a ringing phone, but I was on the verge of doing it anyway when the car bumped into our driveway, sending a surge of relief through me. I hustled to the foyer and pulled on my coat, sliding my feet into fuzzy slippers before I went out to help her.

"Your feet are going to freeze!" she yelled as she popped open the trunk. "You should have on your boots."

"Nah, they're fine. Besides, it's not deep enough for boots yet. I'm saving them for tomorrow." Reaching into the trunk, I hoisted two grocery bags in my arms. "Where were you? I was starting to worry." I paused before adding quietly, "I'm sorry I yelled at you before. I know you're just worried. I shouldn't have taken my own frustration out on you."

"Yeah, I know. Don't worry, mama bear." She closed the trunk and walked next to me toward the door. "Hey, I stopped at the post office to pick up our mail."

"Oh. Good idea." I followed Shelby into the house, pausing to kick off my slippers just inside the door. We both set the bags of groceries on the table, and Shelby shrugged off her coat.

"You got something, Kyra."

"What?" I was rummaging in the bags, separating out the canned goods from what food went into the fridge. "Where?"

"At the post office. You got a letter." There was something in her voice, some barely banked excitement, that made my hands begin to tremble and my heart pound.

"Oh, yeah?" I kept my tone casual. "That's unusual. Who writes letters anymore?"

"Apparently, Prince Nicholas of Great Britain." She opened her tote bag and withdrew a single cream-colored letter-sized envelope. "I mean, I'm guess it's from him. The postmark is Great Britain, the return address says Kensington Palace, and the initials NW are handwritten in the corner. But I guess that could be anyone, huh?" She waved the envelope in her hand. "Anyone at all. I can just toss this, then, with the rest of the junk mail."

"Shelby. Give it to me." I turned my hand palm up and wiggled my fingers. "Please. Now."

"Well, *okay*. Fine." She carefully placed the letter on my hand. "There you go."

"Thanks." I stood still, frowning down as though I

expected the envelope to turn rabid and bite me.

"What're you waiting for? Open it up." Shelby made a rolling motion with her hand.

"Yeah, okay." Pinching the letter between my fingers, I turned around and walked to my bedroom.

"Hey! I meant out here, doofus!" Shelby called after me, but I heard the laughter in her voice.

With fingers that wouldn't stop shaking, I ripped open the envelope.

Dear Kyra,

I'm going to begin by saying that I am a complete ass, and I am so sorry for three things.

First, I am sorry that I let you leave that day. I was confused, upset and afraid, but that wasn't a real excuse. I have none. I shouldn't have done it. I was wrong.

Second, I'm sorry that I spoke to you as I did that day. I was upset, as previously mentioned, because I'd been seeing you change, and it utterly destroyed me to think that you believed you had to do that to win or to keep my love. But I should have moved gently and slowly, and I shouldn't have said the things I did.

Finally, I'm sorry that I didn't write to you before now. I spent several long weeks feeling both sorry for myself and angry at myself. I then convinced myself that you were better off without me, and that your life could go on with less angst and complication if I wasn't part of it. It's idiotic, but then, I never claimed to be that smart. I moped around and made everyone around me miserable, until finally I came to rock bottom and realized that I had to know if we still had a chance.

Ky, I still think you might have a less complicated life without me, but I know that mine could never be as good if you're not in it.

If that makes me selfish, then I'll wear the badge proudly.

I thought about calling you or even coming to see you in person, but I couldn't get away to fly over, and in case you didn't want me back, I decided it was safer to face the possible humiliation of groveling at your feet via pen and paper. Also, I remember you wanted me to write you letters once upon a time. I'm finally doing it.

If you think we might have something to continue discussing, write me back. If you do not, then please accept this as my apology as stated above and as my wish for your happiness in whatever you do.

Love,

Your Nicky

For a long time, I sat on my bed, re-reading his words. Something that had been knotted and aching deep inside me for the past three months began to loosen, and I sagged backward, curling up and simply letting myself be.

And then I jumped up and found a notebook and a pen.

Dear Nicky,

I told you boys write letters. Even boys like you.

Being right about the above fact may mean that I'm also right about the sand castle. I'm just saying it's possible.

Thank you for your letter. I could play cool and aloof and tell you that I hadn't thought about you much since I left London in November, but of course, that would be a huge lie. I could say that my feelings for you have changed and that I'm not interested in seeing you again, but that would also be a huge lie. I could say that I'm mad at you and that yes, I need you to grovel for my forgiveness, but that would be wrong, because I got over being mad pretty quickly and saw my part in what happened.

I've been pretending that I was all right. I haven't allowed myself to feel anything since I ran away from you. I didn't want to let myself feel the hurt and the pain . . . but the truth is that I have been lost and sad.

I wanted to be who I thought you needed. When we were together, just the two of us, it was easy to believe that you loved me for myself and didn't need me to be anything else. But when I saw myself through other people's eyes, I was certain that I could never be good enough. I made the mistake of thinking that eventually, you'd feel the same way—that I was somehow lacking—and although you never once validated that theory, I acted as though you had.

For that, I am sorry, too.

You have never made me feel that I had to be anyone else for you to love me. That all came from within me. I've thought about that fact quite a bit over the last few months.

I've never been worried about fitting in. Or at least, that's been my company line. I tell everyone I'm strong and I'm confident, and my actions bear that out. Until recently, that is.

When I was a little girl, my mother told me that if I was comfortable in my own skin, other people would also be comfortable around me. She said if I was always trying to make other people happy, they'd let me try and blame me if I failed—so it was better to do my best to be true to myself first—not at the expense of others, of course, but because I could be so much more if I didn't let others tell me my limitations and boundaries.

Last year, I let other people into my head, and they were more than happy to whisper about my lacking. I bought into what the press said and how their pictures appeared. I should have only listened to you, because you were constantly telling me that I was perfect for you, that I was exactly who you needed and what you wanted.

Nicky, in case you've been wondering, you are who I want. I don't need you to grovel, and I don't need you to change. But if you want me, I'm here and I'm yours.

I love you.

Ky

PS I don't mean to be presumptuous, but I have to ask for my own peace of mind. Did something happen with you and the French model? It's all right if so. I just wanted to know.

Dear Ky,

Your letter came while Daisy was here with me, and I took it upstairs to read it in privacy. When I came down, she hugged me and said, "There's my brother. He's been gone for months now, but it seems he's come home."

I wanted to grab a suitcase and fly over to you, but the more I thought about it, I decided . . . not yet. You have a semester to finish, and it would be so much more complicated if the world knew we were together again. You'd likely have press camped out on your lawn. And there's the fact that I have a long and complex trip to Africa scheduled for next week. I combined official engagements for the Queen with fact-finding visits for both Waste Not and No Hungry Child. I'm going to be away for quite a while.

I wish you were coming with me. You'd be so excited to meet with some of the farmers. It's because of you and your influence on me that I'm doing this, talking with people who put the ideas of natural farming into place and used the practices of Masanobu Fukuoka to reclaim the desert. Some of the men and women I'll be meeting actually knew him, and I'm not too proud to admit I'm slightly awed by the idea.

One day, I'll take you there with me. One day, we'll go back together, and the trip will be so much fuller and complete then.

Until then, I'll write you letters, so that you know not a day goes by—and not a moment within that day—when I'm not thinking of you and loving you.

Love,
Your Nicky

PS Serene is a friend of Daisy's, and I introduced her to some people when she was over here. She was no more interested in me than I was in her. How could I be when all I see is you?

"I know you're hiding something from me." Shelby crossed her arms and glared at me. "I'm not stupid, Kyra. I know you're holding back, and I know it's because of those letters. What I don't get is why. I'm your best friend. I tell you everything."

I cocked my head and narrowed my eyes. "Do you now, Shelby? Do you tell me everything?" I was mostly bluffing. I'd had a hunch in the last couple of weeks that my friend had met someone, that she herself was hiding something from *me*. I didn't have any hard proof—it was just a feeling.

But watching her face go red and her eyes widen as her mouth dropped open, I knew I'd hit on something.

"You *are* keeping a secret, aren't you? And here you are accusing me. Well, just remember, Shel, I'm rubber and you're glue." I nodded in self-righteous certainty. "Also, when you point a finger at someone, you're pointing three back at yourself."

She rolled her eyes. "Okay. Fine. I won't push the issue. I won't say that I'm pretty sure, judging by the cloud you've been living in lately, that things between you and a certain roy-al hottie are once again hunky with a side of dory."

"I'm not trying to keep anything from you, Shel. I just . . . before, it all played out in front of the world. Now I just want it to be mine for a little while, you know? I'm not ready to share. Not yet."

"I understand. But when you're ready to tell someone, I'll be her, right? I won't have to read about your engagement in the newspaper?"

"Not that you read the newspaper, but of course, I'll tell you. I promise." I hopped off my chair and gave her a tight hug. "Shel, you've been wonderful during this crazy time. You kept me sane when I thought I was going to explode, and you didn't let me drown when I thought my world was ending. I won't ever forget that."

She hugged me back. "Don't worry. I won't let you."

Dear Kyra,

I can't wait to show you photos from this trip. Maybe you're seeing them on line, but there are more that I'm saving to share with just you.

I don't have much time to write at the moment, but I wanted to say something I've been thinking about for a long time. Whatever happens next, I don't want to be separated from you by any ocean or continent. I know it may take some figuring out, but we're going to be together.

That doesn't mean you can't continue with the work I know you're meant to do. We may have to be creative. But I want to wake up next to you every morning and fall asleep with you in my arms every night.

Not sure how we'll make it happen, but we will. Trust me. Believe in me.

I love you~
Your Nicky

Dear Nicky,

I've been following your travels, and the trip looks as though it's been tremendously successful. I can't wait to hear all the details.

Not sure if you need to know this, but I graduate on the tenth of May. After that . . . I haven't made any firm plans. I'm hoping that Honey Bee Juices will approve some funding for me to continue my research into natural farming, so I could work for them in that capacity. I'm going to present my thesis paper and my preliminary findings to them in late April.

I'm not telling you any of this to pressure either of us—just so you'll be informed.

Spring seems to be rolling in slowly this year. We had one last gasp of winter weather last week, but this week, it's been warm every day. Maine warm, you understand—not Florida warm. But I'll take what I can get.

To celebrate spring's arrival and our survival of another New England winter, Shelby and I ate dinner at The Meadows on Saturday. Gav came out to say hello, and he offered his services if I needed someone to, in his very elegant words, 'kick some royal ass' as punishment for hurting me. I told him that he shouldn't believe everything he reads in the papers or hears about on-line. He seemed skeptical, but I think I managed to convince him that I'm okay and that you're not, as he said, 'a stuck-up royal asshole'.

Still, you should probably watch your back.

Speaking of such things, I hope Harold and Tom are well. It also occurred to me that I left Alex and Jake's house without so much as a thank you or an explanation. I want to apologize to them for that. I hope they'll understand.

Honey and Handsome offered to take me with them on the Mediterranean cruise they're planning for the summer. I'd told them no at first, because when they asked, I was still suffering from a broken heart and determined never to go near Europe or the British Isles ever again. And then I said no again last week, because I didn't want to make plans if you . . . or if we . . . well.

By the time you receive this letter, you'll probably be almost ready to leave Africa. If you should decide you want to make a detour to another continent, I'll be here, waiting for you.

Love,
Ky

CHAPTER Twenty-One

"CONGRATULATIONS, KYRA. YOU MUST BE VERY PROUD of yourself." Marietta Jenkins, the president of the Honey Bee Juices advisory board, beamed at me. "I already know your grandparents are. Proud of you, I mean."

"Thank you, Mrs. Jenkins." I returned her smile. "It's been quite a journey, but I think it's been worth the work. And I hope the board feels the same way and will consider allowing me to head up the natural farm research full-time for Honey Bee Juices."

"Well, that's why we're here, isn't it?" She pointed to the experimental plot. "Now, I'm standing here looking at your non-interventionalist plot and thinking that it looks a mess. It's not pruned, it doesn't have the same neat and uniform appearance of the control plants, and it just looks . . . untouched. Wild. And I'm realizing as I think this how much we've been brainwashed to think one way—the man-interference way is so much preferable to letting nature do its thing."

"Exactly." I nodded. "That's one thing we have to be cognizant of as we go forward." I squinted over her shoulder. "Here are my grandparents and the rest of the board. We should be able to get started on time."

"There's my beautiful, smart and strong granddaughter." Honey hugged me. "Look at you, Kyra. You look so grown-up and professional." She stepped back to admire the simple short-sleeved blouse and dark blue jeans I was wearing with my sneakers. For this presentation, I knew I had to dress as though I was both responsible enough to deserve a job with Honey Bee Juices and practical enough to realize that heels and suits were not meant to be worn in the dirt. The new jeans and blouse had been a compromise that worked.

"Honey, you can't hug the job candidates," my grandfather chided. "Kyra is presenting to all of us today. You need to maintain professional distance."

"Oh, bullshit." My grandmother rolled her eyes. "Everyone knows she's our granddaughter, Cal. This isn't an interview with a stranger."

"Fine." Handsome gave in and bent over to kiss my cheek. "Your grandmother's right, sweetie. You look wonderful. And so does this field."

"Thanks, both of you." I raised my voice. "And thank you for coming, everyone. I have an outline of notes for you here, if you'd each take one and pass it along. I'd like to start with a little history . . ."

For forty-five minutes, I took my listeners on a journey from the ancient practices of agriculture to the more modern methods of extreme intervention and then launched into an explanation of natural farming. From there, I moved onto the specifics of our experiment, pointing out the various plants and explaining what the numbers on their outline meant.

Behind me, I heard a huffing and turned my head to glance out of the corner of my eye, to where Ed was jogging over. He'd had a final presentation for another class this morning, and since what I was doing here was for my own future with Honey Bee Juices, it hadn't been vital that he was on hand. But he'd promised to come for the last half of my talk, to answer any questions that I couldn't directly address.

I introduced him to the board, and then together, we continued, finishing up by opening the floor to questions. The few that the board members raised were thoughtful and considered, and Ed and I were both able to provide answers.

"Very interesting. *Very* interesting," one of the older men remarked. "I'm going to go home and order that book on natural farming that you mentioned. I'm not sorry to say I'm intrigued." He offered me his hand. "You already know you have a job with Honey Bee Juices, I hope, but I believe you can consider this project funded going forward. We'll all be eager to see how your work benefits the company's future."

The other four members murmured their agreement, and I felt a mix of relief and exhilaration. All the hours that Ed and I had devoted to these plots and this project suddenly were worth it. We'd done it.

"Kyra, what's over there?" Honey pointed to the hard dirt path that led between the trees. "That's not another one of your project fields, is it?"

I shook my head. "No. That was used by another group—they were experimenting with some new irrigation ideas. I'm not sure if they still have plants growing there now."

"Oh, I'd love to see it." My grandmother enthused. "You know we're always looking for better ways to irrigate." She tilted her head, confiding in Ed, "As passionate as my granddaughter is about food sustainability, I feel the same way about water. It upsets me to think about the waste that goes on."

"Sure, Honey. Go on up and check it out." I waved my head in the direction of the field in question, hoping she'd take the hint and not bend poor Ed's ear about water management through the world.

"Come on and walk with me." Honey held out her hand. "I don't want to trip and break a hip. That would put a real damper on our cruise in the Mediterranean next month."

"It sure would," I muttered, but I obeyed, offering her my arm and walking alongside her through the trees. My grandparents had always been unwaveringly supportive, but even more so over the last year—and especially in the past months. Although they'd never questioned me about what had happened with Nicky, I'd noticed that both Handsome and Honey had been extra attentive, taking me to dinner and showering me with love and attention. I was grateful for them. And given the fact that I was more uncertain than ever now about my future, I was glad that I had the potential for meaningful work settled.

It had been several weeks since I'd had a letter from Nicky. In those first weeks of our correspondence, I'd begun to cautiously believe in the future once again. But I knew he was back from Africa, and I'd been hoping that he would bring up what came next for us. Would he come here after I graduated? Or would I be brave enough to go back to London? I wasn't sure. I held onto my belief in his love for me, trusting that he was working things out, even if I couldn't see it happening.

But I wasn't going to sit around and wait for him to make a move. I'd never been that girl, and I wasn't going to start now. I was moving ahead.

"Honey, remember how you asked me if I wanted to go with you and Handsome on that cruise, as part of my graduation present? I'm thinking about it. Maybe it would be good for me. I mean, I could get away and relax—it's been a hell of a year, and I could use the break."

"Oh, really? Do you think so?" She sounded distracted as she picked her way up the path with me. "Don't you think you might get bored, with all those old people just sitting on a ship in the middle of water?"

I frowned. "Why are they all old people? You told me this was a trip for all ages, not just a senior cruise. And we wouldn't be sitting in the middle of water. We'd be visiting interesting ports of call, like in Italy and Greece and northern Africa. And Spain! I've always wanted to go to Spain. I've heard it's lovely. Think of the history."

"Let's talk about it later, all right?" Honey seemed almost cross now, and I was bewildered. After all, me joining them had been her idea to start. I wondered if she was afraid I'd crimp their style or—ewww—interfere with their romantic trip. That was something that didn't bear thinking about too closely.

"Well, fine, but I might need to—" I came to a sudden halt just beyond the edge of the trees, and my voice broke. My body began to shake, and I was certain my temperature had gone up several degrees, because I was instantly flushed and on fire. My heart thudded so hard that I wondered distractedly how common it was for twenty-five-year old women to have heart attacks.

But it wasn't a heart attack, because I knew why I was feeling this way. Across the field, a mere fifteen or so feet away from me, Nicky was standing. He was wearing jeans—possibly the same ones he'd worn the first day he'd come here to see my gardens—with a snug gray T-shirt and an expression of undisguised hope.

"Ky." He spoke my name—he didn't call or yell, but I heard it anyway. He began to say something else, and then stopped, because his voice was hoarse and trembling.

I was dimly aware that Honey had slipped away from me and was making her way back through the trees, clearly without any worry about needing help. And as I stared at Nicky, waiting for him to talk again, I took in the field in front of me.

Hyacinth. There were rows of vibrant purple hyacinth laid out, but they weren't in neat and orderly rows. Instead, they were in curved lines, although some were straighter. I furrowed my forehead, trying to figure out what it meant.

"I should have thought this through better." Nicky stepped carefully around the flowers, coming toward me, and I thought I'd never seen anything or anyone look more wonderful. "I wanted to make a grand gesture. I didn't realize that you might not be able to see the shape from down here. Not as easily, anyway. But that's a heart in the middle—"

"Oh . . ." I breathed. "I *can* see it. Wow. Oh, it's beautiful."

"And on either side, I spelled out—well, I had another idea, but I also underestimated how many flowers I needed. So it spells out . . . my Ky. I hoped that you'd remember what that means."

I heard the echo of his voice from last summer. *"I'll just have to say you're my Ky, and you'll know that all the other stuff—the intelligence, the goddess, the sexiness—it's all implied in those two syllables."*

"I remember," I whispered. "I remember."

"But what I wanted to spell out was . . . I love you, Ky. If I had all the hyacinth in the world and all the time and space, I would have said, I love you, Kyra, and I never want to be separated from you again. You are my heart, and you own my soul. Life isn't worth living if you're not part of it." He stood close enough to me now that I could feel him, and my entire body was humming with his nearness.

"Kyra, you are my best friend, and falling in love with you is the smartest thing I've ever done. I want us to have a future together. I want you to be who you are, and I want you to know down to your very core that I love you for all of everything you are. I never want you to change. I know we'll both grow and change over the years, but I want us to do that together."

Something wet splashed on my hand, where it was still covering my lips. To my shock, I realized I was crying. Nicky lifted a tentative hand and cupped my cheek, wiping away tears with his thumb.

"I've said a lot about what I want, Ky. Now, you need to tell me what *you* want. Is it the same thing I do? I hope so . . . but no matter what, I'm going to make sure that what you want and need is my number one priority. Nothing else. No one else. Only you. Only my Ky."

I swallowed and moved my hand to cover his where it still rested against my face. "I want everything, Nicky. I want it all. Everything you just said—that's what I want. But when it comes down to it, the only thing in the world I need is you."

Nicky's answering smile was brilliant enough to nearly blind me. He wrapped his arms around me and held me close, both of us clinging to each other. I buried my face in the crook of his neck, and his hands rubbed slow circles on my back as he whispered into my ear.

"Once upon a time, two children—a boy and a girl—fell in love on the sand in Florida. One was very wise, very strong and very beautiful. And the other one was smart enough to know that the girl was everything to him and always would be. On a perfect August night, he kissed her for the first time, and it was magical."

"Did he love her even then?" I murmured.

"He did. But he wasn't old enough to know it fully. Not yet. But when he met her again, ten years later, this time he was old enough, and so was she. This time when he kissed her, he never wanted to stop."

"But he did. And even though it wasn't completely his fault, her heart broke, and she thought she might die of it. She was still strong, but she didn't want to be strong without him." New tears welled in my eyes.

"He felt the same way. He loved her so much that he didn't know how to hold onto her when she thought she had to change for him."

"Silly girl." I touched my lips to his neck.

"And idiot boy," Nicky laughed softly, and then he nudged my head back, and he kissed me as though it was the very first time. And in some ways, perhaps it was, because it was the beginning of our new forever.

A few seconds later, when he lifted his lips from mine, I gazed up into his bright blue eyes.

"Whatever happened to those two children on the beach? The girl who was not quite Cinderella and the boy who was so much more than Prince Charming?"

Nicky brushed my hair back from my face.

"Don't you know? They lived happily ever after."

CHAPTER Epilogue

"Is this box ready to be sealed, Kyra?"

I paused in mid-motion as I bent to place another armful of books into the huge carton in front of me. "Yeah, it should be good to go. Thanks, Shel."

"Phew." She fell onto the couch with a sigh. "When you told me that you were moving to England, I had a mental image. It included uniformed men coming in to pack up your shit to be magically transported across the Atlantic Ocean. It did not include the two of us, sweaty and nasty-smelling, figuring out how to fit all the aforementioned shit into boxes."

"Sorry. Nicky offered some help from professionals, but I thought it would be more fun for us to do it together."

"Fun. Yeah." Shelby rolled her eyes at me. "I still can't believe that you're moving over there. If you had told me when we started grad school that you'd end up deserting me after graduation to go off and be a princess, I would have said you were insane. Yet, here we are."

"Uh, no. Don't jump the gun. I'm not going to be a princess. I'm just moving over there so that Nicky and I can have a real relationship. So we can explore all the . . . possibilities." I stood up and brushed my hands over my thighs. "Okay. The books are done, too."

"What time are the movers coming tomorrow?" Shelby turned her head to watch as I flopped into a chair and rested my feet on the coffee table next to hers.

"About noon." I reached for the beer I'd gotten out of the fridge earlier and took a swig.

"And then you leave the next day." Shelby sniffled a little. "I think I've been in denial. I keep telling myself it's not going to be a big deal. That you're not going to be so far away. But shit, Kyra. I'm never going to see you. You're going to be over there, working for Honey Bee Juices and helping Nicky with his food sustainability projects, and I'll be in New Mexico, where I don't know a single soul."

"Shel, I promise, we'll still see each other." I nudged her foot with mine. "I couldn't lose you. You'll fly over to see me, and I'll do the same."

"Hmmmm." She didn't look convinced. "Will I get the first invitation to the wedding?"

"If there is a wedding, of course you will," I assured her. "And you heard Nicky the other day. He says you need to come to England and make some waffles for him. He's tired of hearing about me eating them all the time."

"Glad to see you ladies are working hard." The man himself strolled into the living room, and I stifled a deep sigh of appreciation. Nicky was wearing shorts and a T-shirt, and damn, my man looked good. I smiled a little; there was something satisfying on a primitive level about knowing that I was the only woman allowed to touch that ass or see him without the shorts and shirt. It might not have been official yet, but I didn't have any more doubts that Nicky and I were it for each other.

"We did work hard." I craned my neck back to gaze at him upside down. "Everything is boxed."

"Hmmmm." Nicky leaned over and touched his lips to mine, sending a thrill of pure need through me. "Then I guess you need a reward."

"I think that's probably my cue to get out of here." Shelby stood up. "We're meeting back at Honey and Handsome's, right? Pool time and pizza?" My grandparents had graciously offered all three of us a place to stay, now that our cottage was packed up.

"Absolutely." I grinned at my friend. "We'll be right behind you."

"Suuuuure you will." She waggled her eyebrows. "I'll just remind you that the beds are already taken down, so any horizontal hootchie cootchie will have to take place on the floor."

I grabbed Nicky's hands in both mine and tugged him down again. "Shel, you're forgetting the sofa and the chairs."

She wrinkled her forehead. "I think *you're* forgetting that I'm taking the sofa and chairs with me to New Mexico. Please don't violate them."

"I make no promises." I winked at her, laughing as she pretended to gag on her way out.

"So." Nicky came around and sat down next to me, draping an arm over my shoulder. "Any second thoughts?"

"About moving? Not one. I loved this place, and I'll always remember it fondly. But it's served its purpose, and now . . . it's time for new adventures."

"As long as those new adventures include me." He wound a lock of my hair around his finger. "I can't wait to live with you, Ky. To wake up every morning, with you in my bed, knowing that we'll end the day in each other's arms. That sounds like the best adventure ever."

"Our very own happily-ever-after," I agreed, snuggling closer.

"Oh, sweetheart." Nicky tapped my chin and kissed me until every part of my body was humming for him. "This isn't an ending. This is just the beginning of the rest of our lives." His eyes gleamed with something secret. "And trust me, I still have a few surprises up my sleeve."

I frowned. "Like what?"

He only shook his head. "Surprises, Ky, by their very nature, are not to be told ahead of time. Trust me, love. I promise, you'll like what I have planned."

"But—" I began to protest, but Nicky stopped me by scooping me into his lap and covering my mouth with his.

And that was the most perfect happy ending ever.

Kyra and Nicky's story continues . . .
The Anti-Cinderella Takes London
and
The Anti-Cinderella Takes On The World

Acknowledgements

When I was a little girl, I loved biographies. One of my favorites was *Majesty*, Robert Lacey's definitive (at the time) book about Elizabeth II. I loved learning not only about the Queen but about the royal family and what life was like within the walls of the palaces. This fascination only deepened years later, when I was thirteen and flipping through a *Newsweek* magazine, came across a photo of a young woman only six years older than me who was being pursued by the press because she was dating the Prince of Wales.

That was the beginning of Diana Mania, and I was definitely a devotee. I ate up every tiny scrap of news, which wasn't that much in those days, before the internet, social media and the obsessive paparazzi that would develop in Diana's wake. Still, I clipped magazine and newspaper articles and poured over any bit of coverage. On July 29, 1981, I got up at three in the morning to watch the Diana and Charles get married.

I had a Diana haircut, I copied her style and I had all the books. For a generation of young women, Diana, Princess of Wales, became an icon and a role model. And even though we soon realized that fairy tales often had a dark side, her tragic death in 1997 was devastating.

For years, I had in mind the story of a young American woman who fell in love with a prince in the British royal family. I honestly had no intention of writing it; this kind of plot line didn't seem to fit with the rest of my books, which always feature strong women. But then I wrote a book called *Fifty Frogs*, and in it, I mentioned the main character's sister Shelby, who was at school in Maine—and one day, I had the image of Shelby's best friend and the outline of her story fall into my head.

I told my cover designer, Meg Murrey, what I was thinking, and within moments, she had this awesome, amazing cover for me. I was in love.

But writing a story that plays on the world's stage rather than simply within a small town or an Army post is very challenging. And things have changed dramatically since I followed the press coverage of Lady Diana Spencer back in the early 1980's. I read about Kate Middleton and Prince William's relationship . . . and then as I was in the opening stages of writing this book, Prince Harry and Meghan Markle announced their engagement. The timing was beyond perfect.

Prince Nicholas is an entirely fictional character. He is not based on any one member of the royal family. He is, however, a member of a very real family; his paternal grandmother is the Queen, and his cousins are the heirs to the throne. This will be a challenge in the next two books, but even so, the focus will remain on Kyra and Nicky, as well as Nicky's immediate family.

A few notes for those who are (like me!) picky about details and precision when it comes to the royal family and aristocracy: first, the styling of Nicholas and his sisters as prince and princesses is entirely correct. It is true that Prince Edward's children (who would be the real-life generational equivalent of Nicky, Alex and Daisy) are not known as prince and princess, but technically they are. Their parents have chosen to have them called Lady and Viscount. The Letters Patent of 1917 provide HRH styling for male-line grandchildren of a sovereign. Second, not all of the extended royals live at Kensington Palace, but it is one place that many of the younger generation do live—which is why I placed Nicky and Alex there.

Masanobu Fukuoka, who is referenced as the modern father of natural farming, is a real person. His books are part of a revolution in the field of agriculture, and I am indebted to my husband and my daughter Cate for their help in understanding Fukuoka's works so that I could explain it in this book.

Of course, a huge THANK YOU to Meg Murry for this cover and to Stacey Blake of Champagne Book Designs for her formatting and for the beautiful teasers and banners. And love eternal to my special beta team, Kara Schilling, Krissy Smith, Christy Durbin and Dawn Line, who have worked above and beyond this year (already).

In writing this book, I feel that I have in some way come full circle, drawing on the dreams of fourteen-year-old me. For all the young women who look at the royals today as role models, it makes me very glad to see the Duchess of Cambridge and Prince Harry's bride Meghan forging new paths for the next generation of a very old family.

]What I have realized in writing this book is that today, princesses aren't helpless girls who need rescuing. Princesses can be strong women who are capable of rescuing themselves and of inspiring an entire generation to compassion and activism.

Long may they reign.

Play List

Our Last Summer—ABBA

Kiss Me—Ed Sheeran

Shake It Off—Taylor Swift

Something to Talk About—Bonnie Raitt

Who I Am—Andrew Galucki

This Kiss—Faith Hill

Andante, Andante—ABBA

Whatever Gets Through—TodayThe Radio

Running on Sunshine—Jesus Jackson

Breathe In, Breathe Out—Mat Kearney

Kisses of Fire—ABBA

Perfect—Ed Sheeran

The Story—Brandi Carlile

Other Books

Career Soldier

Maximum Force

Temporary Duty

Hitting the Silk

Zone of Action

Damage Assessement

Scheme of Manuever

Fifty Frogs

The King Series

Fearless

Breathless

Restless

Endless

The King Quartet Box Set

The Seredipity Series

Undeniable

Stardust on the Sea

Unquenchable

The Shadow Bells

Recipe for Death Series

Death Fricassee

Unforgettable

Death A La Mode

Death Over Easy

Moonlight on the Meadow

The Fox's Wager

Age of Aquarius

Crystal Cove Books

The Posse

The Plan

The Path

The One Trilogy

The Last One

The First One

The Only One

The One Trilogy Box Set

The Always Love Series

Always For You

Underneath My Christmas Tree

Always My Own

My One and Always

Always Our Love

The Love Song Girl

The Perfect Dish Series

Best Served Cold

Just Desserts

I Choose You

Keeping Score

When We Were Us

Hanging By A Moment

Days of You and Me

Not Broken Anymore

About the Author

Tawdra Kandle writes romance, in just about all its forms. She loves unlikely pairings, strong women, sexy guys, hot love scenes and just enough conflict to make it interesting. Her books run from YA paranormal romance through NA paranormal and contemporary romance to adult contemporary and paramystery romance. She lives in central Florida with a husband, kids, sweet pup and too many cats. And yeah, she rocks purple hair.

Follow Tawdra on Facebook, Twitter, Instagram, Pinterest and sign up for her newsletter so you never miss a trick.

If you love Tawdra's books, become a Naughty Temptress! Join the group on Facebook for sneak peeks, advanced reader copies of future books, and other fun.

96212314R00162

Made in the USA
Columbia, SC
27 May 2018